D0857019

the fetishist

ALSO BY KATHERINE MIN

Secondhand World

the fetishist

A NOVEL

KATHERINE MIN

G. P. PUTNAM'S SONS
New York

PUTNAM
— EST. 1838 —

G. P. PUTNAM'S SONS
Publishers Since 1838
An imprint of Penguin Random House LLC
penguinrandomhouse.com

Copyright © 2024 by Min Literary Productions, LLC
Penguin Random House supports copyright. Copyright fuels creativity, encourages diverse voices,
promotes free speech, and creates a vibrant culture. Thank you for buying an authorized edition
of this book and for complying with copyright laws by not reproducing, scanning, or distributing
any part of it in any form without permission. You are supporting writers and allowing
Penguin Random House to publish books for every reader.

Library of Congress Cataloging-in-Publication Data

Names: Min, Katherine, author.
Title: The fetishist: a novel / Katherine Min.
Description: New York: G. P. Putnam's Sons, 2024.
Identifiers: LCCN 2023042356 (print) | LCCN 2023042357 (ebook) |
ISBN 9780593713655 (hardcover) | ISBN 9780593713662 (ebook)
Subjects: LCGFT: Novels.
Classification: LCC PS3613.I592 F48 2024 (print) | LCC PS3613.I592 (ebook) |
DDC 813/.6—dc23/eng/20230912
LC record available at https://lccn.loc.gov/2023042356
LC ebook record available at https://lccn.loc.gov/2023042357

Printed in the United States of America
1st Printing

Book design by Laura K. Corless

This is a work of fiction. Names, characters, places, and incidents either are the product of
the author's imagination or are used fictitiously, and any resemblance to actual persons,
living or dead, businesses, companies, events, or locales is entirely coincidental.

Portions of this book appeared in different form in *River Styx* and the author's website,
katherinekmin.com.

For GCH, who has my back,
and my heart

Either it's going very, very well,
or it's going to be over
very, very soon.

—attributed to Jascha Heifetz

INTRODUCTION

I met Katherine Min at Yaddo, an arts residency, in 2009, when she was fifty and I was thirty-one years old. She was disarmingly warm and direct, a nice surprise in a cliquish residency where writers flaunted their barbed wit over dinner rather than exchanging meaningful conversation. She had short wavy hair that curled under her ears and always wore long silver earrings and bangles and favored silk shawls that she wrapped tightly over her shoulders. Almost immediately, she confided in me about her divorce and her writerly insecurities. I was deeply insecure, too, but I dared not expose it at Yaddo, where writers brought their pretensions with them from New York. I assumed that at fifty, a woman would be over her issues with her racial identity, childhood, and writerly neuroses. Now, a few years shy of fifty myself, I know those issues never disappear and that it takes emotional maturity to be as honest and vulnerable as Katherine was with everyone around her.

Of her writing, Katherine said she was a perfectionist. She polished words like they were jewels. She worked and reworked a chapter of *The Fetishist* while she was at Yaddo. I distinctly recall her reading an excerpt of it during a presentation after dinner. It was the description of a white male musician watching a slim, nubile Asian girl clacking her retainer loose with her tongue. Her writing was exquisite, disturbing, and Nabokovian. *The Fetishist* was a reframing of *Lolita* from the perspective of an Asian fetishist. The idea was so brilliant, I was surprised that someone hadn't already published this book.

I exchanged a few emails with Katherine after 2009 but saw her only a few times before she contracted cancer five years later. On Facebook, she posted detailed entries about life with cancer. She was so persistent, vital, and raw in these pieces that I was sure that she would beat it. It was a shock, then, when she wrote that the cancer reached her brain, and soon afterward, when she said she was going into hospice care.

Katherine finished *The Fetishist* during her lifetime but never sought publication for it. Thankfully, her daughter, Kayla Min Andrews, editor, Sally Kim, and agent, PJ Mark, were able to edit and bring this novel out to the world. *The Fetishist* turned out quite differently than what I had anticipated. Rather than a one-sided delusional monologue of the eponymous male protagonist, the novel is from the perspectives of heroines Alma and Kyoko, as well as the serial fetishist in question, Daniel Karmody—which makes sense. Either erased or hypersexualized, the Asian female is rarely given the chance to share her perspective on being fetishized—at least in mainstream culture—so it's fitting that Katherine would focus on Alma, the beautiful former prodigy cellist who ruefully reflects on her relationship with Daniel, and Kyoko, the punk-rock avenging angel intent on inflicting serious harm on Daniel for using and disposing of her mother, Emi.

Except for David Hwang's play *M. Butterfly*, I can think of no literary works by Asian American writers that deal squarely with queasy questions of desire and politics between a white man and an Asian woman (unfortunately, there are plenty of novels about such relationships by unselfaware white authors). Anne Anlin Cheng, in her scholarly book *Ornamentalism*, writes that under the colonial gaze, the Asian female is "an insistently aesthetic presence that is prized and despoiled." Desire for the "yellow woman" is an aberration or a symptom rather than a preference. Meanwhile, in Western history, her own desires have remained largely unheard until recently. In *The Fetishist*, Katherine brings to life the desires and rage of Alma, Kyoko, and Emi with beauty, humor, and poignancy that will ultimately move any reader. This story is long overdue.

CATHY PARK HONG

AUTHOR'S NOTE

This is a story, a fairy tale of sorts, about three people who begin in utter despair. There is even a giant, a buried treasure (a tiny one), a hero held captive, a kind of ogre (a tiny one), and a sleeping beauty. As with most fairy tales, poison is involved, as is a certain suspension of time (time, a tricky current, medium of buoyancy and stagnation, slick and sticky, fluid, fixative—a prison of its own; an enchanted tower; a strange country once visited, to which we can never return). And because it is a fairy tale, it has a happy ending. For the hero, the ogre, and the sleeping beauty, and for the giant, too. After all, every story has a happy ending, depending on where you put THE END.

the fetishist

failure

KYOKO, THE ASSASSIN

She should have known better. She should have read the signs: the girl, the rain, the crazed quality of light. The sky had been gray, streaked with black, and the rain—backlit in halogen and neon—had fallen sallow green. Why hadn't she seen it then? Nothing auspicious could have transpired beneath such a sky; it was sickly and low-down and regarded the city with a jaundiced eye.

At the time, though, she had read it differently. It had been cold, and damp, and inhospitable, and it had seemed to Kyoko like the perfect evening to kill Daniel Karmody.

She had followed him ten blocks from the enormous brownstone in Baltimore's fanciest downtown neighborhood. He had been performing there for a dying man with his string quartet. It was his pathetic little business these days, playing music for the rich and dying. Kyoko hadn't expected him to come out with someone—a thin, trench-coated female, carrying a violin case (of course! some things never changed!)—and it had enraged her, this added insult, this further blow to her mother's memory. It had seemed like another sign, urging her on toward a justice too long delayed. She had held her umbrella low in front of her face, stopping once in a while to pretend to inspect rain-soaked notices on lampposts, hanging back at crosswalks, maintaining a half-block distance, until the pair had gone up the stone steps of Rafferty's Olde Tyme Grill and disappeared behind its huge wooden door.

Kyoko had waited then, in the shadow of the stone staircase, back behind a line of dumpsters, listening to The Cramps through her earbuds. If you had seen her, you would have thought she looked more Hello Kitty than killer, in her oversize hoodie and size five-and-a-half salmon-colored sneakers. With her heart-shaped face and Day-Glo blue forelock sticking out from beneath her umbrella, she was a bedraggled elf seeking refuge under a mushroom.

But in spite of her cuteness, her size (5′3″, 103 pounds), and her age (twenty-three), Kyoko's life had been deformed by grief; grief, in turn, twisted to hate, hate hammered to anger, until the anger, the hate, and the grief had become grotesquely fused. Kyoko believed that violence would alleviate all three. In fact, she had bet on it.

In the kangaroo pocket of her hoodie, she held the handle of a *yanagi* sashimi knife with a seven-inch carbon steel blade. Forged in Seki, Japan, by the descendants of samurai sword makers, it seemed to Kyoko almost too fine a weapon for Daniel Karmody, whose soft, white belly she had long imagined gutting like a pig's.

The door to the restaurant opened and Kyoko caught a glimpse of the interior: elbows on red-checked tablecloths, the rose flickering of domed candles. Two couples appeared at the top of the stairs, putting up umbrellas, pushing arms through coat sleeves. Kyoko eased her grip on the knife and flexed her hand. *Cramps*, she thought, and smiled to herself; "People Ain't No Good" was blasting in her earbuds.

The Cramps' lead guitarist was one of Kyoko's many idols. Insolent in gold lamé or leopard-skin, Poison Ivy strummed her Gretsch Nashville like she was giving a hand job. Kyoko instinctively pressed the chords into the handle of her knife.

The door to the restaurant opened again, and this time Kyoko looked up to see Daniel Karmody at the top of the stairs with the woman he'd gone in with. Getting a good look finally, Kyoko saw that she was Asian—probably Korean, judging from her sullen features—and much too young for him, around Kyoko's age. Guys like Karmody made Kyoko sick, with their white-male entitlement and their power-trip fetishizing. They viewed Asian women as interchangeable sex dolls, and they never seemed to learn their lesson, never had to pay for what they'd done. But Kyoko was there to make Daniel Karmody pay.

They came down the stairs together, Karmody and the girl. He said something that Kyoko couldn't make out and the girl laughed. "Don't say that," she said. "It makes you sound ancient!" The gray expanse of Karmody's raincoat passed right in front of Kyoko, stopping mere yards away. Kyoko felt a pounding at her temples. Her legs went weak, and her whole body trembled. This was the moment. *Carpe, carpe* the moment! She thought, *Vengeance*. She thought, *At last*.

Kyoko had envisioned her revenge a thousand different ways since the day she had come home from school to find her mother on the bathroom floor. It would be seven years ago in October. Not that Kyoko registered her mother's death as a discrete event, happening at a particular moment. Instead, it was as if each moment since then had been compounded on that one event, accruing around it, so that her mother's death felt ongoing, always, inside a swollen and eternal present, in which Kyoko sat, in a buttered wedge of sunlight, on pale blue linoleum, smoothing her mother's nightgown down around her hips.

Daniel Karmody stood on the curb with one arm up. A blur of headlights passed without stopping. Kyoko depressed the latch on her umbrella, but it wouldn't close. Somewhere deep inside herself, she felt the small prescience of defeat, like the tick of a clock past the hour, but she shook it off. She tried to force the latch, or maybe it was a surge of wind, but the umbrella suddenly bloomed inside out, exposing its thin, silver ribs. Kyoko dropped it to the sidewalk and took a firm grip on her knife. She anticipated the shuddering thrust of the blade into resisting flesh, the *unh-unh* bewilderment of Daniel Karmody's last, grunting breaths.

But whatever it was that Kyoko had imagined for this moment, over the years of plans and schemes, strategies and daydreams, and long conversations with her boyfriend, Kornell Burke—right up until this afternoon's discovery on Facebook and her sudden impulse to action—whatever Kyoko had or could have imagined, this is what happened instead. As she brought her arm out, the knife tip snagged on the inside of her hoodie pocket, unfurling a thin thread of cotton filament. As she struggled to pull the knife free, she brought her foot down on the upended umbrella, her ankle catching between two spokes; she lurched a few steps forward with the umbrella fastened to her leg, like a bear in a trap, before she managed to kick herself free. Whereupon, she tripped, stumbled, staggered, righted herself— poised for an instant, graceful, plumb, like a ballerina *en pointe*— before pitching face forward onto the wet pavement. She felt a stunning smack to the underside of her chin. Tasted metal. Saw red. For a few seconds, she may have been unconscious.

Her rain-blurred eyes opened in time to witness the loathsome culprit, Daniel Karmody, opening a cab door. It seemed to Kyoko, just for a moment, that their gazes locked and he had seen her. But then he turned, and she could only watch, on hands and knees—from the sucker end of destiny—as he guided the girl inside, closed his umbrella smartly, folded himself inside the cab, first one leg, then the other. She heard him murmur a street address to the driver before the door slammed shut.

DANIEL GETS LUCKY

In the cab, they were silent. Daniel snuck a peek at the girl, who was staring straight ahead, a vague smile directed out the windshield. She was lovely, Melody Park, the name itself evocative of carousel and calliope, of geometric grass expanses. *A pretty girl is like a melody* . . . Wasn't that a song?

The cabdriver turned the wipers on intermittent and the world came at them, awash with color and light, in rain-blurred columns and branching rivulets, punctuated by unexpected clarity. He was Southeast Asian, a Hindu or a Sikh, with a dark red turban and thick beard. Daniel wondered if his glance, cast back in the rearview mirror, was reproving, or if Daniel only imagined censure behind the man's stony expression.

Daniel was surprised by his success with the girl. In truth, he'd only been going through the motions, grinding his gears in the worn tire ruts of seduction. He was taking the next three weeks off, to work on some new arrangements, he'd said, but really to try to sort out his life now that Sigrid had finally left him.

And immediately before the gig, there had been the Facebook message from Alma. What timing! At his most vulnerable, newly divorced, running late, checking Facebook to see if the new second violinist could make it after all, and—bam! Out of nowhere. After nearly two decades of silence.

His heart had lurched at the sight of Alma's name, then fallen as he hurriedly read her message. *DK—I hope you're happy and that things are going well for you.* A paragraph of vague niceties, a mention of her illness (which he already knew about, it was common knowledge) and her location (California, which he already knew), more lukewarm well-wishes including the phrase *I'm not angry with you anymore*, then the stultifying conclusion: *Well, take care. —A.*

It had seemed to Daniel so willfully, uncharacteristically, boring. Utterly devoid of the personal—a total repudiation of intimacy, past, present, or future—her message contained no questions, no apparent interest in a response. Why break the silence for this? Seemed a bit cruel. She had also, inexplicably, "liked" a photo of him and the quartet.

Thus, after the gig, Daniel had thought, in a state of creeping panic and emptiness, that a night of romance might cheer him. Instead, he found it all rather unsettling, the rain seeping into the toes of his good leather shoes; Melody's youth, his age; the way her sliced eggs had looked at him, accusingly, from atop her chef's salad. The fact that everything felt like aftermath, like auld lang syne, the memory of desire like a vestigial tail.

The evening had started with a joke. "An Irishman walks into a bar," Daniel had begun, "orders ten shots of whiskey, and starts drinking them as fast as he can. The bartender asks"—here Daniel shifted into his ready Irish brogue—"'Aye, Paddy, why're you drinking so fast?' And Paddy replies, 'You'd be drinking fast, too, if you'd got what I've got.' The bartender says, 'Aye, Paddy, what've you got?' And Paddy says"— here Daniel had paused, *beat, beat, beat*—"'Eighty-five cents.'" Mr. Trask had laughed so hard he started to choke. His wife, who had not laughed, raised a glass of water to his lips, but he waved it away.

What had once been an enormous study had been transformed into a hospital. IV stands and heart monitors, like modern art installations, stood beside the Duncan Phyfe and Hepplewhite furniture. An electric bed presided, like a hulking stage prop, and Mr. Trask, with his translucent face, white hair thinning and unwashed, looked precisely the part of the dying man.

Daniel had helped Mr. Trask sit up straighter and thumped his back. He hadn't thought the joke was funny himself, his timing had been off, and eighty-five cents was clearly not the right amount, but he knew from experience that dying made people less discerning.

"'Eighty-five cents.' Oh, that *is* good," Mr. Trask had said, when he could speak again. The two men had continued to chuckle.

Mrs. Trask looked at them doubtfully. "Easy, Randall," she said.

"Oh, Annie," Mr. Trask said, "what's he going to do, kill me?"

He laughed again, and Mrs. Trask shook her head, miming vexation.

"What shall you play us this evening?" Mr. Trask asked Daniel.

"You're the boss," Daniel said.

"Then *Death and the Maiden*, maestro, please," Mr. Trask said.

"You got it," said Daniel. It was always *Death and the Maiden* for Mr. Trask these days.

"I'm the maiden," he said now, not for the first time.

"Yes," said Daniel. "Yes, you are."

———————

The quartet had galloped to the finish line, riding it, kicking it, skidding so hard on the final D minor that the audience—the night nurse, Mr. and Mrs. Trask, their two daughters, two sons-in-law, and five grandchildren—hadn't realized at first that it was over. Their ears had kept on ringing, retaining the music as memory, as sensation.

Daniel had brought the violin down from his chin and let his bow arm dangle on the back of his chair. The new second violinist sat next to him. She was young and beguiling, her dark hair falling forward onto her pale, serious face. He smiled at her as she turned to put her instrument away.

"Wonderful!" Mr. Trask applauded from his bed, his tufted pink head lolling. His arms were bone and cord, with green-blue tendrils of vein. Daniel smiled and waved his bow.

The only fault Daniel could find with the new violinist was in her chin. Her jaw sloped gracefully to the end of her face, curving toward beauty, already confident of it, and then—precipitously, incomprehensibly, like some eroded stone monument—it just fell away. She was still lovely, Daniel thought, but it was perplexing, this unfinished look of hers, her face coming to such a premature conclusion.

Mrs. Trask walked over to him now, extending her hand. "Thank you, Mr. Karmody," she said.

"Daniel," he prompted her.

"Daniel." Her blue eyes were pink-rimmed. She squeezed his palm. "You've given Randall so much pleasure."

Daniel bowed his head. Mrs. Trask was an attractive woman, considerably younger than her husband, with the blond patrician bearing of a young Grace Kelly. Daniel was aware that he was still holding her hand.

"You're very kind, Mrs. Trask," he said. He waited for her to offer her first name, which he knew to be Anne, but she did not. "Your husband is a lucky man."

"He *was*," she said with surprising vehemence, dropping his hand. "He *was* lucky." She hurried out of the room. Daniel considered going after her, but she had already disappeared.

Just a few weeks before, on a day when Mr. Trask had felt up to it, he'd shown Daniel his prize possession, a thin album of rare stamps locked in vinyl sheets. Errors, freaks, and oddities, he'd called them. His favorite was the Inverted Jenny, a twenty-four-cent stamp, issued in 1918, with an upside-down airplane. He had pointed out a six-fingered President Roosevelt stamp, and one that featured seven legs for four horses. "And this should be of particular interest to you," he'd said, indicating a blue square with his forefinger. "East Germany issued this one in 1956, to commemorate the composer Robert Schumann. Only one problem . . . Look closely at the piece of musical score in the background! Schubert!" Mr. Trask had laughed, a brittle, breaking sound, and Daniel had laughed with him, in the way that the healthy condescend to the dying.

Daniel remembered now that it had been Mrs. Trask who had urged her husband to show Daniel the stamps that day. She had listened patiently to all of Mr. Trask's anecdotes, which she must have heard a thousand times before, and when he was finished, she'd covered his hand with her own for a moment before taking the album away. Strange that he should remember this briefest of gestures, her small, pale hand coming to rest atop her husband's wide, liver-spotted one. Recalling it, Daniel felt close to tears.

One of the sons-in-law walked over to hand Daniel a check. "You're gone the next few weeks, right?" he said.

Daniel nodded, blinking.

"Well, we'll see you when you get back."

"Not likely," Roger, the violist, whispered to Daniel.

"Memorial service," Daniel whispered back. He wiped his eyes with the back of his hand. "Good job, guys," he said, more loudly. Deirdre, the cellist, ignored him. The new second violinist—bless her—smiled. She was their third second violinist in eight months, as Roger kept reminding him. They'd had a hard time getting anyone on such short notice, and until this afternoon Daniel wasn't sure she would show—repeated messages to her cell phone had gone unanswered—but she had posted on Thanatos's Facebook page that she had lost her phone and would be there, which had reassured Daniel that everything would be okay. Though, seconds later, he had discovered the message from Alma.

Against his better judgment, and despite Roger's look of warning, Daniel leaned into the curtain of Melody's hair, which smelled of citrus fruits and coconut, like some tropical rum punch. With one slim hand, she gathered her hair to one side of her neck, and Daniel couldn't help himself.

"You did well," he said.

"Thank you," the girl answered.

"Would you care to get a bite to eat?" He kept his voice low. It was not a general invitation, and anyway he knew that Roger had to hurry home to Nina and the kids, and that Deirdre would rather eat rat poison than go out to dinner with him. He saw a look of uncertainty cross the girl's face, like a dark cloud, but after a moment, she said yes, and Daniel felt almost giddy with relief.

————————

He had taken her to Rafferty's because it was raining, and it was the only place he could think of. He had ordered a Pilsner on tap. She asked for Chardonnay. They had both ordered food.

"So, what do you think?" he asked.

"Of what?"

"This afternoon."

She thought, pouting, her lower lip plump and delicious. "It's sad," she said finally.

Daniel smiled. "Oh, yes, it *is* sad, but you get used to it."

She played with the damp ends of her hair. For a moment, she reminded him of Alma, but then they always did.

"Are you?" she asked.

"Am I what?" Daniel dabbed his brow with his napkin.

"Used to it."

He considered. "I was," he said. "But I'm not now."

"What?"

"Never mind."

She was too young. Daniel could see her collarbone protruding from beneath her skin like a clothes hanger. Her truncated chin disturbed him, made her seem unfinished.

"How old are you?" he said. "If I may ask?"

"Twenty-five."

"Ah, you look five years younger," he said. "That's the wonderful thing about you Asian women," he went on. "You never seem to age."

Melody took a long sip of wine.

"Sorry, I know I shouldn't have said that," Daniel said. And it *was* stupid. He wished the girl would scold him for it. He relished a bit of sparring, like rubbing two sticks together for sparks. He thought of Alma, her dark eyes alight with provocation. "Once Asian, never again Caucasian," she had said the first night they'd spent together. She had meant it as a joke, but—with the exception of Sigrid—it had turned out to be true.

"I'm Irish, you know," Daniel went on. "People call Koreans the 'Irish of the Orient,' though I suppose it should be the other way around, really—Irish, the 'Koreans of Europe.'"

"Oh, why?" Melody asked, though she sounded bored.

Daniel swallowed a mouthful of beer. She had no doubt heard it all before. "Well," he said, "we're both a very passionate people. Sentimental. We like to get drunk and laugh, sing sad songs and cry." He wiped the foam from his upper lip. "And then there's the whole shared history, divided country and all that," he mumbled.

"When my father gets drunk he sings 'Danny Boy,'" Melody said.

"There you go!" said Daniel.

"Then he passes out," she said, and was quiet.

"You're very beautiful," Daniel said.

The girl blushed. "What about your wife?"

He smiled ruefully. "My wife and I were happy for thirty years," he said. *Beat, beat, beat.* "And then we met."

She looked at him sharply. "What does that mean?" she said.

"It's a joke."

"Oh."

Daniel looked down at his plate. "It means she left me," he said. He saw Sigrid picking up the last of her things, a hair dryer, some dish towels, a bottle of shampoo, carrying them out of the house in a wicker wastepaper basket.

Melody stabbed her salad with her fork. "For good?" she asked.

"For better," he answered.

———

Somewhere after the third beer, he decided that all he really wanted was to go home. He'd run out of jokes, or she didn't laugh, or he was exhausted thinking up topics of conversation. A dispirited silence had fallen, which the girl had broached by putting her hand on his thigh. "I have condoms," she'd said. "If you don't."

Daniel had looked around the restaurant, shocked. "And if I do?"

She'd smiled.

And so they had walked back out into the rain.

If he had been going home alone, he would have taken the train. But with Melody by his side, Daniel tried to hail a cab, dimly registering a gloom-faced girl behind him, fumbling with her umbrella. There was a loud, percussive clamoring of rain on metal. The gutters gushed with water. Somewhere far down the street, a car alarm. And standing there with his arm outstretched, Daniel experienced the peculiar brand of despair that comes from getting what you wanted the second you realize you don't want it anymore, and worse, he realized that he had never really wanted it in the first place, and that he hadn't wanted the same thing the last time either, or the last time— a perversion of good luck condemning him to repeat the same mistake, repeating down a corridor of mirrors that stretched many years back, and who knew how far forward? "When the pecker gets hard, the brain goes soft," Daniel's father had been fond of saying. What passed for wisdom from a man who had never had much on offer. But in Daniel's experience, in this one regard, the old man had been right.

So here he now sat, good old Danny boy (. . . *the summer's gone, and all the leaves are falling . . .*), regretting in advance something he had not yet done, something he knew he should not do, but in a faint flush of revelation knew that he would, having narrowly—through the fluke of a defective umbrella latch—escaped a peculiar and meddlesome fate, but not, as it turns out, for long.

Alma and the Miracle Cure

Meanwhile, 2,800-odd miles away, in a cavernous room smelling of cardboard and cabbage, rocking uneasily on an aluminum folding chair with uneven legs, Alma Soon Ja Lee waited her turn. The woman next to her wept discreetly, wiping her nose with a tattered tissue that she clenched in her fist like a rosary. Across from her an Indian man with a walrus mustache pressed his eyes and mouth closed in replicating lines of tightly held pain.

Sitting very still, Alma cataloged her symptoms du jour: the thrumming pain in her lower back, a numbness in her left hand, fatigue like a cairn of stones piled atop her chest. No spasm in her right leg today. No vertigo. No careening roller-coaster headache. Over the years, Alma had learned to survey herself in this manner, eyes closed in concentration, attune to the battery of symptoms that came and went, until she had come to envision her body as one of those old-fashioned telephone switchboards, lighting up and down in a frenzy of incoming calls.

Alma fingered the first few notes of the Franck sonata, humming a little to herself, the fingers of her left hand fanning out to the first extension, reaching for the major third. The problem was that, with the numbness, she couldn't bend her fingers reliably. The impulse to bend them was strong—will and muscle memory—but the translation to action was weak; she had to look to see her fingers tremble in trace compliance. For Alma, the biggest cruelty of her disease was this alienation of mind and body. Like an unhappily married couple, they warred with one another, grew distant, retired to opposite ends of the room, communicating only in stiff, furious bouts.

The building Alma was sitting in had once been a vegetable warehouse. It was cold and drafty, with green corrugated metal walls. A man with a tremendous goiter over his left eye—it hung like a sac above his eyelid—let loose a hacking cough. The woman next to Alma sneezed. Alma considered leaving. She felt stupid being here in the first place, no matter what Rickey had said. She was no dupe, no patsy. She had always prided herself on her rigor, her contrarian's resistance to credence.

"Just go," Rickey had said. "I tell you, the guy's the real deal. And anyway, what do you have to lose?"

"What about my pride?" she'd said.

He'd shrugged. "Didn't you lose that already?"

Alma had nodded. "Somewhere between falling off my chair during a concert in Minneapolis and losing bladder control at an arts fundraiser in D.C."

"You see?" Rickey had said. "Nothing."

———————

D r. Woo finally arrived with an entourage of serious-faced young helpers in brocaded Chinese jackets. By this time there were twelve patients seated in the circle of folding chairs. The last to enter was an elderly couple, the woman supported by the man, both of them wrinkled and droop-jawed, like twin Shar-Pei dogs.

"Okay, let's get started, shall we?" Dr. Woo said, stepping into the center of the circle. He was short and almost bald, with a round, smiling face. His English was British-inflected. He approached the Shar-Pei couple and spoke to them in a low voice, which Alma strained to hear.

"My wife has just been diagnosed with a brain tumor," the man explained. "The doctors say there is nothing they can do."

"I see," Dr. Woo said, taking the woman's wrist. "How do you feel?"

"Ahh," the woman murmured. "A bit of a headache when I woke up this morning, but I took some medicine the doctor gave me and now I have only the slightest edge of pain. Here." The woman indi-cated a spot above her left eye. As Dr. Woo listened to her, he tilted his head, occasionally nodding, like a swimmer trying to drain water from his ear. He said something to an assistant, who began to tap the woman behind her elbow with a tiny silver mallet.

"And you?" the doctor said to the Shar-Pei man.

Behind the man's glasses, his eyes widened and blinked. "Oh, I just came along to bring my wife," he said.

Dr. Woo waited.

"But I do have terrible arthritis," the man said. "In my hands. It's gotten worse, I think, with stress."

Alma watched as Dr. Woo consulted with each patient, always with the same birdlike inquisitiveness, asking one or two questions, responding with a nod, leaving an earnest assistant behind to attend to the mechanics.

Stage IV lung cancer. Lupus. Severe head trauma. Leukemia. The complaints were dire, the patients in distress, the building a warehouse of suffering, smelling of vegetables. Alma began to feel lucky by comparison. Her pain was intermittent, scattered and various; she could not honestly say that it was too much to be borne. What *was* too much, and here Alma half rose in her chair, were the things she had lost to the pain, the things that the pain was replacing. She thought of Jacqueline du Pré, her predecessor in both vocation and disease. The irony was that early on in her career, Alma's playing had been compared to du Pré's. *Brilliant, passionate, barely controlled.* They had both made names for themselves playing Elgar, and they had both married conductors. When Alma was diagnosed, she'd been incredulous. She was seven years older now than du Pré had been when she died. People might interpret her illness as an eccentric career move, some grim, misguided homage.

At last Dr. Woo made his way to her. When he asked what was wrong, Alma, suddenly superstitious, didn't want to name it. "I have this pain in my lower back," she said. "And I'm always tired." The doctor took her wrist. She could feel her own pulse against his fingers. He put his hands on the sides of her head and pressed.

"What is wrong with your hand?" he said.

"What?"

"Your hand," Dr. Woo said.

"It's numb."

He gave her the sideways scrutiny. His face was smooth and flat, with a dusting of small moles.

"Are you Chinese?" he asked.

"Korean."

"Ah." He nodded, as though this clarified something. "Born here?"

"In Seoul, but moved to the U.S. when I was four," said Alma.

Dr. Woo nodded again. "And how long have you had MS?" he said.

Alma was startled. "I was first diagnosed twelve years ago."

"And it's moved to the secondary phase?"

Again, Alma tried not to register her surprise. "Yes."

"Since when?"

"Nine months ago."

Dr. Woo tilted his head, stroking his chin between a thumb and forefinger. Alma felt a small sense of pride that he was taking more time with her than the others. He spoke with an assistant, a young Caucasian woman with multiple facial piercings. She tapped Alma's wrists with a mallet in light, even movements. "After this," Dr. Woo said, "your MS will go into remission." His tone was matter-of-fact. Alma was surprised once again.

"What did you do?" she asked in a subdued voice.

Dr. Woo waved his hand, his wrist relaxed, two fingers extended. Alma had no idea what it meant. "Anyway," he said, moving away, "this is the case."

Rickey had told her that she would be astounded. He knew people with an assortment of maladies, including cancer, who claimed to have been cured by Dr. Woo and his silver mallets. Perhaps, Alma thought, it was a matter of faith after all. That Dr. Woo was Asian made a difference to her somehow. Eastern medicine, ancient and incomprehensible, reminded her of the smelly black herbal balls her grandmother used to swallow, the tiny seeds her father used to press into the inner curl of his ear. It seemed entirely possible that

Western science, in its infinite hubris, had missed something, had failed to take into account, simply because it could not explain them, the uncanny results of so arcane a knowledge. There was also the matter of payment. Dr. Woo didn't charge for his treatments. "He says it's bad karma," Rickey had said. "No one knows how he does it." And, in the end, after countless hours, days, weeks, running into years, of hassling with insurance companies, hospitals, doctors' offices, the Italian health system, and her ex-husband, which had left Alma exhausted and broke—more than broke, in debt, disheartened, desperate—it was this that had convinced her to come.

Alma got up from her chair now. She breathed deeply and gathered her purse. She was hyperconscious of her body, her mind scanning for interventions. The pain in her back seemed to be gone; the numbness subsided. She flexed her fingers, played a bit of Bach, her hands out in front, moving in midair. The music, sounding in her mind's ear, was energetic, joyful. It was possible that she felt less tired. Alma sent a quick text to Rickey.

The Shar-Pei couple was leaving. She waited for them to shuffle past, the old woman with her watery, opaque eyes, the man holding her elbow with his hand as though it were a rudder. The man nodded to Alma as he steered by, wattles bouncing sadly, and for a second she saw in his eyes an expression that must have mirrored her own: doubt and astonishment, fear, and the fragile ignition of hope.

"It's not common," said Dr. Mehta, three weeks later. "But it's not completely unheard of either." She was referring to Alma's "remission," which she would not call a remission. "Think of it more as an 'intermission,'" she said. Alma imagined her disease as a recital. *Alma Soon Ja Lee, barely live and in concert, performing "MS in A Minor by a Vengeful God" (with a brief intermission)*.

They should send them to comedy school," Alma told Rickey later. "They should have to wear rubber noses."

"Like Patch Adams," said Rickey.

"Who?" said Alma.

"Never mind." Rickey should have known by now that Alma rarely got pop culture references, a combination of not having been born in the States and having had no life outside of the cello. She was proud of what little she did know, which was mostly music from the '70s and '80s. "I used to be in a band," she'd told him, as though this were widely known. It was Talking Heads' "Swamp" that they were listening to now. Rickey bopped his head, and Alma waved the knife, and when it got to the chorus they both sang, *"Hi, hi, hi, hi, hi, hiiiii . . . Woo-ooo."*

Rickey and Alma had been best friends since the night he had knocked on her door three years ago to borrow fish sauce for Vietnamese spring rolls. Not only had she had some but kimchi besides, and a special bond had formed. Nowadays Rickey cooked for Alma whenever he could, curries and stir-fries, and soups that he froze in small containers so she could microwave individual servings. He also bought her groceries. "Whole Foods had a sale on cheeses," he would say. "I couldn't resist." He pretended he was just being neighborly, and she pretended it was no big deal, though her pantry was stockpiled for the apocalypse, with cans of tuna fish, baked beans, and soup, bags of trail mix and Oreos, cases of condensed milk, ramen, and bottled water—and in this way Rickey could continue to save Alma's life without the burden of her gratitude.

Ever since her "intermission," though, Alma had been cooking again. She was making her mother's famous *japchae* now. "My mother always parboiled the carrots," Alma said, "but you don't have to." She poured the carrots into a colander and ran them under cold water. Her face was flushed from the steam, but also, Rickey thought, from the giddiness of unexpected health. She was beautiful in that particularly soft Asian way, her long black hair, with its mirror shine, her sloe-eyed gaze, and long, slender fingers, occupied now with julienning carrots. Her cheekbones were high and sharply angled, and though it gave her face a look of severity, a modern art aspect, like a cubist Picasso, Rickey thought it was this that most committed her to beauty, the way that most beautiful things could seem freakish, even ugly, from certain angles, because beauty was strange and singular, and often unsettling.

"The thing is," she was saying, "that I feel kind of better than normal. I mean, for a long time. Like I'm souped-up or something. I have all this energy." She was onto the scallions now, fingers moving adroitly back behind the speeding knife blade.

Rickey was about to take a sip of his Chianti. "Whoa there, A.," he said.

Alma stopped, pushed the scallions into the *japchae*. "Done," she said. She wiped a hand on the front of her apron and took up her wineglass. "Santé."

"*Geonbae*," said Rickey.

Alma leaned across the counter to give him a kiss. She smiled in a shy way, her dark eyes shining. "Sometimes I wish you were straight," she said.

"Sometimes I wish you were a guy," he said.

"Sometimes I wish you were a woman and I was gay," she said.

"Sometimes I wish I was a woman, and you were a guy, and we were both straight," he said. They laughed.

Alma reached over to hold Rickey's hand. "Sometimes," she said, "I wish it would always be like this."

Five hours later she woke from a dream about an earthquake, only the quaking did not subside. She spent rude seconds in violent tremor, lying on her side, her left leg pedaling the bedsheets as though riding an unseen bicycle. "This isn't funny," she said to the empty room. Her sheets were soaked in sweat, her left leg still now, feigning rest.

She went into the bathroom and turned on the light. Her face in the mirror was mushroom-colored, sunken-cheeked, with dark, rubbery circles under her eyes, her loose, damp hair sticking out in all directions. She looked like Caravaggio's head of Medusa, a Gorgon monster with writhing hair. Some wild, defeated thing.

It was unfathomable how quickly her life had changed. One minute she had been worrying about her recital gown—whether the skirt was too long, the front too plunging—the next minute she'd been hoping that she could hold her cello upright for an hour. She had first noticed a tingling in her bow hand. That was more than thirteen years ago now. The tingling had been quickly accompanied by extreme weakness in her left hand. It became harder and harder for her to press her fingers forcefully enough into the cello strings. She'd gone to a massage therapist trained in the Feldenkrais Method. He had taught her some exercises. It was not uncommon for cellists to feel pain in their neck, back, and shoulders, and Alma had a standing prescription for a kick-ass pain reliever. But this had been different, more ticklish than painful, and accompanied by a disproportionate fatigue, as though she had pitched nine innings instead of practiced cello for five hours. Soon, the tickle and fatigue had been accompanied by a slight tremor, and soon after that she started to fall down, her legs buckling as she got up from her chair, sliding out from under her as she negotiated the pavement. Her vision went blurry, or she'd see two of everything. An arm or a leg would stiffen. She'd go numb. They did tests, made diagnoses. *She was under stress. She had a vitamin deficiency. It might be a brain tumor. Rheumatoid arthritis. Possibility of a mild stroke.*

She had been in the early stages of divorcing Paolo, slated to record the Franck in L.A. When they said MS, she had been doubtful—they had been wrong so many times already—but all other contenders had fallen away, and retesting had confirmed it.

Paolo, impatient to be divorced but trying, in his way, to be considerate, was upbeat. "This is good news, *cara*," he'd said, and when she hadn't responded, he'd added, "I mean, it's not can—" He was speaking to her via speakerphone from his office in Milan. She could picture him perched on the corner of his desk, absently picking lint off the cuff of one of his crisp, custom-tailored suits—solid navy or navy pinstripe—and glancing at his watch, wondering how fast he could tactfully end the call. Right there on that desk, there used to be a photo of her, in an engraved silver frame, backstage at the Teatro Comunale in Florence the summer they had first met. In it, she wore a red halter evening gown with a black leather belt, her hair swept up into an impossible architecture. It was one of the few photographs she liked of herself, something about the way the dress swirled around her as she strode forward, the expression on her face looking through the camera, beyond it, as though she defied it to fix her in the moment. There was something prescient about that expression, Alma had always thought, as if she had been gazing out toward her future self, as if she had known everything that was going to happen and had still chosen to go forward. And in the background you could just make out Daniel, half his face cast downward, coming off the stage, and Alma knew it was no accident that Paolo had chosen this particular photograph for display—the trophy of his wife's triumph, of course, but more importantly, of his own.

Alma wondered now what had happened to that photo. And what photo had replaced it. "I am coming to the States in June, *cara*," Paolo had said. "I promise to come see you. *Ciao, bella*, I have a meeting."

And then her whole life had simply stopped, like a broken-down car by the side of the road.

A lma, knowing that she would not get back to sleep now, went into the living room. Her cello stood in the corner, to the side of the stereo cabinet, in its hard carbon fiber case. It was a 1732 Francesco Goffriller that Alma called "Franny." She had stopped playing it altogether six months ago when she had fallen out of her chair and nearly crushed it, her bow hand shaking uncontrollably, beating a manic rhythm on the floor. Since then it had stood unmoved, like a strange sculpture, or, as Rickey had dubbed it, "the proverbial elephant in the room."

When Alma had first stopped playing, she had listened to music obsessively, lying on the couch for hours with her eyes closed, and while she listened, she dozed, dreaming about the time she had heard this particular piece in London, another performed by Barenboim, another still in Boston with Daniel. But it became gradually more difficult to listen—the more beautiful, the more transcendent, the harder a hot stone pressed against her chest. She was like an exile looking at photographs of her native country—all the familiar land-marks, the sacred places that had been burned into memory, lay life-less and shrunken, because they remained inaccessible.

Alma had been eleven when she became obsessed with the cello; she had been playing for six years by then, but had been too young for it to feel like a choice. At eleven, though, something had hap-pened. She didn't need her parents, or Mr. Felsenfeld, to scold her; she wasn't motivated by competition or recitals. She didn't give a thought to pleasing anyone, to becoming better, or really to achieving anything at all. She just felt compelled to keep her cello close to her, to move with it, to listen to it, until the cello had become a part of her, or, more precisely, she had felt a part of it. It was very physical, more like dancing than playing an instrument, and all her life Alma had felt this weirdly mystical sense of her playing as moving through physical space, the notes like steps, like gestures, the music like breath, like breeze, and the feeling of wide-ranging freedom, of expanse and embrace, and of always ending up somewhere else. It was a compul-sion that kept her fingers pressing imaginary strings, her bow hand moving even as she was solving algebra problems or sitting in English class. It was not something she was proud of or that she felt she owned, and it was mystifying to her the way her mother bragged about her—the trophies and ribbons that accumulated on the shelves of the living room and in the store, the judges' lavish praise in com-petitions, the murderous envy of the other mothers and their cowed and driven children—all of that was simply by-product to her, a kind of sausage that resulted from the steaming entrails of her obsession.

Now, Alma lifted her cello from her case. She drew the bow from its velvet bed, rosined up in short, swift strokes, and sat down, hefting

Franny's beloved, familiar weight. She looked down the length of the four strings—A, D, G, C—architecturally suspended above the f-holes, to the delicate bridge, then down the gleaming spruce, to its ebony tailpiece. She brushed back her hair and straightened, bringing her hands into position. Alma felt sweat bead on her upper lip. She paused. Her right hand shook. She forced herself to play a few notes. D, F-sharp, B, G-sharp. The opening of the Franck. She stopped. Tried again. D, F-sharp. D, F-sharp. She couldn't get her fingers to stick to the notes. They kept sliding off, skidding sideways. D, F-sharp. Her hand shook more violently and Alma started to cry, tears of frustration at first and then harder. "Fucking shit!" she yelled into the darkened room.

DANIEL, DEFLATED

He was embarrassed by the living room. Sigrid had cleared out all the art she'd collected over the years. A trumpeting angel cut from wood, by Howard Finster; a painting of a blue head by Mose Tolliver; one of Henry Darger's Vivian Girls collages, from *In the Realms of the Unreal*; and—Daniel's favorite—a Milo Kretz, done in bright, enamel bicycle paint on the back of a barn door.

The painting had hung above the sofa for so long that its absence registered as a bright white rectangle against the duller white wall. Sigrid had picked it up just the day before, bringing along four moving men and a truck from the gallery. Daniel had watched in bitter silence as the men had swaddled the Kretz in blankets and carried it out the door like a body. "Easy, easy now," Sigrid had said, guiding them, moving her arms like semaphores, and "Gently, gently," down the stairs.

Untitled #172, by Milo Kretz, depicted an alligator-headed man fishing in the blue waters of the Yazoo River, a catfish-headed woman in a white dress behind him, with her hand on his shoulder. Leaping up out of the water, at the end of the man's line, was the baby Jesus, with a catfish body and a hook in his mouth, and all along the river-bank a crowd of catfish- and alligator-headed figures dressed in over-alls and yellow sunbonnets bore witness. Around the painted trompe l'oeil frame, in wobbly cursive letters, gold and black, were the words, "And they rejoiced, for the infant Baby Jesus was an abundant catch that day. Hallelujah! Hallelujah! Milo Kretz, 1974."

The painting had always seemed to Daniel to be too bold for the living room, and all the tiny figures in it, the catfish heads and the alligator heads, in their gingham and floral prints, against the prima-vera green of the riverbank, the white-topped turbulence of the water, and the gold rays of divine light shooting out in all directions, had teemed with such vitality that whatever real life had been lived in that room—the *living* room—felt pallid and dwarf-sized in com-parison.

Recalling it now with Melody Park, Daniel felt the loss of the painting (more than the loss of Sigrid) like an aching hole in his chest, as though his life, like the wall, were newly blank, its ghostly outline traceable as a slightly paler shade of what remained. To calm himself, Daniel put on John Coltrane and poured two small glasses of port. "My wife took some things," he said, but Melody, who was fiddling with her phone, did not reply.

"Who is this?" she inquired, tilting her head toward the music. "I only listened to classical growing up."

Daniel sat close to Melody on the couch and undertook a brief introduction to jazz, to which the girl seemed attentive. Of course it was Alma who had first introduced him to Coltrane. *Listen up, DK, this will change your life!*

"Tell me, Melody, do you have a boyfriend?" Daniel asked after an awkward silence.

She looked at him from beneath her bangs. "I don't like men my own age," she said.

"Why not?"

"They seem . . ." she said. "I don't know . . . they seem silly."

"Silly," he said. "Silly, how?"

A look of impatience crossed her face. "Silly in the way they're unsure of themselves," she said.

"I see," Daniel said, sure of himself as he leaned in to kiss her. He parted her lips with his and ran his tongue across her teeth; she bit the underside of his lip. Daniel winced and tried not to feel silly. He thought of the old Groucho Marx line, "A man is as old as the woman he feels." Cupping the girl's breast beneath her blouse, he felt his cock inflate, like a clown balloon, lurching drunkenly against the crotch of his boxers. *Silly*, he thought fleetingly as he pushed her skirt up her thigh.

Later, when Daniel had her laid out on the bed, her body partially illuminated by the light from the hall, he was overwhelmed by her beauty—so strange after Sigrid's familiar—brown where Sigrid had been pink, slim where she had been ample, her breasts small, skin creamy. Daniel knew from experience that the strangeness could not be separated from the beauty, that it was, in some measure, the same thing. Sigrid had been the exception. The rest had all been like Melody—the same slender bodies and hairless legs, with a small thatch of hair at the crotch. Daniel kissed her there now, darting his tongue inside, as she groaned.

"Oh, oh," she said, pressing her hand down against the top of his head. She moaned and pulled hard at the roots of his hair. Daniel tried to get up, feeling suddenly panicked, but she held him down, and just when he thought he might suffocate, she released him, her arms thrashing the air for purchase, and he was up and on top of her, as agile as a wrestler. He pushed his way inside her, felt his cock enveloped in her warm sleeve. Wrapping an arm around her narrow waist, he grabbed ahold of her ass and pulled her closer. The hard mound of her pelvis bucked up to meet him. The girl's eyes were closed, and Daniel was aware of the sounds she was making, encouraging, breathy yeses and ohs, in escalating rhythm.

All this should have registered as ecstasy, as ratcheting excitement, but it felt to Daniel curiously distant, like poor cell phone reception from some remote location. The harder he fucked the girl, the less he felt her. She dissolved beneath him, fading to transparency like a coy ghost. He fucked her, and there was Sigrid with the moving van. He fucked her, and there was Alma on the Ponte Vecchio. He fucked her, and fucked her, and there was the broad white wall, minus the Milo Kretz, and it was no longer the girl who was dissolving, but himself.

"What's the matter?" Melody said, surfacing.

"I don't . . . I don't know," he said.

"Can I do anything?" Her hand came up to help him.

Daniel poked her half-heartedly, half-revived. "This has never . . ." he said, feeling sick to his stomach. "I mean . . . before . . . It's . . ."

"It's okay," the girl cooed. "It happens."

"No, it doesn't," Daniel lamented. "Not to me."

"Relax," she said. She started to knead him in her small fist, and though Daniel appreciated the gesture, it was no go. Humiliated, he took her hand and kissed it. "I'm sorry," he said, rolling onto the bed beside her. He stroked her hip. "It's not you," he said. "You're perfect."

She turned away from him then, and Daniel nuzzled into her back. "I'm going to fall asleep for a little while," he mumbled, "and when I wake up, I'm going to fuck you properly."

"Mmmm," she said.

B ut in the middle of the night, he awoke to the sound of the front door clicking shut. He heard a brief blare of a radio, the soft thud of a car door. He got up to look out the window, peering down at red taillights as they moved along the sleek, wet street. The world was shadows and hulking shapes, darkness hung with rain.

Daniel was relieved the girl was gone, but stricken by his failure with her. Horrifying to think of himself, flopping like a sock puppet, his erection (so reliable, so ubiquitous) behaving with such low-down, slinking disloyalty. He stayed at the window a long time, looking out. The rain had either stopped or fallen off to fine mist. Something in the sky, a plane or a satellite, winked a slow trail across the clouded horizon, and on the window a spatter of raindrops, like a hundred tiny ejaculates, mocking him. Was a time he could go three, four times a night. With Alma. She had liked anal, it made her come the hardest. They had used those beads. Blindfolds. Handcuffs. Once— Daniel felt himself blushing—she had peed on him as he climaxed, the warm, wet rush making him come like a jackhammer. She would take fistfuls of her hair and rub them over his cock, stick her little finger up his asshole. *Oh! And now it appeared, the traitor! Too late, too late . . .*

Daniel couldn't help thinking that things could have turned out differently. *If only he had . . . If only he hadn't . . . If only . . .* That dreary middle-aged *ostinato*, in a requiem for lost youth and missed opportunity. Daniel was a sentimental man, with a tremendous capacity for feeling. The Irishman in him had always liked that about himself. But more and more these days, this tendency manifested as self-pity, the sentimentalist's lowest corkscrew contortion, and this he could not abide.

Timing, Daniel had come to believe, was the most important thing—in comedy as in music—a matter of knowing when to come in and when to get off. "A ham, an egg, and a biscuit walk into a bar, and the bartender says"—*beat, beat, beat*—"'Sorry, you'll have to go someplace else. We don't serve breakfast here.'" There was nothing worse for a man than an awareness of his own obsolescence, the ticking of his heart marking time, like the second hand of a clock—mechanism of duty now more than desire, of memory more than moment.

Daniel found himself shaking, gently at first, then harder, until his knees gave way and he sank to the floor. He had broken into a sweat but felt freezing cold. There was a sharp pain at his temple. His chest was pounding. It was bodily sensation, involuntary, peristaltic, overcoming him with violent physical force—a heart attack? a seizure?—but then it receded, like a tide, and Daniel felt the residue in his spirit, or whatever it was that was not-the-body. He got out his phone and wondered who to call, what to say. *I'm sick? I'm dying?* Who—*banish self-pity*—was left to care? It was not Daniel's finest moment, and he started to cry, to keen, bare and crumpled at the base of the bedroom window. This, too, felt like seizure, like violent physical force, his whole body juddering with each sob. He lay on the floor, as the crying subsided into hiccups, and for a little while after, and when he was done, he got dressed and went downstairs.

Which brings us to Daniel in the garage, on the driver's side of his 2005 Suburu station wagon, with the motor running. Three times he had settled himself, only to jump up with a start and rush back inside—once to grab his violin, the nineteenth-century Rocca, which he couldn't bear to leave behind; the second time to fetch a CD; the third, to retrieve the notes he had written: to Sigrid—*Don't blame yourself*—and to Roger—*All bookings and receipts are in a manila envelope. . . .*

Finally, he adjusted the seat and settled back. Alma Soon Ja Lee played Bach's second Suite in D Minor, and at the sprightly crossings in the first minuet, Daniel pictured her clearly, long hair swept to one side, falling loose above her bow arm, eyes closed, brow creased, mouth slightly open. It was severe, this look, almost tortured, and she shook in the vibrato like an autumn leaf.

Daniel would have done anything to hear Alma play live again. That was what he longed for most. No vapid Facebook messages, which were worse than silence. No computer-mediated mind games. He didn't have it in him to craft a response, couldn't even bear to read her message again—the pain was too great.

Losing Alma was the biggest regret of Daniel's life. He could see that now. It had been the pivotal point at which everything began to change for him, when everything in his life had turned to shit. How was it that Daniel had let it happen? He saw again the Kretz-less white wall in the living room, broad and blank, pristine with loss. The impulse to cry rose in him, but he did not give in to it. *Nothing easy*, he told himself. *Nothing cheap*. If he had not lived with dignity, he would at least try to die with some. Daniel swallowed hard. He would try to manage that, at least.

KORNELL TO THE RESCUE

He didn't mind the work, the long hours, the rush, the heat, scrubbing food scraps off plates, loading trays of dishes, the smell of fish guts and rancid oil. Point of fact, there wasn't much Kornell did mind, outside of being woken up too early in the morning or being treated like an idiot. He was big (6′3″, 295 pounds), Black (dark, with a high blue sheen), and not much of a talker (not shy at all, but quiet, watchful), and some people thought this added up to slowness, as though a big Black man who looked you in the eye without speaking had to be a fool—either that or a menace, which Kornell preferred, because at least then they left him alone.

He liked working at Yoshi's Sushi Bar because the Japanese, though they were as racist as anyone, admired hard work, and Yoshi had caught on early that Kornell was fast, efficient, and reliable, and beyond this, that he was naturally gifted in the kitchen. So, when things were slow, as they had been tonight, Yoshi showed Kornell how to prepare the rice, which he rinsed three times in cold water through a bamboo sieve, shaking it from side to side, like he was prospecting for gold, then soaked in spring water for thirty minutes before steaming it in an electric rice cooker. In a saucepan, Yoshi dissolved sugar and Japanese sea salt into rice vinegar over a low flame and then, turning the rice out into a large cypress *hangiri*, he mixed the rice quickly, with a bamboo paddle, finally covering it with a cloth to let it cool. The last few nights, he had let Kornell help with the side dishes, slicing *takuan* and plating eggplant, turnip, and lotus root pickles, which were served with every meal.

What Kornell loved about Japanese food, as much as the taste, was the way it looked on the table: the symmetry, the color, the economy, and the elegance—yellow daikon on a flat white plate, ginger dipping sauce in a pale green saucer, clear soup in a red and black lacquer bowl. He was attracted to the simplicity of the presentation, the emphasis on beauty and balance. *Wabi-sabi*, Yoshi had taught him, the aesthetics of austerity, of restraint.

"Ahh, Burke-san!" Yoshi liked to joke. "You are Black man, but you are Japanese, in here." He would try to tap Kornell on the chest, in the vicinity of his heart, but he was too short, and his hand would land nearer Kornell's midsection.

Kornell's heart swelled with pride. It was weird, but he did sort of feel Japanese, as though some of Kyoko's aura had transmitted itself through proximity. It was through her, of course, that he had first learned about Japanese culture, starting with manga and anime and extending to food. On their first date, they had watched Miyazaki's *Spirited Away*, and Kornell had been mesmerized.

"*Godzilla!*" Jiro, the boldest of the waiters, called to him now. Haru and Tadashi laughed uneasily, and Tadashi cuffed Jiro on the arm, but Kornell didn't mind. He took off his apron and tossed it in the laundry bin. "Ruawwwrrrrr!" he roared, striking a Godzilla pose, with clawlike hands. The waiters laughed and clapped.

Yoshi followed Kornell to the back door with a plastic bag. "For Kyoko-san," he said, bowing. Kornell smiled and bowed back. He knew it contained *tonkatsu*, *tamago* sushi, or *donburi* with chicken, all foods that Kyoko didn't eat. Despite Kornell's repeated attempts to explain that Kyoko didn't eat meat, eggs, fish, or even milk, Yoshi didn't seem to understand. She had been with him when he got the job, and Kornell was convinced that Yoshi only hired him because she was Japanese. "Ahh, Burke-san, she is your girlfriend?" Yoshi marveled, looking from Kornell to Kyoko and back to Kornell again. "Very good, very good," he'd said, though he'd shaken his head and giggled.

Kornell walked down the sidewalk carrying the bag of food. The rain felt good on his face, cooling the sweat from the steamy kitchen. There weren't many people out, and the ones who were crossed to the other side, though Kornell barely noticed. He couldn't wait to tell Kyoko that Yoshi was teaching him how to make sushi rice. And how to describe the thrill of tasting *umeboshi*—the bracing sourness mixed with the salty? He wondered if she was still working on the new song. He had gotten them a gig at Holey Shmoley's and he'd been hoping to have it ready by then. Last night she had gotten frustrated and had thrown her guitar onto the bed, almost on top of Sumo. Kornell had thought it sounded great. He hoped she was in a better mood tonight. He'd tell her about Yoshi and the boys, do his imitation of Godzilla.

More than anything, Kornell loved to make Kyoko laugh. He found himself doing the stupidest, most ridiculous things, like wearing her underwear on his head or opening his mouth when it was filled with food.

"Hey, Kyo, what do you call a headless man with no arms and no legs?"

Kyoko would smirk, not answering.

"Chester."

"Kyo, what do Eskimos get from sitting on the ice too long?"

Kyoko would roll her eyes.

"Polaroids."

Eventually, she would laugh despite herself, a low bleat of mirth, almost silent, located in the rhythmic hiccup of her shoulders. Her whole face would change, would soften, and Kornell would feel something in his chest clench, then open—knowing what a hard life she had had, how alone she had been, and how much she still struggled—and he would already be scheming how to make her laugh the next time.

Kornell opened the door to a silent house. He was surprised because there was always music playing, either Kyoko practicing or her iTunes, or sometimes the TV or radio blaring. He put the food Yoshi had given him on the kitchen counter. "Kyoko?" he called. "Kyo?" He glanced into the living room, which was a mess of amps and mike stands, stand-up drums, sound mixers, and thick, snaking electrical cords on yellow carpet. There were a few large pillows on the floor, two metal tables that held equipment, and a low stool for the drums. But no Kyoko.

Kornell checked the bedroom. Sumo looked back from the bed with wide green eyes. "Where is she, Su?" he asked. She was curled up next to Kyoko's guitar, her tail dusting its neck. It was a black Gibson SG that Kyoko had bought after her mother's death, along with the used Econoline and some recording equipment. It had been her one extravagance, Kornell knew, though Emi had left Kyoko a ton of money. "My consolation prize," she called it with sardonic emphasis. "Woohoo, my mother's dead! Check out my new guitar!"

Now Kornell heard a drip of water from the bathroom. "Kyoko?" Kornell opened the door. "Kyo?"

She was sitting in the half-filled tub, her arms around her knees, which were scraped and bloody. Her short hair was slicked back, and she was shivering. "Kyo? What's the matter?" Kornell said. He knelt by the tub and saw that she was crying. Kyoko hated to cry, and the only way Kornell could tell she was crying now was because her face was scrunched and contorted from trying so hard not to, each begrudged tear slipping stealthily into the bathwater. "What's the matter, baby? Tell me." Kyoko gulped and said some words Kornell couldn't decipher. She was shaking harder. There were goose bumps on her arms and legs, and her lips were purple.

"Let's get you dry." Kornell grabbed a towel, and Kyoko stood obediently, like a small child, while Kornell dried her off. He wrapped her up and carried her into the bedroom, but when he tried to get her in bed, she sprang up and started pacing.

"I fucked it up, Korny," she said. "I don't know why . . . Tonight I tried . . . I tried . . . God, I'm such a fuckup!"

"Whoa, slow down, baby!" Kornell said. "What? What did you fuck up?"

"I saw . . . I saw on Facebook—on Daniel's group page—Alma! Alma liked a picture! Why can't she just leave it alone?" Kyoko had been enraged at the banality: internet-Alma casually swooping in to internet-flirt, as if nothing in the past meant anything, a further defiling of her mother's memory. Then she had seen the most recent post, from someone named Melody—*Lost cell phone. Sorry. C u @ 109 Magruder @ 4:30*—and had taken it as a sign.

She told Kornell how she'd gone on a whim, wanting simply to see him, but had taken the knife at the last minute, just in case; how she'd stood outside the brownstone mansion and followed him to Rafferty's, making up her mind to kill him on the street there and then, never mind the girl; how she had botched it, tripping over her umbrella and falling; how she had watched him slip away, then stumbled home in the rain.

"But I heard his address! He said it to the driver!" she said. "We've got to make it count, Korny. We've got to do it now. Like we'd planned. Tonight!" Kyoko was pacing now, and something about her agitation made Sumo jump from the bed and leave the room.

Kornell watched as Kyoko squatted naked in front of the dresser, pulling things out from the bottom drawer. "I know they're here somewhere," she said. "Now, where are they?"

Crouched down on her heels, she was tiny, like one of her mom's netsuke on the mantel, the wooden frog or porcelain rabbit. Kornell imagined he could hold her in one palm. He loved her so much, this strange, sad girl with the murderous intention, and though he knew that her plans were crazy, he also knew that he would do anything to help her.

In college, Kornell had made a short film, a repeating loop of Kyoko walking naked out of a pond. It was the visual equivalent of a stutter—first her head, neck, and shoulders, then her breasts, torso, and legs—rising up from the water in continuous iteration. At a little over a minute long, it had won second prize in a college-wide arts contest, and it had captured something about Kyoko that Kornell could never express in words.

By coincidence, they both thought of it now: Kyoko distorting it, playing it backward, seeing herself hitting and re-hitting the sidewalk in slapstick perpetuity, her foot tangled in wayward umbrella spokes, her body in spastic motion, flailing, stumbling, falling, getting up only to fall again; while Kornell saw her emerging, naiad from a river, water streaming off her naked body, golden and glorious, rising, rising.

Alma, in Cyberspace

Rickey had insisted Alma get on the internet, had forced her to join Facebook. "Hello! It's the twenty-first century!" he had said when she demurred.

"I'm not sure that's a recommendation," she had replied, but had allowed him to fill out a Facebook profile for her.

"'Interested in . . . ?' *Men*," Rickey said, typing.

"Not anymore," Alma said.

Rickey ignored her. "'Relationship status?' *Single*."

"Wait, why is that necessary?"

"'Religion . . . ?'"

"I don't see why that information needs to be . . ."

Rickey kept typing. "'*Badass Buddhist*,'" he read. "You can change it later."

Alma professed disinterest, but she soon realized what an incredible resource the internet could be for shut-ins, agoraphobics, invalids, and the socially averse (i.e., for her). She started paying her bills online—very convenient. She ordered a couple of books on Amazon, began reading the *New York Times* website, got a subscription to Netflix, started browsing *Slate*, *Salon*, and *The Huffington Post*. She would StumbleUpon, YouTube, and eBay; play word games with strangers, FarmVille, and Bejeweled Blitz.

For a long time, Rickey was her only friend on Facebook, but people soon came out of the woodwork—people she'd gone to conservatory with, people who remembered her from music festivals, fans who wondered what had happened to her, a few childhood acquaintances, friends of friends. She never posted anything, never "liked" or commented, but she found herself lurking more and more each day, following threads of comments from strangers about babies, cats, tomato plants, and the Supreme Court. She viewed photographs of other people's vacations, gap-toothed grandchildren, plates of wild mushroom risotto, dogs in sunglasses (doggles!), sunsets over the Grand Canyon; watched videos people posted of baby pandas with hiccups or diapered toddlers lip-synching Elvis; read articles supporting gay marriage, gun legislation, and health-care reform. *"Like" this and save the rain forest. Sign this petition. Give to this cause.*

All the while, Alma would feel superior to these people, the ones who earnestly revealed themselves, the ones whose status updates included heartache, cancer, job loss, and death. How pathetic, how sad, how tragic and boring. Alma, sitting at her desk with a cold cup of tea, still in her pajamas and bathrobe at two in the afternoon, clicking on links, following threads, disappearing down the rabbit holes of other people's lives, cast judgment on all that passed before her until, from weakness and fatigue, she would put her head down on the cool wooden edge of the desk and acknowledge that she was the stupidest, saddest, most pathetic of all—because this was life, all of it, the stupid and weird and precious, and because she was apart from it, doubly removed; not even a spectator, but a tracker of spoor, a voyeur of aftermath, a specter.

Now, at a little after two a.m., on the night her symptoms returned, Alma found Daniel's Facebook page. Not his, personally, but for Thanatos, his string quartet. They played for the dying and the newly dead, and Alma thought how sad it was that Daniel should have ended up this way—a rent-for-hire fiddler for affluent terminal cases. Nero for a perpetually burning Rome.

People had left comments, touching testimonials. *"Thanks for easing Mom's pain at the end. You guys were great. I can't think of a more beautiful way for her to have gone." "My father-in-law always loved that Haydn piece. How fitting that it was the last thing he heard."* There were nineteen likes, a few links to videos. And a photo. Daniel, a balding violist named Roger Ellingworth, an unhappy-looking female cellist named Deirdre Burns, and a young Asian second violinist named Huiliang Chiu, whom, Alma was sure, Daniel was screwing. Something in the way she leaned toward him slightly, in her austere black dress, and the way he leaned slightly away, in an exaggerated gesture of refutation and false dignity, the way that he had seemed to lean away from Emi that summer in Florence.

Alma begrudged Daniel his good looks, his apparent health and libido, the way he seemed essentially unchanged despite the inevitable thickening at the waist—when there was nothing about Alma that had stayed the same. She clicked off his page, annoyed with herself for being close to tears. She clicked back on, enlarged the photo to try to glean more information: Daniel's violin (the nineteenth-century Rocca that he had called Rocky), held at a jaunty angle, the corresponding jauntiness of the Asian violinist; the violist, bespectacled and put-upon; the doughy disapproval of the cellist.

She googled Daniel and received a lot of additional information.

He was still on the faculty at the conservatory in Baltimore; he had moved there shortly after Florence. There were press releases about recitals and master classes. He had taught at Aspen, Yellow Barn, and Tanglewood. Several years ago, he had been at Verbier. Two years ago, he had been invited to Beijing. There were Google images of him with groups of students, smiling at banquet tables, hands folded, in a line of dignitaries. Alma had heard about his marriage to a Swedish art dealer. She had kidded him about being an Asian fetishist, but she hadn't thought he was one—until, suddenly, he was. Turns out Alma had been a mere appetizer, the first of a veritable smorgasbord of Asian delights. But when she had heard about his Viking bride, it had felt like repudiation. And here was a blurry photograph of them to-gether: a tall blonde with upswept hair, solid, patrician, her thin mouth downturned, Daniel beside her, his hand on her shoulder.

And this, unexpectedly, from an Italian newspaper: a photo of herself with Daniel and the pianist Archie, onstage at the Maggio. Alma had winced, as though the image had struck her in the face. Their hands were joined, Alma in the middle, in a gown that she remembered as blue, but that appeared in the photograph as black. She was beaming at the audience. Archie's head was lowered—he hated curtain calls, could never get off the stage fast enough—but Daniel was looking at Alma, gesturing with his free hand toward an unseen destination, and on his face, it could not be mistaken, was a look of naked adoration.

When Alma looked at the clock again, it was close to four. It had been nearly nine hours since she had cooked dinner for Rickey, but it felt like years. Years since she had woken up in spasms, since she had sat in the living room with Franny dead in her arms. The last day and long night had been a mocking encapsulation of Alma's last twelve years: from health to illness, better treatments, worsening symptoms; hope to despair, to hope, and back again. She was furious with herself for having gone to Dr. Woo, furious for having allowed herself to believe, for one moment, that he could affect some mysterious Asian juju cure. The anger, she knew, was mainly pride's injury, masking, as anger always masked, something truer and more tender.

Alma felt a deeper sense of exhaustion than she had ever known. It was in her bones, like a cancer, and she did not think she had the strength to carry the weight of it one more day. She took off her reading glasses and put her head down on the desk. Strange how it could come down to this: forty-nine years old, tired, sick, stalking an ex-lover in the middle of the night, finally admitting to yourself that you did not want to go on. Alma tested this out. *I don't want to go on.* She said it out loud. It didn't sound melodramatic or hysterical, or like something hypothetical that you might say just to get a reaction. To the contrary, it felt neutral, clear, like the answer to a math problem she had been working on. The one barb of pain was when she thought about Rickey. *Please don't hate me. It all came back tonight and I just couldn't. I hope you know how much you meant to me. I couldn't have gotten this far without you. Love, A.*

She went back to the Thanatos page and stared at the photo of a middle-aged Daniel, a Daniel she had never known, conveyed from her memory of him at thirty, to this stranger at fifty, as though two decades had gone by in a span of minutes. She couldn't say why, but she clicked Like under the photo. Then she clicked Message and began to type.

RICKEY HAS A PREMONITION

R U up?" he texted from work. He had twenty-nine new emails, twenty-two of them from Cecily, the new art director, who was, Rickey was discovering, a micromanager. She didn't like the design for the Head Rush logo and had to tell him so—twenty-two times. Never in a million years could Rickey have imagined himself working for a surfboard company—Christ, he could barely swim!—but here he was, eight years down the line, having absconded to Southern California from the Upper Peninsula of Michigan. "That's what you get for leaving winters, *dude*," his sister in Marquette had admonished him. "It makes me feel butch," he had told her. "And you can keep your winters!"

Rickey fiddled with his X-Acto knife, scraping the tip against his thumbnail. There was very little mock-up work anymore, but he liked to keep the tools around for nostalgia's sake. He glanced at his phone and sighed. He had recently taught Alma how to text so they could communicate throughout the day. He had even taught her a few standard acronyms—OMG, IMHO, LOL, LMAO—and they had made up some of their own. SIH (Spider in House)—because Alma was an arachnophobe and Rickey had to come squash them for her; INADB (I Need a Drink Badly)—one of Rickey's most frequent messages, for when he was in an interminable meeting or a coworker was being a dick; KOP (Korean on Parade)—so Rickey would know that Alma was taking her daily walk on the beach; BBB (Blah, Blah, Blah)—when either of them was feeling bored or self-pitying. "IJSMITH," Alma had proposed, as they had laughed, coming up with ever more ridiculous examples. "I Just Shot Myself in the Head." She had usually texted him a few times by now.

Rickey spent the morning at the computer, tweaking Head Rush, per Cecily's suggestions, though he thought she was dead wrong and the whole thing looked too busy, slightly hysterical, with the dude in the middle and the waves coming out of his hair. In a down moment, he texted Alma again. "Need anything?"

"Hey, Rickey!" Melissa popped her head up from the other side of their divider. "Want to go to lunch?"

Rickey stared morosely at the screen. He shook his head. "How the hell did I get here?" he said.

Melissa gave him a sympathetic look. She was a copywriter at Surf's Up and Rickey's best friend at work. "I know, baby," she said. "Let's go get In-N-Out."

Rickey looked down at his phone. He raised one finger toward Melissa, flipped the top, and pressed 2—only his sister was ahead of her now that Chas was out of the picture. He listened to the phone ring and imagined the "March of the Toreadors," from Bizet's *Carmen*, playing in Alma's apartment. She had accused him of being stubborn as a bull, so he had made it her ringtone as a joke. The phone rang and rang. "Hello, you've reached Alma . . ." Rickey flipped the phone shut. "She's not answering," he said. He felt a weight in his chest, a weird breathlessness, as though he'd just run a great distance.

"Alma?" Melissa said.

"Yeah," he said, shutting down his computer, slipping his phone into his pocket. "She's probably fine. I'm just going to run home and check."

"Mother Rickey," said Melissa, sounding a little sour. He shrugged in apology and grabbed his keys.

Driving over, Rickey tried Alma again, and again it went to voice mail. "Hey, A., it's me," he said. "Coming home to feed Gustav. Up for a quick lunch? I've got leftover *japchae*. Oh, that's right, you sent me home with it, didn't you? So you probably know that already . . . Anyway, I'll stop by in a minute. Okay, bye." He knew that Alma would find it suspicious that he'd come home in the middle of the day just to feed Gustav, who grazed all day from an endless mound of kibble, but off the top of his head, he couldn't think of a better excuse.

Rickey tried his best to conceal it from Alma, but he was really worried about her. During the three years he had known her, she had suffered longer and deeper bouts of depression that had corresponded with more frequent and severe symptoms relating to the MS. A few months ago she had stopped doing all the things she loved the most— playing the cello (she said she couldn't anymore, but Rickey was doubtful), listening to music, going out to eat. Most days, she wouldn't even change out of the yoga clothes she wore as pajamas—this from a woman who used to put on makeup to walk on the beach! More and more, he had had to push her to get out of the apartment.

And now, suddenly, this "intermission," which Rickey should have been thrilled by. He had, in fact, been thrilled at first. After all, it had been his idea for Alma to go to Dr. Woo in the first place. But there was something about the way she'd been acting lately, rushing around, buying things, cooking elaborate meals. What had she said last night—about feeling souped-up? He recalled the way she'd cut the scallions, the rat-a-tat machine-gun sound, the blur of her hand on the knife. "Santé," she had said, clinking her glass against his, the glint in her eye like defiance.

* * *

Rickey used his spare key after buzzing twice and getting no answer. "A.?" he called out. "Wasssabi, girl?" It cracked her up when he used surfer lingo. "Pula Kahula, you asleep?"

The apartment was dark, but the stereo lights were on, and Franny, out of its case for the first time in weeks, lay on its side on the floor. Rickey, who knew Alma to be fastidious about her cello, felt a weird sense of déjà vu, not of having lived this moment before, exactly, but of having watched himself live through it. He walked around to the front of the white leather couch and there she was, curled sideways on the carpet with her hair across her face. Above her on the coffee table was a blue bowl with some pills in it and four empty water glasses. A fifth glass was half-empty. Half-full, Rickey corrected himself, and was stricken by the humor, even as he was certain Alma would have found it funny.

He moved the coffee table so he could get in close to her, and his sense of detachment vanished. "Alma! Wake up!" He shook her by the shoulder. "Oh, God! A., what have you done?" He called 911 while he knelt beside her, pushing the hair off her face. Her skin was waxen, blue-tinged; there was white crusty drool at the corner of her mouth. He checked her pulse at the side of her neck. Mercifully, there was one, though it felt slow. He tried to count, but he couldn't stay with it. The emergency dispatcher instructed him to be sure the paramedics could get into the building. He called Mimi, who lived on the other side of him. He didn't tell her about the pills, just that Alma was unconscious.

"Oh, dear," Mimi said. "Is she going to be okay?"

"How the hell should I know?" Rickey snapped, and immediately regretted it. Mimi was a retired schoolteacher and a dear old lady, but . . . What did Alma call her? *Babo.* A dummy.

"Sorry, Mimi," he said. "Just go wait in the lobby, okay? Thanks."

He checked Alma's breathing again. She made an abrupt noise, a kind of half snort. Rickey leaned in, but the noise stopped as abruptly. "Alma, you shit," he said. His hands began to tremble. He lay down on the carpet beside her. "You better not fucking die," he said, balling his hands into fists. He wanted to throttle her, to smack her. He was trying not to cry. *Don't be gay!* he exhorted himself. Another joke Alma would appreciate. He moved in closer, breathing in her innate essence, her sweet Alma scent, but with a sourness underneath like yeast. Her hair got in his face, dark, wiry strands; he took some between his teeth and chewed.

Old *CSI* episodes came back to him, scenes from *Law & Order,* and other crime shows. Bodies lying open-eyed, staring at nothing, mouths forever closed, unable to give their testimony. Janet Leigh at the end of the shower scene in *Psycho.* Why did everything remind him of a movie or a television show? God, how pathetic was he? But he knew that Alma would have understood.

Rickey was crying now. He couldn't stop himself. He had lost lovers; he had had friends who committed suicide, died of an overdose, of alcohol, and each time he had felt the guilt of not having been able to save them. With Alma, it had been different. They had saved each other every day. When Chas had broken up with him, Rickey had raged and cried and eaten all of Alma's Oreos, and she had just sat and listened. She hadn't tried to make him feel better by saying catty things about Chas or offering philosophical perspectives on heartache. She had just listened. When Alma had tripped and smashed a Crock-Pot of Italian wedding soup all over the kitchen floor, it was Rickey who had cleaned up the mess, picking the shards of orange ceramic out of the meatballs and orzo and then ordering a pizza. When Alma woke up in the middle of the night and couldn't swallow or see out of one eye, it was Rickey who drove her to the ER, leafing sleepily through old *People* magazines until it was time to pick up the prescriptions and drive her home.

Rickey put his arm around Alma now, gripped her at the wrist. He loved her so much, though he had come upon it sideways— not from sex, or fear, or some misguided sense of loyalty, but out of devotion—loneliness, yes, but also true friendship, which he'd thought himself incapable of, though it seemed now that he might be—much good it did him, and perhaps too late.

limbo

KYOKO AND KORNELL
GO BACK TO PLAN A

By the time they arrived at the top of the hill, headlights off, on the curb beside Daniel Karmody's house, Kyoko had invented a thousand scenarios for how it might go down. She imagined Kornell dragging him from bed, a naked Daniel flailing to keep his hands over his genitals, the girl having to be hit over the head to keep from screaming. Or Daniel would be sleeping, and Kornell would just pick him up and sling him over his shoulder like a sack of potatoes. Or he'd be surprised while pissing and come peacefully (pissfully?), in bare feet and cotton pajamas, his gaze on the floor. She even allowed herself to imagine the plan gone awry—Daniel on the phone with 911, Kornell flung to the wall, rendered unconscious, Kyoko captured in a humiliating fashion.

But she was not prepared for what they did find. After just a few minutes, a light went on in the garage and they could see Daniel moving around inside. He disappeared for a few minutes and then reemerged, crossing close to the window in back of the car. He did this a couple of times, and Kyoko thought he was preparing for a trip.

"What should I do if he starts to drive away?" Kornell asked, adjusting his ski mask.

"Follow him," Kyoko said, though in truth she wasn't sure. "What's he doing now?" The light in the garage had gone off finally, but the garage door didn't open and Daniel's car didn't come out. They waited for what seemed a long time. Kyoko counted three minutes—*180 Mississippi.*

They crept the van closer, parked it in front of the house, and got out. Kyoko held the clothesline, gag, and blindfold, Kornell, the knife and Maglite. They were both wearing all black, with matching knit ski masks that Kyoko had found at Goodwill. When they got up to the garage window, they could see wisps of smoke milling their way up from the exhaust pipe. There was music coming from inside the green station wagon, a deep murmuring of strings, and there was Daniel in the driver's seat, bawling like a baby.

"Shit," said Kornell, his tone reverential. "Dude's trying to off himself!" He pulled off his ski mask and looked at Kyoko. "We don't have to do a thing."

"Put that back on," Kyoko hissed. "We have to get him out of there."

"But, baby," Kornell said, "there's no point."

"There's no way. He can't . . ." Kyoko's teeth were chattering. She felt a swooning heat. "He can't just do it *himself*! Not after what he did. Not without being held accountable."

"But—"

"I swear to God, Korny," Kyoko said. "You said you would help me. You said you had my back!"

Kornell stared at her, his eyes wide. It was a defining moment, he knew. He could end this now or he could commit completely, not to Kyoko, to whom he was already committed, but to her insanity, which until tonight had felt entirely abstract to him, or if not abstract, then internalized, an insanity of thought and not of action. Kyoko was looking at him, her eyes visible only by their whites, floating in black knit, her mouth a small pink O. There was something monstrous in her sincerity, her blank-faced plea. He put his mask back on. "Okay, Kyo," he said. "I got this." He smashed the Maglite into the side-door window of the garage and unlocked the door, then they were in. He grabbed a groggy Daniel out of the car, Kyoko coming up behind him and cutting the engine. Kyoko handed Kornell the clothesline and tied the blindfold while Kornell bound Daniel's wrists and ankles. A gag hardly seemed necessary, but Kyoko wrapped a roll of duct tape around his mouth twice and Kornell cut it with Yoshi's knife.

Having settled in for his grand exit, Daniel had a hard time taking in what was happening. He wondered if death could possibly be this literal: a large figure in black coming to take you away. Alma's playing lingered in his head, the second Bach prelude, fiercely played. He was oddly cooperative as his arms and legs were bound, mustered only a feeble blub-blub of protest before his mouth was sealed, and had fallen unconscious by the time he was carried down the drive, fireman's style, and thrown into the back of a van.

DANIEL IN CAPTIVITY

"Who are you?" Daniel demands, sounding to himself like a character in a melodrama. "What do you want?"

The hulking figure in the balaclava—Daniel first thinks "baklava," before recalling that "balaclava" is the headgear and "baklava," the pastry—just points to a thin wall of paneling, behind which Daniel will eventually discover a toilet, a narrow shower, and a sink.

"Listen, I don't have any money. I'm a musician, for Christ's sake! Why have I been brought here?"

The black-clad figure points to a thin mattress on the floor.

"How long—?"

His guard turns and goes back up the stairs, and Daniel is left alone.

———

A little while later, Daniel is surprised to wake up. Surprised because he hadn't realized he was asleep. Surprised because he was under the impression that he was already dead. Instead, he finds himself sunk deep in a cracked Naugahyde recliner in a dank, cluttered room. His head throbs dully. He tries to pay attention, but despite his best efforts, he keeps losing his train of thought, which has become less a train than a single car, a caboose with no precedent—one of those handcars that requires two people to seesaw it into motion, when now there is only one.

The strange events of the last few hours register for Daniel like elements of a dream, fragments of image and sensation. The best Daniel can tell, he has been kidnapped by a silent behemoth and—though she has disappeared—a tiny, low-voiced sylph. The former, with his mute gestures and hunched posture, reminds Daniel of the Ghost of Christmas Past. Something about that faceless, shrouded figure had deeply frightened Daniel as a child, the way it floated in the night, pointing to Scrooge's grave with an insistent white-bone forefinger. Daniel pictures the cartoon version: Mr. Magoo, trembling on his knees before the Ghost. "Of all the specters I have seen, I fear you most!" he exclaims. Daniel struggles to get his thoughts back on track.

There he'd been, the motor running on the Subaru, Alma on the CD player—reclining on the seat with his eyes closed, thinking that he could smell the carbon monoxide, though he knew carbon monoxide to be odorless; thinking it smelled like sweat and upholstery, wondering who would find him now that Sigrid had moved out, wondering how she would feel when she heard the news, whether she would weep or sigh or simply shake her head in pity, wondering what death was really like and if there was a special circle in hell for impotent, middle-aged philanderers with an impulse to self-slaughter;

thinking of the Woody Allen joke "It's not that I'm afraid to die. I just don't want to be there when it happens," wondering if this would be his last thought, a joke, and someone else's, someone funnier, more famous, who had ended up having an affair with the adopted Korean daughter of his girlfriend, wondering if it was true that the heart wanted what the heart wanted or if, as his father had suggested, it was just that the dick wanted what the dick wanted, which had been Daniel's sober experience—when, all of a sudden, there had been a smashing of glass and muffled voices, then a huge gloved hand had reached in and dragged him out of his car. He'd been gagged, blindfolded, tied up, and thrown into a van, where he had landed, belly-first, against some rolled-up padding, the kind they used to move furniture.

He'd struggled to sit up, feeling around with his bound hands. There had been a tangle of cords and some heavy piece of equipment that kept sliding around in the downturns. Something metal had crashed to the floor by his head, scaring the hell out of him. A cymbal? Groggily, he had tried to process this. Musicians? He had been abducted by a rival string quartet. The Emerson or the Kronos. But drums? A rock band then. Daniel had tried to think of the name of a single contemporary rock band. Nirvana? Green Day? It had been dark inside the van and he'd been blindfolded, but Daniel had perceived light sweeping across his face at regular intervals, and the vehicle had stopped a lot. He'd made a mental note: city driving.

When he was a boy, Daniel had loved the Encyclopedia Brown mysteries with their brisk, boyish narratives and sensible solutions. The broken fish tank, the melted icicle. He had tried to pay attention to clues. Was that a fire engine? Were they on the highway now? The carbon monoxide, or maybe the port, had left him woozy. He had tried to take stock. He had been kidnapped. Which meant his life meant something to someone. Daniel had felt a small swell of unreasonable pride. But why? And to whom? Daniel wasn't rich, he wasn't political, he wasn't involved in controversial activity (though there *had* been that collaboration with an Israeli orchestra two years ago). He was a classical musician, which was tantamount to being irrelevant to everyone (a fact that had driven him to suicide in the first place), and his sense of pride quickly turned to depression.

The fact that Daniel was now afraid for his life, when only a few hours earlier he had fervently wished to die, was an irony not entirely lost on him, though it was somewhat misplaced. For, of course, there was a world of difference between wanting to die and wanting to be killed—between sitting in an idling car listening to your ex-lover play Bach and being dumped into the back of a van by masked intruders. It was the difference between judging oneself and being judged by others: a matter of sincerity, of degree, and of self-governance.

The ride had seemed to smooth out after a while, and there had been no more stops and starts. Definitely the highway. But in which direction? And how long had they been driving? Fifteen minutes? Half an hour? Daniel had strained toward voices in the front of the van, but all he had been able to make out was the sluicing of tires—it had still been raining—and the rattling of metal on metal. He had struggled to stay awake, twitching and sinking, from wakefulness to sleep and back again, but the steady vibration of the van had lulled him into a rough slumber.

Rickey During Visiting Hours

Rickey visits Alma every evening. He brings her small presents: two rose-scented candles, a bottle of Kiehl's lotion, a terrarium of moss and ferns, and lots of flowers—orange poppies, bearded irises, birds-of-paradise and a pale pink orchid. He pulls a chair up to her bed, holds her hand, and talks nonsense to her, whatever comes out of his mouth.

"That young nurse, the one with the mole on her nose? I think her boyfriend is that horrible janitor—the one who yelled at me for using the bathroom he'd just cleaned? You remember! I saw them together just now in the cafeteria downstairs. I think she's Russian or maybe from Ukraine. She could do much better, don't you think? He looks like a perp, like Ratso Rizzo with a mop. You know. That greased-back hair and his face all shiny? Oh, I forget, you have no idea what I'm talking about, do you? *Midnight Cowboy*, sweetie, one of the iconic movies of the seventies. Or was it the sixties? We should watch it together sometime. You'd love it! Anyway, do you think I should warn her? Is her name Mesha or Masha? I can't remember. Because she's really sweet, she helped me out the other day when I didn't have any change for the Coke machine, and she's gentle with you, and I really like her voice. Sort of soft and breathy. You know who she reminds me of? I just thought of it! Juliette Binoche in *The English Patient*! Yes! That's it! And she was a nurse, too, come to think of it. The way she gave Ralph Fiennes morphine injections . . . And when he pushes all the ampoules toward her! God! That scene always kills me. You have to watch it with me, A. And if you aren't bawling like a baby by the end, then your little yellow heart is made of stone. You hear me? Hard. Cold. Korean. Stone."

Sometimes there are other visitors, the wild-haired conductor from Los Angeles, Kristophe, who had once been Alma's lover; a few fellow musicians, mostly from the West Coast, and one from as far away as Vancouver. They never stay long. Rickey makes sure of it. As far as he is concerned, they had all turned their backs on Alma when she had gotten sick, and he is not going to let them so easily assuage their guilt by stopping by with a box of fancy chocolates and a down-turned mouth full of pity.

"She's in a coma," he says when Kristophe arrives with Godiva chocolate. "She doesn't need candy."

The man raises an eyebrow at Rickey. "And who are you, may I ask?" he says in an insolent German accent.

"Oh, didn't Alma tell you? I'm her husband, Rickey Marchand. We got married over a year ago. You didn't get an invitation?" Rickey ushers him toward the door. "I'll be sure to tell her you looked in."

"I can't believe you fucked him, A.," Rickey says, after Kristophe leaves. "More than once, anyway." He rubs Kiehl's cream on Alma's hands and forearms up to her IV tubes. "I could have told you the guy was a rice king the minute I laid eyes on him. Saved you a lot of trouble." He bends low to Alma's face, feels the warmth of her breath from around her NG tube, and kisses her, lightly, on the cheek.

ALMA AND THE MARCH
OF THE RICE KINGS

And what of Alma? Where is she? Far away and close at hand. From deep inside a well she hears the words, *rice king*. The syllables swing and sway inside her head—*ri-i-i-ssss kk-iii-ngggg*—a bit of nonsense sound, loopy and reptilian. She is tethered to her body, but her mind is floating free, or if not free, then bobbing like a balloon against the upper limits of the ceiling, like the balloons that really do bob on her ceiling—shiny Mylar with Get Well messages in primary colors, attached to tangles of curling ribbon tied to the base of her bed. She is blind to them, as she is to all her sensible surroundings, but she is not altogether blind, for on the smooth, black wall of her coma-slowed mind, there has begun a strange tally.

Many of the names she's forgotten, but the names are not important. Nor are the faces, though she remembers some of these. Too close, too loud, booze-flushed, hot-breathed, brow-cocked, bloodshot—five-o'clock shadows lengthening, like blue ink spilled across blank pages. What Alma does not forget, what remains fiercely emblazoned across her hippocampus like graffiti on a subway train, are their strategies, a taxonomy of seduction ploys, of opening gambits. "Hey, baby, baby!" "Hey, hot mama!" All of them—every one—curiously confident, unabashed, proclaiming their intentions as though they were calling out the winning lottery numbers for the jackpot of her heart.

Johnny Appleby had been the first. Tall, with listless blond hair and a fuzz of mustache. Senior to her freshman. Clarinet to her cello. In a leather vest, with fedora and suspenders, he fancied himself a dandy and was, or what passed for one in regional youth orchestra. Backstage during a rehearsal of Bizet's *Carmen* Suite, he had leaned into her, his clarinetist's embouchure grazing her ear, tickling the tiny hairs of its inner channel. "Oriental girls are so sexy," he had whispered, and walked away, never to utter another word to her again.

But the damage had been done. Johnny Appleby had sown his seed, impregnating her with his five-word pronouncement of immutable destiny. "Oriental girls are so sexy." Blush of pleasure at the implication. She, Alma Soon Ja Lee, flat-chested, twig-legged, scale-practicing daughter of greengrocers, was Oriental (like a rug!) and therefore she was . . . sexy? Was it true that all Asian girls—here Alma took a quick survey: there was cross-eyed Charlotte Koh, Audrey Park with her underbite, Tina Chun, whose ears stuck out like the handles on a sugar bowl—surely not all Oriental girls were sexy? She thought of her mother—not a girl, but once was—her uniform of fuchsia sweatpants and matching quilted jacket, and Mrs. Kim, whom her father called Pig Lady, surveying the turnip kimchi through half-moon glasses while slack necklaces of flesh cascaded to her bosom.

And even if it were true, what solace was there in being part of a throng, a teeming corridor of button-nosed, black-haired girls with sallow skin and narrow hips? If they were all sexy, then they were all the same. And if they were all the same, then in what sense was she, Alma Soon Ja Lee, ninth-grade cello prodigy, a distinct and disparate entity worthy of individual attention?

And yet. The possibility had emerged out of nowhere, from the hot clarinetist's breath of a boy she had barely noticed, the possibility of sexy, and who cared, really, where it had come from? Alma, at thirteen, was ready to hear the news. Circumscribed by freakish musical talents, presided over by a coterie of grimly dedicated adults, jam-packed with lessons, recitals, and competitions, Alma's life had been carefully scaffolded in discipline and obedience, and only recently had the stirrings of adolescence intimated to her that this whole elaborate construction, this edifice-life, might not be all there was.

Johnny Appleby had been a messenger from that other, as yet unknown life, a bearer of tidings from her future self. "Oriental girls are so sexy," he had whispered to her in a conspiratorial aside, casually, but with a whiff of portent that kept on whispering, kept on conspiring, until it became a kind of scaffold of its own, the spring platform from which to launch herself into a brash and glamorous future.

Here, from within her coma, Alma ruefully congratulates herself from the other side of that life—reaches back, with tenderness and knowing mockery, to chuck her younger self under the chin. She could offer advice—*Beware what you wish for, sister*—or solace—*You'll have fun!*—but in the end, all she can do is nod her head to acknowledge the moment—retrospectively recognized and reinforced by repetition—when the promise of allure had first been offered, at the cost of self-erasure, and the twisted roots of racism had become so deeply embedded in desire that she could not dig them out, could not, in truth, distinguish them from the healthy roots.

And so Johnny Appleby had yielded to Brian Kolota, who told her he liked her "Chinky" eyes; followed by Mr. Higginbottham, briefly her cello teacher, who kept a photo of the famous Chung sisters in a frame on top of his desk; succeeded by Arvin Bergmann, the dashing guest cellist at music camp, who, under the guise of adjusting Alma's fingering position, bit her, hard, on the shoulder, only to apologize later by explaining that his Taiwanese girlfriend had recently broken up with him; quickly followed by Eddy "Black Belt" Grossman, bassist and student of tae kwon do, who tried to impress Alma with his handful of Korean phrases, including *sarang hae*, which meant "I love you," which he murmured in her vicinity for the duration of that summer, winking suggestively and twirling his large instrument.

And because being in a coma means having a lot of free time on your hands, and the vagaries of the human brain are such that you never know what will pop into your head at any given moment, Alma finds herself surveying the fetishists she has known over the years. *Ri-i-i-sssss kkk-iii-nggggs*, rice chasers, Asiaphiles, victims of that mysterious incurable disease known as Yellow Fever. Every Asian woman knows the generic type, but Alma, classical musician, world traveler, and unconscious taxonomist, breaks them down into three subcategories:

1) The cultural ambassador. Recognized by a pedantic tendency and messianic glint. Accessories may include: Chinese character tattoo—usually "love," "honor," "courage," or something meaningless copied incorrectly from a fortune cookie; Buddha beads or Korean War bomber jacket; or, in the home, joss sticks and an electric rice cooker. Writing of haiku optional. One cultural ambassador, a big-money symphony donor, had been eager to show Alma his chopstick collection; another, the bonsai trees he'd brought back from

Japan. The cultural ambassador's shtick went something like this: "I deeply respect and honor your people and your culture. *Ni hao.* I could tell you were Thai right away. Yeah, I can always tell. Oh, you're Korean, that was my next guess. I took a course in Mandarin Chinese, I have a black belt in karate, I love Vietnamese food, I think Kurosawa is the Asian Spielberg, I do yoga, I'm thinking of becoming a Buddhist. Did you know the first geisha were actually men? You have such pretty hair. Your skin is so smooth. Can I touch it? Can I kiss you?"

In Alma's opinion, there was something almost endearing about the cultural ambassador. In his eagerness to prove himself a connoisseur of all things Asian, Alma read a paucity of confidence, saw the great white void against which was projected this false authority. It was a ransacked specialness he was after, distinction by proxy, and the longing for it moved Alma, even as it annoyed her.

2) The carnal colonialist. This subcategory was far worse in Alma's opinion. Worldly, where the cultural ambassador was naive, charismatic rather than boorish, insinuating as a serpent rather than bumbling like a bear, the carnal colonialist was, in Alma's experience, altogether more sinister. Once, at a party, a somewhat famous violinist had approached Alma. She had been wearing an evening gown with a low back, and he had laid a chilly hand on her bare flesh, breathed scotch into her neck, and asked if she might please join him in the men's room in five minutes. "You're ravishing," he had exclaimed. "I can't help myself!" When Alma had turned him down, laughing, really, because it was so absurd, the somewhat famous violinist had shrugged. "My dear, I'm devastated," he had said, his eye already roving to Selene Kawanishi.

The carnal colonialist lived in a fantasy world of triple X–rated movies—*Oriental Sex Kittens, Wild Chinese Babysitters, Hong Kong*

King Dong. They collected erotic Asian art, woodblock prints of the Floating World, obscene netsuke of copulating couples; were aficionados of pink films, Japanese soft-core porn. In her younger days, Alma had succumbed to a few men of this type, and she knew from personal experience that they wore kimonos instead of robes, favored doggie-style, and kept ornate sex gear in the bedroom. "Speak dirty to me in Korean, baby! Oh yeah! *Hanguk saram choayo!*"

3) The rational revolutionary. Unlike other rice kings, who were almost exclusively white, rational revolutionaries were Black, or Latino, or either kind of Indian, and their modes of seduction were politically formulated. Alma had encountered many rational revolutionaries on tour in South America, in parts of Africa, and in the Caribbean. They were trim, dark men with narrow mustaches; or puffed-out, with pomaded hair; in crisp guayaberas with khaki pants or natty three-piece suits; encountered on terraces overlooking sunsets on water or at buffet tables in hotel ballrooms. "My dear, you have simply not lived until you have had an Egyptian/Ghanaian/Senegalese/Dominican lover!" Said with hands a certain distance apart, as though denoting the proverbial fish that got away. "You don't . . ."—eyes suddenly piercing with indictment—"have anything against men of my race, do you?"

A cultural attaché with the Nigerian embassy had grown angry with Alma when she'd declined the offer of his company for the night. "Do you know what you are, Miss Lee?" he had told her. "I regret to say this, but you are what they call a banana: yellow on the outside, white on the inside. Yes, I am certain this must be the case."

Rubbing their palms together, smiling with only their mouths, rational revolutionaries made discussing politics into earnest foreplay. "Sleep with me, and together we will strike a blow against the evils of American cultural and economic hegemony!" This was their rousing pickup line. Spurning their advances was not a mere personal matter, then, but a deliberate turning away from all that was good, a repudiation of the struggle of oppressed dark people everywhere.

A parade of rice kings wherever she went, lecherous, treacherous, beseeching—enfolded like origami, bent like bonsai, draped in silk, and embellished with *hanzi*—presenting themselves like gifts to a foreign bride. The Other as envoy, as smitten colonizer. Like an heiress with a fortune, then, Alma has learned to be suspicious of all suitors lest they should desire her solely for her luscious yellowness. Whether for cultural status, sexual conquest, or racial solidarity, she would be no one's Tiger Lily, China Doll, Geisha Girl, Baby San, Miss Saigon, Suzie Wong, Me Love You Long Time, goddamn Madame Butterfly!

Except. Except, and here is the thing that even from the depths of coma Alma finds hard to face, from Mr. Steinhart, Eric, Vincent, Kristophe, Paolo, and even Daniel—echoing all the way back to Johnny Appleby in ninth grade—there is a part of her that believes that she is, in fact, all these things, a part of her that believes this is what she has to offer. For how do you separate out the race from the girl, the singular desirability of an individual from the menu of collective traits? It was trickier than one might think.

"Once Asian, never again Caucasian," she had teased Daniel after they slept together for the first time. It was meant to be a joke, a way to downplay the seriousness of what was happening between them, a way to show that she was in on it, that she had control. Only it had turned out to be true.

DANIEL DEFENDS HIMSELF

In the bowels of a basement, Daniel tries to figure out what has happened to him. He checks the doors and window, looking for weaknesses, for possible escape routes. The one narrow window is at ground height, half-painted over, and only big enough for one of his arms to get through, if he could get it open, which he can't. He racks his brain trying to think of who would want to kidnap him, and to what purpose. He can't shake the feeling that it has something to do with Alma, the person in all the world with the greatest cause to hate him. Though it makes no sense, of course. Why arrange for his capture after sending a just-saying-hi Facebook message? Part of him hopes it *is* Alma, logic be damned—hopes she still hates him, because that would mean she still cares about him, which would be far better than hey-how-you-doing banality. Hope roils in his stomach, sickening him with its utter unlikeliness, his pathetic desire to still matter to a woman he lost two decades ago.

But here is proof of synchronicity: at the moment that Alma, in her coma, recalls her words to him, Daniel recalls them also.

Once Asian, never again Caucasian," she had said. Daniel had taken it as a kind of marking, like planting a flag on terra incognita. *I claim this white ass in the name of Asian women everywhere.* But it was funny how quickly what started as a joke became a running argument between them.

"How can you sit in judgment, but not turn the mirror on yourself?" Daniel said. "How can you say that a white guy has an Asian fetish and not that you have a white-guy fetish? How does that work? I mean, you've never dated anyone but white men."

"It's different," Alma insisted.

"How is it different?"

"It's about power," she said. "The fact that guys like you call all the shots. You're in all the top positions, on the movie screens, on the billboards, in the boardrooms . . . White men—white American men—rule the world. So when white guys seek Asian women from the position of power, they're acting like coloniz—"

"Wait, wait, wait!" Daniel held a hand up. "That's total bullshit!"

"Let me finish!" Alma glared at him as if to say, *This is exactly what I'm talking about.* "I'm saying that part of the attraction is this myth of Orientalism that goes way back, and it's . . ." She put her own hand up. "Let me finish! It's predicated on the whole notion that Asian women are demure and subservient, these exotic little geisha—"

"And I'm saying," Daniel said, "that that's bullshit. You just can't accept that a white man could be attracted to an Asian woman in the same way that a white woman could be attracted to . . . to a surfer dude. As an aesthetic choice, a mere matter of preference."

Alma shook her head. "You're so naive," she said. "Where do you think aesthetic choices come from?"

Daniel pretended to consider. "From the aesthetics store?"

Alma made a face of disgust. "You started this conversation, mister," she said. "Don't think you can just weasel out of it."

Daniel grabbed her hand.

"Sometimes . . ." she said.

"Sometimes, what?" He put her hand to his lips.

"Sometimes . . . I'm not really sure I like you."

Daniel pulled her toward him. "I'm the big, bad Asian fetishist," he growled into her neck. "And I'm coming to get you!"

"Get off me," Alma said, but she was laughing, and Daniel chose to interpret this as victory.

Kyoko procrastinates

Upstairs, Kyoko works on *Willy*, the girl samurai manga she has created. She uses tracing paper, masking-taped to Strathmore 300 Series Smooth Bristol board, at an Alvin WorkMaster drafting table that she bought on eBay for 150 dollars. Willy's face, as it emerges from feathered pencil lines, is vertiginously sloped—high forehead and carved cheeks, swooping eyebrows and vicious widow's peak, small mouth pressed thin in a Morse code dash, hard eyes black-irised, and a flag of black hair unfurling as she hunches over her Mongol pony, Dastard. Willy is the apotheosis of Kyoko's series of manga heroines, dating back to her first attempts at age twelve—an androgynous crew of tomboys, spindle-legged and flat-chested, with silver-hooped ears and studded noses, whole-sleeve tattoos of dragons and swords and purple ideograms for honor and death—whose sworn vengeance against the murderers of her family is two parts Chinese folk legend and one part Western gun-slinging myth.

Kyoko draws, head bent so close that her cheek almost rests on the page. She tries not to think about the man in the basement, her own personal revenge project. For, whereas Willy has tracked down and slaughtered five of the gang who killed not only her family but her entire village—two by decapitation, two by impalement, and one by vertical cleaving—Kyoko has managed only to secure her victim in the basement, and having felt a great measure of satisfaction at getting this done, she has yet to muster the inspiration to finish him off.

Or perhaps it is not inspiration she is looking for, exactly, but a certain rightness of gesture, having so recently failed at crude, hacking spontaneity, following years of obsessive planning that yielded nothing but big talk and reverie (picture Daniel Karmody writhing with electricity, picture him gut-shot, stabbed to death, garroted by piano wire, convulsed with poison) and some compulsive late-night cyber-stalking.

Kyoko has some ideas. Here, she shakes her head and rubs her eraser vigorously over Willy's uncertain features—eyes, nose, mouth retracting back into white nothing. The truth is, now that she has him, Kyoko doesn't mind letting Karmody sweat. Make him wonder why he was there, what was going to happen to him. She blows eraser crumbles off the page and across the table, brushes the rest away with the side of her hand.

It makes perfect sense to Kyoko, the way everything in her life has built to this, the past an armature, a meticulous pencil sketch. When she was eleven, she found a book of Japanese erotic woodblock prints on her parents' bookshelf. Men and women wrestling, dressed in gorgeous robes, half-covered by intricately patterned blankets or posing in front of folding screens, slick hair piled high upon their heads; peeking beneath their robes, rounded bottoms, jutting breasts, giant penises. The angle of the couples' heads in relation to the torque of their bodies, the size of their genitalia in proportion to their arms and legs—all were anatomically preposterous—and yet the prints had held such a curious vitality. Although the couples' faces remained impassive, the contortion of their embraces, the clutch of their hands, created an air of urgency, as though their frenzy had been suspended only for the moment of the viewer's gaze. The discovery defined Kyoko in two ways: it caused her to fall deeply in love with her Japanese heritage, and it made her determined to become an artist.

By the time her parents separated three years later, she had become something of a connoisseur. *Miyazaki, Kurosawa, Hiroshige, origami, ikebana.* The very words were incantations to Kyoko, the work exquisitely melancholy and macabre. The conflation of sex and death, in particular, seemed wholly Japanese in flavor, like wasabi or pickled ginger. Sex, death, and folded frogs. Art became a buffer. Kyoko would sit at her makeshift drawing table and create worlds, like planets, galaxies away from . . . First, the fighting, the sibilant intensity of her parents' voices in Japanese, sounding to her like characters in a Godzilla movie. *Shkk-kka-kk-shkkta. The monster is loose in the city.* Then, after the separation, from her mother's late-night crying jags, the newspaper clippings on the kitchen counter, and the pile of boxes that kept arriving in the mail.

Around this same time, Kyoko had heard "Holiday in Cambodia" by the Dead Kennedys for the first time, and it had blown her mind. She had saved up for an Aria Pro II and taught herself to play. The first song she ever wrote was a punk ballad called "Boffo for Bashō" based on one of the seventeenth-century poet's haiku. *Fever-felled halfway / fever-felled halfway / Marching, marching / Into a hollow / Into a hollow land.* As Kyoko's playing improved, her songs got wilder, fueled by a seismic anger that heaved to the surface in clotted waves, stoked on a dark and troubling energy, words smoking in her mouth, music seizing up from inside her emptiness, dropping it down into new chasms, through new canyons, containing more anger and more emptiness, until it seemed Kyoko could never use it all, but only detonate a small amount at a time and cache the rest, her infinite supply of hollowness and fury.

One evening, when Kyoko was sixteen, she had been sitting in the living room with her mother. The television had been on—they were probably watching *House* or *CSI*, which had been Emi's favorite show—when the phone rang and her mother went to answer it. Kyoko had been putting the finishing touches on a drawing: two women looked on as a samurai soldier in a gold robe plunged his sword so deep into his own belly that it came out the other side. From the kitchen, Kyoko could hear her mother's voice. "Oh, Daniel," she said, laughing. "Thank you for getting back to me. Yes, it has been a long time, hasn't it? You haven't forgotten me?" There was a pause while Emi listened. After a few seconds, she laughed.

Kyoko colored in the blood that sprayed out in all directions, across the faces of the onlookers and onto the floor, seeming, with a trick of perspective, to spill out of two dimensions toward the viewer.

"I need to see you," she heard Emi say. "Will you meet me?" She giggled. "Of course, Daniel," she said. "I remember."

Kyoko worked on the women, whose expressions were impassive, their kimonos green and pink. They could have been the samurai's courtesans; they could have been his wife and daughter. The samurai, in the throes of his last conscious moment, regarded them with mixed emotions, as though he could not decide, in the midst of extreme pain, and at the risk of great dishonor, if they wished him well.

Kyoko walked into the kitchen. "Okay, okay," she heard her mother say. Emi looked up at Kyoko, noticed her hands, which were smeared with marker, and indicated with her eyes toward the sink.

"Umm, I have to go," she said. That high, anxious giggle. "All right. Yes, of course. I will."

Kyoko turned on the tap and waited for the water to get hot. She grabbed the bar of Ivory and scrubbed her hands. She knew all about this Daniel. He was a face in a wedge of light in her bedroom doorway once when she was small. He was words printed on a concert program, a dark figure on a bright stage. Kyoko had heard his name from her father's lips, like something rotten spat out, and in her mother's mouth, like luscious fruit. She associated it with a blue suitcase and a pair of high-heeled shoes, her mother sitting in the hallway like a punished child. Barbed silences, stretched like concertina wire, late-night outbursts, the sound of footsteps clamoring down the stairs. Kyoko coming down in the morning to find her father asleep on the couch beside an empty glass, a note from her mother on the counter with three dollars for lunch. Once, years ago, she had snooped in her mother's things and found a half-filled journal with a painting on the cover by Caravaggio, a still life of fruit on a table that her mother had bought in the Uffizi. It said so on the first page. Emi had been somewhat discreet, but Kyoko had known enough to figure out who D. was, and could guess well enough what the little asterisks had meant by the calendar dates.

"I really have to go," Emi said, eyeing Kyoko warily. "Okay. Of course I know . . . I will. Yes. Goodbye." As she hung up the phone, Emi's face remained illuminated by some lingering joke.

"Who was that?" Kyoko asked.

"An old friend," her mother said. The light flickered and died.

"Daniel," Kyoko tested.

Emi nodded, turning to wipe the counter. "We used to play together."

A face behind her mother's shoulder, peering in from the hall.

"'Play together,'" Kyoko said, weighing the words.

"Yes," her mother said. "That's right."

Three months later, she was dead.

Kyoko had moved in with her father and his new wife and baby, where no one even pretended to want her there, even as a babysitter—Michiko no doubt worried that Kyoko would suffocate the newborn. It was a weird-looking child, with a huge head and squinty eyes, and Kyoko felt no kinship. Her father tried to keep the peace, but Kyoko saw clearly how it was.

"Gen," Michiko would say, her eyes wide with anger. "Someone tracked in dirt!" "Gen! The music is disturbing the baby!" "Gen! She left her dishes again!" She never referred to Kyoko by name and almost never spoke to her directly, and Kyoko began to follow her lead. "Dad, tell her I *did* wipe my feet!" "Dad, she's being totally irrational!" "Dad! I would do them if she'd just leave them alone!"

Gen would look at Kyoko, then at his new wife. "Please, Kyoko," he would say, his voice mild and thin, in the same exact way he used to talk to Emi, "you're upsetting Michiko." And Kyoko would give up and leave the room.

Her new school had been less demanding than St. Elizabeth's, and Kyoko barely had to work. She spent all her time listening to music, and drawing, and thinking about her mother. Gen suggested that Kyoko go to counseling, but in this she and her stepmother were in agreement—Michiko, because she didn't want to spend the money, and Kyoko, because she thought it would be a waste of time. In Kyoko's mind, it was clear that the root source of Emi's unhappiness—the cause of her parents' problems and subsequent divorce, Emi's escalating depression and subsequent suicide—was her affair with Daniel Karmody. Proof came from a childhood of clues—eavesdropping on arguments, spying in her parents' room (where she had found the Caravaggio journal), paying attention to Emi's stories, and piecing together early memories. *Kyoko in bed. A widening swath of light. A tall figure in shadow behind her mother's left shoulder.*

A mantra began to form in Kyoko's head. "Daniel Karmody must pay. Daniel Karmody must pay." Kyoko whispered it to herself in chemistry class, in the lunch line, while the other kids jostled and chattered, at home, as her stepbrother wailed and Michiko complained. Somewhere along the way, the mantra had changed to "Daniel Karmody must die. Daniel Karmody must die," and Kyoko began to think in earnest how this might be managed.

Preliminary reconnaissance uncovered Daniel's whereabouts. He was teaching at the conservatory. He performed regularly with the Guilford Quartet. A couple of times she found herself standing outside Griswold Hall on the night of a concert, just waiting for a glimpse of the man her mother had loved. She was in no hurry. It was enough to be in proximity, to see Daniel's bland face pass by without suspicion. White men seemed bloodless to Kyoko, insipid—and she couldn't stand the arrogance, the casual self-regard, as though they actually believed they pissed gold and shat diamonds, that the world was indebted to their piss and shit. She couldn't understand her mother's attraction. Daniel might have been handsome by *People* magazine standards, but to Kyoko, her smaller, darker father, with his sad, sympathetic face, was infinitely more appealing.

Kyoko could forgive her father's spinelessness, his ineffectuality. Gen had loved Emi, and though Kyoko didn't understand why, he seemed to love Michiko. She could forgive Emi her fragility, her childish preoccupations and fretting self-pity. But Daniel Karmody... Daniel Karmody she could not forgive. Far from forgiving, Kyoko began to devise a plan that would force him to confront what he had done to her mother, a plan worthy of any manga heroine.

And six years later, here he was.

Daniel establishes a routine

In the absence of a clock, Daniel relied on his own circadian rhythms. He woke when the light shone through the tiny window. Because the cot sagged, he slept in the Naugahyde recliner, which was not very comfortable but was more comfortable than the cot. It took him a moment to remember where he was, and the recognition was quickly accompanied by a feeling of incredulity, as though he had woken to a further dream.

Daniel, who would never deliberately choose prolonged solitude for himself, knew that he needed a routine or he would go crazy, so as soon as he got up, he did what he thought amounted to an hour of calisthenics—a combination of exercises he remembered from a Pilates class he had taken with Sigrid a few years ago ("Pulse, pulse, pulse! Work that core!") and old-fashioned boot-camp exercises, jumping jacks, push-ups, and ab curls.

After his workout, he took a shower in the tiny capsule in the bathroom, which was like a vertical coffin. The water was tepid at its hottest and came out in a disconsolate trickle so that Daniel had to turn around to get both sides of his body wet. Without shampoo, he would just pass the virulent green bar of soap over his hair and growing beard. Luckily, the mirror in the bathroom was clouded, pocked with white and green spots, and when Daniel peered into it, he could barely make out his face. It looked far away, peevish and mistrustful, like the face of a dim ancestor.

He would change into one of the few outfits he had to choose from, an assortment of clothes that looked and smelled like they had come from Goodwill—a maroon polyester tracksuit, a pair of too-small brown corduroy pants, and two striped, long-sleeve polo shirts. Because it was cold in the basement, and he was always sneezing (Daniel suspected he had a mold allergy), his captor had recently given him a massive orange-and-yellow plaid hunting jacket.

Daniel had taken to calling his captor—the one he saw—The Big Guy. He would bring Daniel's breakfast along with his lunch—a piece of toast with peanut butter and a banana, or a bowl of mushy cornflakes with a glass of OJ. A cheese sandwich on white bread with mayo, sometimes with a piece of ham or bologna, a glass of milk, and an apple. Daniel tried to goad The Big Guy into conversation, and though it hadn't worked thus far, he liked to think he was making inroads.

"Do you know that white bread has almost no nutrients?" he would say. "Any chance of switching to whole wheat?" "You know, I left my medications behind. The next time you're at a CVS, would you mind picking me up some Claritin? And I could really use some fish oil."

After breakfast, Daniel "practiced" the violin on a piece of wood paneling from which he had fashioned a violin neck, with drawn lines for strings, and a narrow piece of corrugated cardboard, which he used as a bow. He practiced double- and triple-stops from the fastest movements of the hardest violin concerti he knew, Britten, Ligeti, Beethoven, straining toward the music, sometimes humming it, sometimes just hearing it in his head, trying to keep his mind on the rote discipline, the routine and muscle memory. At times he was successful, but at other times he just went through the motions, his fingers moving like crazed pistons.

The bulk of Daniel's time in captivity was devoted to the boxes of junk that were stacked up in columns almost as high as the ceiling like massive walls—gray plastic storage bins with blue lids, see-through plastic storage bins with clear lids, cardboard boxes from liquor stores and supermarkets with pictures of palm trees and oranges on the sides, overflowing wicker laundry hampers, a rolling clothes rack, and piles of freestanding newspapers and magazines.

He had started out searching for clues. If he knew who was holding him prisoner, he was sure he could find a way to obtain his release. Daniel, either out of egotism or common sense, could not think of anyone who might dislike him so much as to go to these lengths, though there were many who might have been unhappy with him at one time or another—some husbands, a few spurned women. His thoughts kept returning to Alma.

He was also looking for a weapon or a tool—anything that could be used to escape or to get a message out. When he had first thought he was alone in the house, Daniel had tried jimmying the lock to the door upstairs and the one that led to the outside; he had stood at the top of the stairs and yelled for several minutes, banging and kicking on the door, but none of these efforts had seemed in the least productive. He hoped that somewhere in the hoard of boxes, he would come across a box cutter or a knife, a staple gun, a string of Chinese firecrackers with some matches, or something heavy, like a glass globe paperweight, which he had once seen used as a murder weapon by a character in a movie.

Quickly, though, he had forgotten his agenda, and instead of looking for anything in particular, he became absorbed in the sheer variety and volume of what had been amassed. It was like perpetual Christmas morning—a bizarre and bountiful Christmas, presided over by a lunatic Santa Claus. One box was, in fact, filled with Christmas things: angel ornaments, and stars, and colored balls of frosted glass; long tubes of wrapping paper in greens and reds, with mittens on them, and sledding children, and candy canes; plastic bags of bows, and to/from stickers, coils of green wire, clusters of fake holly berries, Styrofoam spheres, and spools of gold ribbon.

In one box, Daniel found unopened packages of bedsheets (queen-sized and twin), towels, and underwear (three-packs of Fruit of the Loom women's briefs, six-packs of socks). In another, Kleenex boxes, paper towel rolls, bags of microwave popcorn, wasabi peanuts, and chocolate lover's trail mix.

There was a container filled solely with products advertised on late-night television in unopened blue packages: Ageless Sleep Pillow, Magic Hands, Odor Assassins. In this container, too, silver and gold earrings in tiny, resealable bags, a cascade of free-floating necklaces and pendants, and some giant scarves from QVC and HSN. Daniel had taken long chains of gold links and hung them around his neck. He had unfolded a scarf and fastened it over his head like a do-rag. Picking his way through the jewelry, he found some huge silver hoop earrings, which he unpackaged and hung around his ears, and a silver spoon shaped as a ring, which he fit onto his little finger.

Daniel marveled at such wanton consumerism—the peculiar brand of industry that had gone into ordering and buying all of it in the first place, and the resulting mountain of objects that seemed to have meant less in physical realization than it had in the abstract con-figuration of desire. Who was this deranged pack rat? Did Daniel know her? (It seemed obvious to him that it was a she, considering the preponderance of evidence.) And what had propelled her to hoard all this stuff? Daniel made a pile of things that he thought might come in handy and hid them in a box at the back of the farthest column.

Before it got dark, dinner would arrive. A sandwich, or a salad of iceberg lettuce and limp tomatoes with hard croutons and Italian dressing. Daniel would read a paperback he had found, *Tales of the South Pacific* by James Michener. Just before pulling the string that turned off the buzzing fluorescent light, he would make a hash mark on the back blank page of the book to indicate the day passed. One mark, two marks, three. It felt like a lot more. And each night he would fall asleep, after considerable struggle, to the sounds of ghastly music coming from upstairs.

KYOKO WRITES A SONG

Kornell held Sumo in his arms, one hand curved along her plump backside, the other stroking downward from her neck to her tail. The cat's eyes opened and closed lazily.

"Play it for me again," Kornell said now. "I dig it."

Kyoko was almost finished with a new song. One she liked for a change. She strummed the intro. B-flat, D, A-flat, C. *"Mi-ya-za-ki, Ku-ro-sa-wa, O-zu,"* she sang softly into the neck of her guitar. "Wait, I messed up. *'Mi-ya-zaki, Kur-O-sa-wa, O-zu / Ba-shō-ba-ba-ba . . .'* Work that out later. Then the chorus . . ."

Kornell nodded his head. "That's nice, baby," he said. "Good strong hook. I feel it." Sumo, to the contrary, chose this moment to jump out of Kornell's arms and saunter out of the room. Kornell picked at the gray cat hairs on his pant leg. "Hey, baby?" he said.

Kyoko started over from the beginning. Something didn't seem quite right. Maybe better to go A-flat, E. "Mmm?"

"You're going to do something soon about that man down there?"

Kyoko looked up. "Yes," she said, trying not to sound defensive. "Yeah," she added with more enthusiasm. "I'm on it. It's gonna be good."

Kornell had been administering to Daniel Karmody on his own since they'd abducted him from his garage three days ago. Kyoko didn't want Karmody to guess who she was. She almost couldn't believe that he was really down there, after all this time. Kornell would come up the steps with a half-eaten bologna sandwich, or a dirty glass, or she would hear the toilet flush, the creak and whoosh of the plumbing, and she would marvel: Daniel Karmody was in her basement; Daniel Karmody was her prisoner, defenseless and alone. Finally, Daniel Karmody would pay.

Kornell looked pensive. "Because he's starting to act kind of crazy."

"Crazy? Like how?"

"Like getting into your mom's shit. This morning he was wearing one of those blankets with arms. You know what all's in those boxes down there. There's all kinds of crazy shit."

"Nothing dangerous? That he could use, I mean?"

Kornell shook his head. "No, I checked before we brought him down. No knives or scissors or anything sharp. Just a lot of junk. And the dude never stops talking. He's a chatty motherfucker."

"You haven't told him anything?" Kyoko said. She put the guitar down.

Kornell gave her a look. "Baby," he said. "Who do you think you're dealing with? I don't talk to him at all. I'm stone cold."

"Good. Let him act crazy. Means he's suffering." Kyoko stretched out on the bed, her hands on her stomach.

"Well, look here now," Kornell said, moving closer. Kyoko was wearing the ratty 5.6.7.8's T-shirt she liked to sleep in. Her legs were bare, the tops of her thighs barely wider than her calves, and she wasn't wearing underwear. Kornell smiled and put two fingers under the hem of her shirt. "Mm-mmm," he said, slowly raising the hem higher.

He worked the shirt up with his fingers, concentrating on the gold of her skin, the smooth curve of her thighs, and the triangle rise at the top, which he cupped in the palm of his hand. Kyoko tensed and sighed. She was so thin, so small, that Kornell had wondered how they could possibly make sex work between them. The first time, he had been careful to go slow and not put his full weight on her. Even so, she had screamed in pain and bled all over the sheets, and Kornell, feeling like a monster, had apologized miserably, convinced that he had hurt her in some deep, irrevocable way. But she had surprised him, scared him, actually, with the intensity of her response over time. She was small but strong, and she had liked the pain.

Kornell pulled her shirt off and plucked at her nipple with his thumb and forefinger, felt it harden like a nut against his touch. He leaned down to take it in his mouth. His hard-on bumped against her, and he shifted his weight to get to the other breast. But, as lithe as she was, she slipped out from under him and got up to turn the camera on. Kornell turned onto his back, and Kyoko climbed on.

Kyoko liked recording their fucking, though they seldom watched it later. It turned Kornell on, the notion of an audience, of an archive. Looking up at her now, he was overcome by the mix of emotions he always felt when he was with her, the mix of emotions that he had come to know as love, though the word was a subway token, a casino chip. Her small, bud-like breasts were dark at the nipples, and he could see the rack of her ribs as she arched above him, the flat plane of her stomach, with its dark mole just above the belly button. Her short hair spiked forward from her face, and her eyes were closed as she teased him, rocking slightly, so that just the tip of his cock could wet itself inside her. Kornell groaned from the frustration of it.

She enclosed him in her tiny fist and rocked more vigorously, positioning herself so he slipped from the tight enclosure of her hand to the tight enclosure of her pussy, still only halfway—but the sensation of tightness, of wetness and warmth, was overwhelming. He grabbed her by the hips then—she couldn't stop him—and pushed inside her, and still he could not seem to fully reach her, so he pulled her off him, turning her over in one motion, and took her from behind.

He heard her cry out. She grabbed the top of the mattress and braced herself, lifting her ass higher in the air. He was blind with excitement, with brute pleasure and the rush of feeling, and something in him wanted to break her, to tear her apart, even as he loved her and wanted to protect her. It was her separateness he meant to destroy, her distance, which was his own separateness, his own distance, and the fact that no matter how hard he fucked her, or for how long, they would not merge.

Kornell placed a hand on the back of Kyoko's neck and pushed her face into the bed, already regretting the ebbing of sensation as the blood pulsed all the way from his root to his toes and temples, and at the tips of his ears. Kyoko shuddered as Kornell crested the wave, rode it out as far as he could, helpless to stop himself, even though he could already feel her slipping away.

loss

DANIEL DREAMS

Daniel woke from a dream in which he had been making ice cream for all the women he had ever made love to, all of them clamoring to be first in line. In the dream, his arms had ached from cranking the old-fashioned ice cream maker; the rock salt worked its way into tiny cuts between his fingers, and he kept switching arms, but still the ice cream would not turn. Sigrid had been there; a couple of college girlfriends; Polly Minter, from high school; Amy Feinstein, the girl who had taken his virginity; Alma, of course; Jiang Jiang; Sophea; Emi; Nhu; Marisa; and Fusan—all crowding around, pushing one another out of the way.

"I don't know what's happening," he had said. "It was supposed to be vanilla." He kept on cranking, but the women were clearly disappointed. They began to drift away, until only Alma remained, standing on the other side of the ice cream maker, regarding it with a doleful eye. "Daniel is an anagram for Denial," she had said then, and from both inside and outside his dream, Daniel had denied it.

It was something Alma had actually said. First in connection to an argument they'd had about whether or not he was angry with Dorothea for assigning him an advanced violin class at eight in the morning.

"I'm not angry, I just wish she'd listened to me," he'd said.

Alma had made her cute, exasperated face. "Admit it, you're angry! You're pissed off because she's passive aggressive, she lords it over you, and she doesn't listen."

Daniel had smiled. "Darlin'," he said, "we've been through this before. I'm not angry."

Alma had shaken her head. "Daniel is an anagram for Denial," she'd said, and soon after, she said it any time he did something she deemed an evasion, a willful, masculine U-turning away from emotional truth. Even Daniel started saying it. "Well, I wouldn't know about that," he'd say. "'Cuz Daniel is an anagram for Denial."

That Alma had appeared to him in a dream, that she had said something she used to say to him in real life—all this made Daniel wistful. From the bowels of his imprisonment (in the parentheses between death, self-administered, and death, outsourced), it felt as if the significant events of a certain crucial period of his past had kicked back into motion, like some rude, ancient machinery. He had woken from the dream with a massive hard-on—the lingering scent of Alma, the overwhelming feeling that she had just recently left the room. He remembered the early days when she used to come home from school and get undressed for him, leaving her clothes cocooned in the middle of the room, the way she would emerge from the shower and sit at the edge of the bed, her long hair dripping, her thighs spread, while he got down on his knees before her. Daniel had masturbated then, for the first time since he'd been captured, retreating to the bathroom and pawing himself with a mitten of toilet paper, almost sobbing with the release of tension, but also with a sense of loss that Daniel, in denial, could not account for.

ALMA REMEMBERS

Alma emerges from the Uffizi courtyard into the shadow of the Palazzo Vecchio and finds herself on the loggia, among the group of sculptures that she and Daniel referred to as *Women Being Fucked Over*. Topless Polyxena in the clutches of Achilles, who beats back her mother with his sword; boastful Perseus bearing Medusa's severed head like a lantern; Giambologna's *Abduction of a Sabine Woman*, the nubile maiden spiraling helplessly above the Roman captor who holds her aloft while her father cowers beneath them in shame.

Under the loggia, Alma is spared the full assault of the sun, and yet she is flush with heat. She senses Daniel beside her, though she does not see him, his physical presence asserting itself like a disturbance, a displacement of Florentine molecules. Is it a dream? A memory? The random snap of synapses in a brain gone fizzy with pharmaceuticals? Or a sloughing of electricity, like some cerebral moraine? No matter. It is enough that she has returned, that she can feel the paving stones beneath the thin soles of her Italian sandals. She is twenty-nine.

*　*　*

They fought the whole time: walking single file on the narrow stone pathways by the River Arno, vital points lost to the revving of motorcycles and the high, bright laughter of tourists; gesticulating with gelato spoons as they sat outside a café in the Piazza della Signoria; standing on the second floor of the Uffizi Gallery, lowering their voices before a bevy of Madonnas—grim, grinning, stately, plump, aloof, aloft, alluring: Madonnas electric, dyspeptic, melancholic, myopic, dowdy, dreamy, and delicate—ranging from buca to loggia; sputtering in and out of leather shops, through churches and palazzos, between market stalls of zucchini flowers and porcini mushrooms; waiting backstage to perform at the Teatro Comunale, the Verdi, or in the sacristy of Orsanmichele; pausing momentarily in convivial wonder over shared forkfuls of broad pasta with wild boar ragù and chocolate hazelnut torta, distracted by the flavors and the atmosphere, the company and the candlelight, the corny accordion player outside playing "That's Amore" and the vendor of cut roses passing; resuming full force over bottles of Nozzole, chilled glasses of *limoncello*, and tiny decorated cups of espresso, their voices becoming slurred, overlapping, lapsing for full minutes into drunken, recriminating silences; and later at night, preparing for bed, moody over washcloths and dental floss, cold cream and contact solution, tending to wine stains on cuffs and lipstick removal; listening abstractly to the percussive sputter of Italian plumbing, the ardent, aggrieved rhythm of passing street conversation, and the distant brassy strains of Gershwin issuing from a tourist spot near the Ponte Vecchio—both of them weary of their own positions, forgetful of them, almost willing to give them up if it weren't for the principle, the responsibility to truth, to reason, until the only recourse was a furious, fast fucking that wasn't so much truce as it was transliteration, the struggle stripped clear of civilized discourse and smarty-pants articulations, stripped bare and rocking in almost catatonic frenzy, the yielding and the pushing, insinuating and subsuming, the pouring in and crying out, conceding nothing.

And what did they fight about? This wasn't so easily determined. It was, of course, the continuation of the argument they'd been having during the five years they'd been together, not so much an argument as an undertow, a countercurrent, the same argument that runs swift and dark beneath every romance—the argument against. An irrefutable movement, after the tidal knocking, closer, the lulling waves of intimacy, the moony directional pull toward the same soft shore, gravity's shadow impulse—away.

From deep inside her coma, Alma's brow furrows. Even unconscious, riven with disease, drug-embattled, intravenous-fed, she frowns at the imprecision. Because what they had fought about had been entirely singular.

They had been performing piano trios with Archie that summer. Daniel's Italian was atrocious, and Alma winced whenever he opened his mouth. "It's not *grazie* to rhyme with *Nazi*," she had to tell him repeatedly. "It's *grazie-eh*."

"To rhyme with *Nazi-eh*?" said Daniel.

"Not funny."

It wasn't that Alma spoke Italian fluently, or that her vocabulary progressed much beyond his, but she was proud of her pronunciation, which she knew wasn't perfect, but which she took painstaking care to reproduce correctly. She fancied herself something of a linguistics expert by virtue of the fact that she had had to learn English at an early age, and because Daniel, by comparison, was so lame. "You know what I love about Italian?" said Alma. "I love that everything has a gender."

Daniel frowned. "How do they decide if something is masculine or feminine? It seems completely arbitrary to me."

Alma held up her spoon. "Paolo says you just know. This, for example, *il cucchiaio*, is masculine." She pointed to her cup of espresso. "And this, *la coppa*, is feminine."

"You see? Completely arbitrary."

"Really?" Alma opened her mouth and slowly, deliberately, licked the back of *il cucchiaio* with the tip of her tongue, then slowly, deliberately inserted it inside *la coppa*. She smiled. "*I* think it's sexy."

"You think Paolo is sexy." Daniel was trying to sound casual, but Alma heard the anger that masked the vulnerability, that posed as judgment. She wasn't in the mood tonight to reassure him.

She brought the cup to her lips. "Paolo is our host," she said.

"He's Italian," said Daniel doubtfully.

"Precisely," Alma said.

Paolo, the impresario, the opera composer, cosmopolitan, the disarmingly charming Paolo. Handsome in a tux, tall and dark, with wild antennae eyebrows and thick waves of hair that never seemed to muss or move, reminiscent of Michelangelo's *David*. Paolo, who loved all things American, including the New York Yankees, cheeseburgers, and Bruce Springsteen. People said he was a prince, one of the last of a long line of Florentine royalty that included a Medici or two and at least one pope, and it wasn't hard to believe it, though he graciously waved aside any direct inquiries into his ancestry. "My dear," he said in his charmingly disarming English, "you see, the problem in Italy, we look too much to the past. I like your American way better. Look to the future!"

Daniel was naturally suspicious of Paolo, in the way that he was suspicious of any man to whom Alma paid more than a cursory attention. "I think he's got Yellow Fever," he told her after they'd first been introduced.

"You think any man who flirts with me has Yellow Fever," Alma said. "What does that say about me? That no man could possibly just find *me* attractive?"

Daniel had taken Alma's hand. "No, baby, I'm saying that every man who sees *you* comes down with a case of malaria."

Alma and Daniel on the terrace of Paolo's palazzo in the Oltrarno, newly arrived from a private concert in the Basilica di Santa Trinita. The guests were mostly stuffed shirts and women with ponderous bosoms, and the waiters, who seemed better dressed—spiffier, anyway—in white dinner jackets and black bow ties, circulated among them with service trays of prosecco and Chianti.

"Uh-oh, don't look now, Count Luigi at twelve o'clock," whispered Daniel.

"Shh," said Alma, cuffing him on the arm, "he'll hear you."

"*Ciao* there, Paolo!" said Daniel loudly, extending his hand.

Paolo nodded, barely deigning to shake.

"*Buonasera*," Alma corrected Daniel. "Sorry," she said to Paolo.

"What'd I do?" Daniel said.

"You were too familiar," Alma said.

"It is all right," Paolo said, shrugging, "we are all friends here."

"Americans don't understand levels of formality," Alma explained. "In Korean, the honorifics are in the verb endings. You say *kahmsamnida* to your elders, *kahmupsumnida* to your equals, *kumupda* with children."

"And it means, this word?"

"Thank you."

Alma felt Daniel's anger like a furnace beside her. It fueled her own, and their heat rose and roused something in Paolo.

"Ahh," said Paolo, "fascinating!" He turned to Daniel, gesturing minutely with his wineglass. "You Americans have no honorifics, I think?" he said.

"No, we're a democracy."

Alma shot Daniel a look. "Americans have no respect for their elders," she said.

"Americans give respect where respect is due," said Daniel. "And anyway, what's all this 'Americans this, Americans that' bullshit? You haven't lived in Korea since you were four years old."

Alma ignored him, smiled steadfastly into Paolo's cool, patrician face. They were in sync, allied against Daniel and all his fatuous compatriots, and the thrill of her small betrayal blossomed in Alma like a night-blooming flower. Daniel's pale Irish complexion, freckled lightly along the bridge of his nose, seemed too fair, too telling, in this historied city of deadly plots and shifting alliances; it simply gave too much away.

"There are some people I wish you to meet, *cara*," Paolo said now, steering Alma away by the elbow. His own expression was hooded, eyes cast down, and though he spoke to her, he seemed to be addressing Daniel, who, pink-cheeked and scowling, stared after Alma with a cast-iron hatred that caused her, for the first time that night, to sense the danger of the game she was playing.

"Oh, Signora Lee," a grating American voice cried out, "we just loved your performance!"

"*Brava!*" someone called.

W hy did you do that?"
        "Why did I do what?"

"Let's see . . . embarrass me in front of Paolo. Act like a total bitch. Ignore me all night like I'm nobody to you."

Alma looked at herself in the mirror, at Daniel behind her. "I don't know what you're talking about, babe," she said.

"Oh, cut the crap!" Daniel brought his fist down on the nightstand a little harder than he'd intended, causing it to jump off the floor. Alma flinched. "You know exactly what I'm talking about, *babe*. Why don't you just fuck him and get it over with?"

"Me!" Alma threw her hairbrush across the bureau. "You're the ones who act like you want to fuck each other, always circling around sniffing each other's assholes."

"What are you talking about?"

"You know. You read D. H. Lawrence."

"That's sick." Daniel twisted the elastic band of his wristwatch but did not remove it. "That's just—"

"—because we both know you're into some freaky shit."

"Oh, that's . . . !" Daniel clapped his hands. "Me? When you're the one who, who . . ." He stared at her for a moment. "Okay, then, why not a threesome? You, me, and Machiavelli."

Alma's mouth felt devoid of moisture, as though she could spit sand. "He doesn't want to sleep with me. He just likes to get your goat."

Daniel shook his head. "He had his hands all over you tonight."

"Don't exaggerate."

Daniel took a step toward Alma, his hands on his crotch. "*Cara! Bella!* Come here, *cara!*" He pitched his voice high, rolling his *r*'s, exploding his *l*'s, imitating Paolo's open, insinuating diction. "*Bella, bella, cara mia, bella!*"

"Stop it!"

"Here it is, *cara*. I call it my *ba*-ton!"

Alma stared at Daniel, who was holding his cock in his hands, sticking it out from his unzipped pants. It was partially erect, and he bobbed it up and down in exaggerated three-quarter time, and Alma had to admit that he'd nailed the accent, captured the effeminate lilt of European refinement. It was late and she felt herself losing the edge of her drunken belligerence; she was exhausted from performing earlier and then the party after. It had been a long day. And here now was Daniel with his penis out, mincing about the room, conducting his idiot's symphony, and the only possible response was to laugh, and once she started, Daniel joined in, until they couldn't stand up from laughing so hard, and fell onto the bed, clutching their bellies, wiping their tears, and Daniel went soft and grew hard again. Laughter ceasing, he grabbed Alma around the waist and pulled her under him—as Paolo still or as himself, Alma wasn't certain, nor did she know which aroused her more, though she was aroused. He pulled her panties down, grabbed her ass where it was fleshiest, and pushed his way inside her until she could feel his pelvic bone slamming against her, *bam, bam*—she pictured a car hitting a retaining wall, something hard, something fast, something out of control—and here she was coming, arching up to meet him, reaching back to pull him deeper, *fuck me, baby, harder,* like a porn-star queen, and she was not at all sorry that she had capitulated or that she had made him suffer; she was glad of it, if it had led to this, this igniting, and whatever else Alma felt or previously thought—because she was not thinking now—she was most certainly no longer mad.

A nd in her dreams that night, Alma feels herself held aloft, carried in strong arms, hot against her back, a calloused hand pressed against her backside. At her feet, a man crouches, one arm flung up in lamentation, just like in Giambologna's sculpture. She is terrified, but also excited, to be in the Roman aggressor's grip. It is akin to exultation, laced with contempt, a feeling all the more seductive for being unkind. For it is thrilling to be aligned with the victor, to be held up like a prize, exalted and desired, while the weak are left to gesture in the dirt. The Sabine women bore Romulus a nation, and in her dream, Alma smiles at the notion.

DANIEL REMEMBERS

Daniel sits in the Naugahyde recliner, fiddling with a pipe cleaner. He winds it round and round his left index finger, his hands emerging from the fleece sleeves of his Snugli. Dreaming of Alma has made him horny—but a strange kind of horny, mixed with rueful nostalgia, a vague, vast, unfulfillable desire, that is the only kind Daniel seems to have left. That last summer in Florence was so painful a memory that he had spent a decade trying to fuck it out of his mind. Alcohol hadn't helped. It dulled the memories but left the pain. Marrying Sigrid hadn't worked—her cool Swedish minimalism providing only a light, temporary numbing. Even music, Daniel's lifeblood, hadn't helped; the memory of Alma lived inside the music. He thinks of the Elgar, he thinks of the Franck. Somehow, Daniel feels closer to Alma down here. He tries and tries to recall the exact words of her Facebook message but can only remember that they felt dismissive. He wonders if he may have misinterpreted her tone, hoping against hope that she still thinks of him as he thinks of her. Little things are starting to come back to him, memories involving that summer that he can recall with fondness—fondness, and wonder—the way you can look back at a time in your life and say with certainty, "Here, I was most alive."

* * *

They had argued about the Medicis, whom Alma despised. "The vanity! The ego! The false piety!" she'd scoffed. "Just because they had money to buy all this art and build these buildings . . . Hooligans, murderers, and double-crossing backstabbers, and they *still* thought they could buy their way into heaven."

"Some of them were actually very forward-thinking," Daniel said, wielding his dog-eared guidebook. "They had a vision for what Florence could become, and they implemented that vision for the good of its citizens. And whatever else they were, you can't deny they were shrewd businessmen."

Alma screwed up her face in a look of profound objection. Daniel was aware of the dryness in his voice, the condescension. "Besides," he added before Alma could jump in, "if it hadn't been for the Medicis, putting all their wealth into art instead of some war chest somewhere, we wouldn't have all this to look at."

"Well, I am grateful for that," conceded Alma. "But that doesn't make them any less despicable. The Renaissance was supposed to be all about humanism, but really it was just about replacing God with the wealthy and the powerful. Look how they paid artists to paint them into crowd scenes. You saw Masaccio's *Tribute Money*, all that bullshit propaganda about God wanting them to pay their taxes; it was so self-serving. Everything they did was in the name of posterity."

"And what's wrong with that?" Daniel challenged. "Doesn't the notion of posterity account for all great art?"

Alma frowned. "The Medicis weren't artists. True artists engage in the moment; they live in the here and now. Michelangelo might leave behind the *Pietà*, but the fact of its survival is incidental to his creating it. It's great precisely because we feel the vitality of its creation, the life inside it. Same with Beethoven. Yes, he left behind the Ninth Symphony, but what makes it so great is the life within the work."

Daniel shook his head. "You can't tell me that Beethoven wasn't thinking about posterity when he composed his music, or that Michelangelo wasn't concerned about what he was leaving behind when he painted the Sistine Chapel."

Alma gave him a pitying look. "What I'm saying is that whether or not they thought about posterity is beside the point. It's the creative life force *in the moment* that makes the work endure." She pursed her lips. "All this thinking about posterity—it's so typically male, don't you think?—this preoccupation with end product, with legacy? What is history anyway but a bunch of penises on parade?"

"It's not just men," Daniel protested, but Alma had already launched into the topic of patriarchy, Italian and beyond.

Daniel can't remember now where this particular discussion had taken place—in the Medici Chapels, the Uffizi, or at the Pitti—because there had been similar conversations in all these places, and more, and because, from so far a distance in time, the points have become blunted, the edges filed down, the thrust and parry recalled only as an intricate dance, no longer as a dangerous duel or high-stakes game. Everything mattered to Alma, everything had consequences; each argument fed into the next, like the continuation of one big argument, and wherever they argued, Alma's hands inscribed emphatic angles in the space around her; her dark eyes sparked flint and steel, and her long hair, loosening from its perch, floated in black tendrils across her cheeks.

And here, the tip of his finger turns blue where the pipe cleaner is cutting off his circulation, and Daniel feels the blueness down to his balls.

Daniel wears oven mitts

When Kornell comes down with breakfast the next day, Daniel is wearing a suit coat that is way too small for him and a pair of lobster-claw oven mitts. "Good morning, sir," he says, waving a claw cheerfully. "What have you brought me today? Ahh, white toast with grape jelly and a glass of Sunny Delight. The Arkansas Brunch Special, I see."

Kornell puts the plate and glass down on the crate beside the chair. He doesn't know what to do about Daniel ransacking the storage bins. It was all stuff Kyoko's mother had hoarded over the years—sad, crazy old-lady shit. Kornell had looked through it quickly, and as he'd told Kyoko, he didn't think they contained anything dangerous. Meanwhile, dude seemed to think he was hilarious, a regular stand-up comedian.

"I see you're looking at my new coat," Daniel says, looking down at himself. "I know. It needs to be let out a little. The sleeves . . ." He holds his arms out in front of him, revealing several inches of white flesh above each quilted mitt.

Kornell tries not to laugh. Dude was corny, that was for sure. He is about to turn to go when a pair of red claws latches onto his nearer arm. Instinctively, Kornell rears back. Instinctively, Daniel brings his claws up.

"Don't—"

"Get off me, man!" Kornell snarls at Daniel from behind his mask. The first words he has spoken.

"I . . . I didn't mean to . . ." Daniel, still with his arms in the air, sinks back into the recliner. Its mammoth seat seems, more than ever, to suck him down inside it. "It's just . . ." He looks sadly at Kornell. "I know who you are. Or I don't know who *you* are . . . but I know this has something to do with Emi Tokugawa. That it might have something to do with her daughter."

Kornell is startled. He isn't sure it matters, but he wonders how Daniel guessed it.

"Are you . . . are you going to hurt me?" Daniel says. "You can just nod your head yes or no. I was going through some stuff and . . ." He stops. "I mean . . . I mean . . . Please don't hurt me."

These last words come out in such a strained, desperate whisper that it physically pains Kornell to hear them, pains him as a fellow man bearing witness to another's naked fear. But it is to Kyoko that Kornell has sworn allegiance, and he does not know how to begin to weigh the pain of Daniel Karmody's miserable life against the pain of Kyoko's mother, who had died alone, in the upstairs bathroom of this very house, or against Kyoko's pain, which is his main concern.

Daniel takes off the lobster mitts and sets them, one atop the other, on the arm of the recliner. In the too-small suit jacket, he looks like an overgrown child waiting for his mother to pick him up after school. Kornell takes one last look to make sure he is staying put, then turns and goes back up the stairs.

Earlier that day, Daniel had been looking for things he could add to his stash of potentially useful objects. This is what he had amassed so far: a hot glue gun, a roll of green craft wire, three cans of Wilson tennis balls, a package of pipe cleaners, sixteen electric hair rollers in a steam tray with an assortment of bobby pins, a box of glass Christmas ball ornaments, a box of paper clips, a folding tripod, and a bag of assorted-size rubber bands.

As he'd worked, he had listened for the door, ready to throw the lid back on the box, jump back into his chair, and cover himself with the blanket. Because of the way the stairs were situated in relation to the basement, the view obstructed by the wall, he had a few seconds before The Big Guy, descending, could see where he was.

Daniel thought of what he was doing, somewhat grandiosely, as stockpiling parts for his very own weapon of mass destruction. It made him feel better to be doing something cumulative, something involving planning, inventiveness, and hope for the future. Of course, he had no idea what he was actually going to *do* with all the items he was collecting, but he refused to think about that. *Daniel was an anagram for Denial.* He had been trying to move a giant stack of newspapers and magazines when he had made the discovery. What an idiot he was not to have figured it out before! Someone had cut out the address labels on all the magazines, but at the very bottom of the pile, they had missed one. And there it was: *Emi Tokugawa, 55 Guinevere Ct., Baltimore.* Daniel had taken a deep breath. Emi! But Emi had been dead for years. Archie had emailed him. He had read her obituary online. So how . . . ?

Daniel had searched his memory for anything that would make sense to him. In truth, he had not thought about Emi Tokugawa in a long time. When he moved back to Baltimore for a teaching position, brokenhearted after Alma, he and Emi had played together occasionally. They had even slept together a few times, though it lacked the intensity it had had before. Then their paths had stopped crossing. Several years had passed. Through mutual acquaintances, he had heard of her divorce.

Emi was one of the people that Daniel had tried hardest to forget. Bad memories all around. When he had heard about her death, he had been stricken, because he somehow knew without being told that it had been suicide, and because when she had reached out to him that final time, he had not helped her. But, really, how could he have? He was married to Sigrid then, and trying, unsuccessfully, it turned out, to be a good husband. And there had always been something about Emi that scared him, an instability that bordered on hysteria, but which, he had to admit, had also excited him for a time.

Here, Daniel stopped riffling through the pages of the magazine— "Seven Summer 'Dos You'll Love," "When Husbands Cheat," "Five Steps to Flat Abs"—and closed his eyes. The last time he'd seen Emi was in a Thai restaurant in the city. The place with the elephants out front and the mango shrimp curry that made your eyes water. She had called him up out of the blue, and they'd had an awkward conversation with a lot of giggling on her end and a lot of blustery male courtesy on his. She had asked to see him, and Daniel, who had reason to be wary of her, considered refusing, but he always had a hard time saying no to women, and it was a mix of obligation, vanity, and compassion that had made him say yes.

He had been shocked by how much she had aged. Or not necessarily aged, but how pressed down she looked, as though someone had placed an invisible anvil on her head. The bright, quick look that had been in her eyes was gone, replaced by a duller, more furtive expression. She had cut her hair very short, and one of the first things Daniel had said to her was that it suited her, but that had been a lie. She was still pretty, or the ghost of pretty still hovered about her face, and she had obviously made an effort. Daniel recalled red lipstick, dangly earrings, some kind of fancy scarf. But her hair had grown thin in the back, where there was a gray whirl of a cowlick—he had tried not to stare at the mirror behind her head—and she had been perspiring a lot, her upper lip beaded with sweat, which she kept dabbing with the edge of a napkin.

"Can you help me find work?" she had asked in a low tone, looking at him, then down at her plate. "I need something to do."

He had heard about her being laid off at Longbourne but hadn't thought much of it. In Italy, she had told him she was an heiress, her father one of the big technology moguls to emerge after the war. Daniel hadn't known whether or not to believe her, but then she had bought him the Bulgari. Daniel pushed away the memory.

He gave Emi a few names that day, though he wasn't confident any of them would hire her, and he never got around to contacting them to vouch for her. In his vanity, perhaps, he assumed this was a pretense and not the true reason for the lunch. At one point, he mentioned Sigrid, awkwardly, and Emi bobbed her head in disconsolation.

The conversation had come around, in the end, to that summer in Florence. He hadn't wanted it to, and he had gotten the feeling that she hadn't wanted it to, either. Nevertheless, they talked about it, and Emi said something that struck him, and that he remembered now. "The thing is," she had said, "the thing I regret most isn't the affair, or telling Gen about it, or that you didn't want me after Alma left you." Daniel had looked at her sharply, wondering where this was going. She had looked away. "It's just that nothing that's happened since seems as real."

Daniel strained to remember more of their conversation. Emi had mentioned her teenaged daughter. A toddler back when they'd been in Florence. (What age would that make her now? Midtwenties, maybe?) At lunch, Emi had said something about her being very gifted but listening to terrible music. (And hearing it, Daniel thought he could now confirm.) Because Daniel was childless himself, he tended to zone out whenever people spoke about their children. Was it possible that this same daughter had gone through the trouble of kidnapping him, locking him in the basement with her dead mother's stuff? But why? What had Emi told her? For a moment he even entertained the idea that Emi wasn't dead, that it was she herself who had detained him, ready to pop out of her hiding place at any moment, like something out of Poe.

Daniel's head had hurt, and the chill of the cement floor had seeped into his bones. It had been four days. Wouldn't they have done whatever they were going to do to him by now? What were they waiting for? Daniel wasn't confident they even had a plan. It scared him more somehow, this partial knowledge—Emi Tokugawa's grown-up daughter and her accomplice, playing fast and loose with some misguided revenge fantasy. Daniel honestly did not see how he could be made culpable for Emi's fate. It was absurd. And yet there he'd been, and sitting with the magazine in his lap, boxes of Emi's things all around him, Daniel had had to admit that his conscience was not entirely clear.

THE YUKIO MISHIMAS GO VIRAL(ISH)

This is how it happened: Kyoko—restless with murderous anticipation, seeking distraction from a creeping sense of shame that she had not yet done the deed—created a video of their band, the Yukio Mishimas, and posted it to YouTube.

She had done this before, recorded them performing, sometimes with primitive animation she had created, sometimes with snippets of video Kornell had made, of Sumo in the litter box or Kyoko sleeping. This time, though, Kyoko had used pieces of their sex tapes—nothing graphic—grainy close-ups of shadowed movements, shots of Kornell's back as it rose and fell, the darkened outline of her breast, sidelong glimpses of haunch and hip. She had interspliced these images with a performance of their song "Seppuku." Kyoko, with freshly spiked hair, in black jeans and Shonen Knife T-shirt. *"Was a time I thought I loved you,"* she sang softly. *"Was a time I thought I cared / You gave your love to another / I don't know how you dared / You broke my heart in pieces, left them torn and scattered on the floor / Now you say you want to make up, don't know why you say that for / 'Cause I got a few words for you, and then a few words more . . ."* Kornell upped the tempo in a short drum fill to cymbal crash, and Kyoko leaned into the chorus with a scream. *"Sssssep-pu-ku, sep-pu-ku, I wanna com-mit sep-pu-ku / Just need to get the fuck away from you / Sep-pu-ku. Sep-pu-ku! / Fuuuuck you!"*

Kyoko's singing voice was an adequate rasping alto, the most marked feature of which was its volume, but her peculiar talent as a performer was her disquieting ability to unravel during a song, to come apart, a deep psychic unspooling that was simultaneously riveting and hard to watch. *"Watch my guts spill / Cut off my head! / Watch my guts spill / Cut off my head! / Watch my guts spill / Cut off my head! / Disemboweled, and now I . . . and now I . . . and now I'm dead."* Kyoko would have described it as an involuntary purging, like vom-iting or shitting, a hot hazardous waste dump of hate, anger, grief, and fear, the violent force of which nearly rendered her unconscious every time. The camera had recorded Kyoko's furious energy as she homed in on the mike, then jumped and spun away, her child's face contorted in multiplying expressions of private suffering—and be-hind her, steady on the drums, Kornell was a bald, benevolent genie in a worn undershirt, laying down the groove for her pain.

On the fifth day of Daniel's captivity, Kornell called Kyoko over to the computer screen. It took Kyoko a few moments to register what she was seeing or what it signified. She liked to make things—music, art, video—but once she was done, she lost interest. It was the process that mattered, the making; the product was incidental. In this, she was a true artist. Posting video on the internet, for Kyoko, was like dumping it in the trash. If someone found it on the other side, dug it out of the massive scrap heap of other shit, then fine, they could have their own experience with it, but Kyoko was done.

So she was genuinely astonished by what Kornell was showing her.

"Holy shit," she said.

"I know," Kornell said, laughing. "Can you believe it?" He clicked the trackpad, and Kyoko heard herself, in mid-fury, her voice raw with words. There was Kornell, his head glistening with sweat, reverent on drums, and her in her yellow T-shirt with the sleeves rolled up, thumping power chords on her Gibson SG. *Sssssep-pu-ku, sep-pu-ku, I wanna com-mit sep-pu-ku!*

Then a slender thigh, a black arm bracing, darkness shaded into lighter darkness, moving to a slower rhythm. Her own voice again, higher, softer, and Kornell's response, lush and low. *"Baby, that's good, just like that, just like that."*

Underneath the video were the band name, song title, and running time: *The Yukio Mishimas—"(I Want to Commit) Seppuku" 2:51.* And to the lower right, in smaller font: *72,363 views.*

ALMA IN BOBOLI GARDENS

Now Alma is walking in the Boboli Gardens with Paolo. She is struck by the differences between him and Daniel. There is the obvious: Paolo is a good three inches taller, is dark-haired and has Mediterranean coloring; Daniel's hair is also dark, but he has the fair skin and freckles of his Irish ancestry; Paolo dresses impeccably, in bespoke suits and pointy leather shoes, while Daniel favors a casual American uniform of polo shirts and khakis, with Jack Purcell tennis shoes; Paolo's English is practically fluent, and even when he stumbles, his Italian accent is refined and adorable, while Daniel's Italian, what little there is of it, is execrable. There is the readily apparent: Paolo is rich, with a palazzo in the Oltrarno, a Ferrari, and a villa outside Siena; Daniel splits the rent on their apartment in Back Bay, drives a 1983 Subaru, and owns a 1970-something Kawasaki motorcycle that doesn't run. And there is the subtle: Daniel is highly changeable emotionally—storms pass through him with frequency—but he is equally emotionally transparent; there is never any doubt about what he is feeling; he is stubborn, funny, smart, and he indulges Alma, she knows, in ways that are crucial to her. Paolo, whom she knows less well, feels more like a grown-up. He is shrewd in business, powerful in the world—managing the Teatro and the Opera, zipping from Florence to Rome to Milan (here Alma thinks, uneasily, of the Medicis)—courtly in manner, opinionated but not contentious, intensely ambitious, supremely confident, and though he is charming, he is one of those men who can seem quite open and confiding without, in fact, revealing anything about themselves. Alma senses a coldness at the core, his heart inaccessible—guards at the gate, a high fence, and a daunting security system—and this is what intrigues her the most.

They have come to the Knight's Garden, Alma's favorite spot in the Boboli, with its terrace of roses overlooking the Tuscan hills. Paolo has been talking about his new opera, which is based on the *Theogony* by the Greek poet Hesiod. Alma has only been half listening, distracted by the brilliance of the day and the gardens, and Paolo's courtly attentions, but from what she can make out, Gaia, the earth goddess, had mated with her son, Uranus, and had a lot of kids that Uranus killed, which made Gaia angry, so she got their son Cronus (who was also her grandson) to castrate him. Cronus, in turn, married his sister Rhea and swallowed all their babies at birth, except the one time she tricked him into swallowing a stone.

"Imagine, *cara*," Paolo says now, "what Freud would make of it. All this marrying sisters and mothers . . . *come si dici* . . . in English?"

"Incest?" Alma ventures.

"Yes, exact! Incest. Only my idea," he pauses significantly, even looking over his shoulder, "is to set the story in your American South. In . . . how do you call it? The trailer village?"

"Trailer park?" Alma says.

Paulo nods his head excitedly. "Just so. In the trailer park!"

Alma tries to look encouraging. This is the kind of thing for which Paolo is known, combining his fascination with America with classic stories to make original operas. He wrote an opera set during the California Gold Rush of 1849, loosely based on the *Orestia*, and another based on the story of Judith and Holofernes that took place in a New England whaling village.

The man had vision. Alma would give him that. And she is indulgent of people's passions, no matter how odd or seemingly misplaced, because she understands that nothing great has ever been achieved without it, and because, for Alma, passion is everything in life. She thinks of Bach's *St. Matthew Passion*, of the *Pietà* by Michelangelo, and does not discount the suffering. No, the suffering is an inextricable part of it.

The view of the landscape from the garden is muted, in variable green and earth tones. Alma loves the cypress trees especially—thin, dark green columns—and the shorter, silvery olives. On the other side of the terrace lies Florence. She recognizes the Palazzo Vecchio by its tower. So much beauty, in the museums and the churches, in the buildings themselves, beauty created by men, passionate in their creation—and here in the garden, overlooking the hills, natural beauty—color and curve, and shade and light.

Directly below the terrace, Alma's eye catches something she hasn't seen before, a tiny ramshackle building with a caved-in terracotta roof. She hasn't noticed it before because it is almost completely overrun by spidery gray vines and small trees with feathered leaves sticking out from the holes in the roof. A faint breeze lifts the stray pieces of hair that have come loose at Alma's temples, blowing them sharply across her face, and she feels suddenly overcome—by nature, by passion, by history and human striving, and the sense of impermanence that gives it all a particular piquancy.

"Cara," Paolo says. "Why do you cry?"

Alma brushes away tears and laughs. "It's just so beautiful," she says, and having said it, the beauty recedes to a manageable proportion.

"I understand," he says. "It is like this when I heard you play the Franck the other night. Sublime."

Alma shrugs. "Not my best, I'm afraid," she says. "Too much prosecco the night before. That was your fault."

Paolo looks at her strangely. "I think, *mia amorata*, if I may say so, you are a very beautiful woman."

"You may say so," says Alma lightly.

"You think this beauty is on the outside," Paolo says, "and yes, you are certainly beautiful that way, *cara*, but your true beauty is deep inside. I think that you do not know how deep."

Alma shivers and looks down at the half-buried house. She thinks about Daniel, wonders what he is doing. "You Italians," she says. "Such seducers."

Paolo makes an impatient gesture. "Okay, so you do not accept it," he says. They are silent. The sound of distant bees buzzing and, more distantly, the clacking of construction.

"A beautiful woman should have whatever she wants in life," he says finally. His voice is dreamy. "Tell me, *cara*, what is it you want?"

Alma laughs. "And I suppose you're going to tell me you can get it for me, is that it?" she says.

But Paolo is serious. His dark eyes hold the question, and Alma has to look away.

"What do I want?" she says. She turns toward the city and fans her hands out wide. "This," she says. "This is what I want."

Paolo's eyes narrow; he nods, as though Alma has passed some crucial test. "Of course," he says. "You want it all." He strokes her hair. "*Bene.* I will help you." He leans down to kiss her, but Alma moves away.

"You forget I'm with Daniel," she says.

Paolo shrugs. "I'm not jealous," he says.

Alma wonders what it would be like to fuck Paolo, his wild-haired eyebrows teasing her nipples, tickling her belly, feeling their way blindly in the dark. Would he be a brute and throw her on the bed, take her from the back and pull her hair? Or would he be sensitive, kiss her all over with his sensualist's lips, at the moment of climax cry out "My darling!" before collapsing onto her breast? She has been with Daniel for five years, and though there is a tacit understanding that they will get married one day, Alma is growing impatient. She hates to cleave to stereotype, the twenty-nine-year-old spinster angling for a proposal—in fact, with her career, she is not even sure she wants children or anything that smacks of domestic arrangement—but it irks her that Daniel should seem so unhurried on the subject, so complacent in the status quo. Alma, who is much admired, highly sought after by men who fall in love with her stage presence, her musicianship, her angular beauty, is offended by it.

They walk back through the garden together slowly, Paolo tucking Alma's arm into the crook of his elbow, and by the fountain with the fat dwarf riding on a turtle, she lets him kiss her, his tongue in her mouth tasting of garlic and Chianti. She feels no guilt, but also, strangely, no arousal, and is eager to get back to the hotel to find Daniel.

Kyoko recalls her mother

At first Kyoko was upset that Daniel had discovered who she was, but Kornell convinced her it didn't matter. "What good does it do him?" he said. "This way he has some time to think on what he's done." The image of her mother on the bathroom floor came to Kyoko, the way it had hundreds of times before, not just the image but a full flashback time reversal, wrenching her backward to the day of her mother's death, to the shock, the numbness, and the grief of the moment when she had found her.

It made Kyoko furious that this was the moment that kept returning to her, that the memory of her mother dead had become more vivid for her than any memory of her alive.

Emi: the dreamer, the schemer, the hoarder, the holder, the martyr, the lover, the mother. Sweet, delicate, deluded, and magical Emi. When someone dies, our impulse is to flatten her out, to press her between wax paper like a leaf, or to fix her in amber like a bug. Death as capture, death as collected works. But death is a false terminus, one moment only. It seems more significant because it is the last moment, the most recent, when really it is the smallest and least telling. Life is the plumpness of all directions, of surprises and contradictions, of impulses, mistakes, duplicities, and redemptions. While the vanishing point on the horizon line is a dot, a blip, the same for us all.

K yoko was having a hard time working. Or, rather, she was working fine, but she despised everything that resulted. Willy had tracked the overlord responsible for her family's deaths to an inn in the southernmost prefecture of Japan, and Kyoko had envisioned a scene where the realization hit Willy that this was the evildoer, while he ate and drank with his henchmen, unaware. It was going to be a full two-page spread, with an oval inset of Willy's shocked and excited face, and a rectangular flashback panel of her family's murders, but Kyoko had sketched and re-sketched, drawn, rubbed out, redrawn, rubbed out, until the surface of her sketchpad was raw and abraded and covered with pink crumbles.

Kyoko should have been excited about their unexpected YouTube popularity, and she had been, for about five minutes. But at the moment she was feeling dull and ineffective. The simple act of drawing a line seemed beyond her capability. She kept going back to her worst humiliations, like the other night, in the rain outside Rafferty's, when she had been stalking Daniel. She would dwell on the moment her foot had gotten caught in the spokes of the umbrella, with an obsessive attention that bordered on nostalgia. Squish, squish, oof!, and the taste of her own blood. Squish, squish, oof!, and the wet asphalt smack to the underside of her chin.

Mostly, though, Kyoko was thinking about her mother. Finally having Daniel Karmody in her custody forced Kyoko to reflect on what exactly she was avenging. Her mother's suicide, certainly. The despair Emi had felt when she realized Prince Charming was never coming to the rescue. And before that, the swollen regret of her divorce and her husband's remarriage. Staying in bed. Losing her job. Mugfuls of coffee with Bailey's in the mornings, then the afternoons and the evenings; the potpourri of pills—Xanax, Ambien, Klonopin, Prozac. Newspaper clippings laid out on the kitchen table when Kyoko came home from school—of rapes and murders, earthquakes and oil spills, bridge collapses and terrorist attacks—"Read this, Kyoko! Read what happened! It's terrible!" Her QVC addiction—USPS, FedEx, and UPS showing up at the house each day with brown packages of all sizes and shapes; the accumulation of objects, the amassing of paper, plastic, wood, metal, and glass, piled into closets, rooms, and boxes—until they had to navigate a narrow labyrinth from room to room.

As Emi had grown more and more withdrawn, depressed and mistrustful, Kyoko had adopted a false persona of cheer and optimism. She had had no choice. She was terrified. "They're so beautiful," she would say, pulling out evening gowns from Emi's closet. "Will you wear this one for me? What about the purple? I bet you look stunning in this one!" while her mother lay in bed, in the maroon velour robe and Lanz nightgown that had become her constant uniform.

On good days, she could get Emi to dress up for her, to sit at the vanity and do her makeup the way she wore it for recitals, with Cleopatra cat eyes and bright crimson lipstick. "This is the dress I wore when we played for Zubin Mehta in Florence," she would say. "Did I ever tell you what he said to me?"

"No," Kyoko would lie. "Tell me."

"He said I was a vision in white. Like a beautiful dream."

On bad days, Emi would lie in bed and cry. "I *was* beautiful once," she would say, turning her face to her pillow. "But look at me now! I'm hideous and old!" Her voice rising high, then cracking. "No wonder Daniel doesn't want me. I could never be like *Alma*." Pronouncing her name like a curse. "Why couldn't I be like *Alma*?" Pronouncing her name like a doomed prayer. Kyoko would rub her back and listen and make sympathetic noises that were no longer words.

Now, as Kyoko contemplated ripping her sketchpad pages into tiny pieces and eating them, she tried to remember further back, to when her mother was whole and strong. To blame Daniel Karmody for her mother's pitiful decline was one thing, but to concede to him the entirety of her mother was another, and Kyoko would not do it, even if she had to struggle to reclaim her.

The truth was that it was Emi who had been Kyoko's biggest supporter. "Oh, such a wonderful picture!" she would say, as ten-, eleven-, twelve-year-old Kyoko would be coloring at the kitchen counter, never commenting on the bloody depictions of grotesque hara-kiri deaths or imitation *shunga* with oversized genitalia. "So advanced! Look, Gen! Isn't Kyoko so talented?"

"Ah, very nice!" She would clap her hands as Kyoko played the last trembling note of her latest composition, back when she still played the violin. "That one sounded to me like the brook in the forest where I used to play as a child. I could hear the birds singing!"

One of Kyoko's earliest and fondest memories of her mother was of the bedtime story she had told her every night for years. It was about a poor, elderly couple that lived in the remote mountains. The man would go out every day to gather sticks for firewood, and the woman would wash their clothes by the river. One day, when the woman was washing clothes, a giant peach came floating down the river toward her. The woman brought the peach home, delighted by such bounty, and when the man came back from gathering firewood, she cut into it with a knife. "Don't cut me," exclaimed a voice, surprising the old man and woman, who were even more surprised when a small boy popped out from the peach pit. "I am Momotarō," he said, "and I have been sent to you from Heaven in answer to your prayers for a child." The old couple was overjoyed, and Momotarō grew up strong and dutiful. When he was fifteen, he asked for permission to go on a long journey to Ogre Mountain, to kill the evil monsters that were terrorizing the land. The old couple reluctantly agreed, and Momotarō traveled for years, across water and mountains, and with the help of some animals he enlisted along the way, he defeated the ogres and carried their treasure home to his parents, where they lived in peace and prosperity for the rest of their days.

Emi would tell the story—which Kyoko didn't know was a Japanese folk tale until years later—with different twists and embellishments each time. It was what Kyoko loved most, catching the changes, the added little details, within the cozy familiarity of the story's basic structure. Sometimes Momotarō would emerge naked and sometimes wrapped in yellow robes, sometimes it was a dog and a monkey who helped him and sometimes a dog and a cat. The number of years his journey took would be seven, or ten, or thirteen. But always, the reunion, the treasure, and the happy ending.

K yoko remembered one night—she must have been around six or seven—asking her mother how old the couple had been when Momotarō first came to them. Emi considered. "Around sixty," she said.

Kyoko worked out the math. "So that means when Momotarō went to fight the ogres, they were seventy-five."

"Yes, that sounds about right," Emi said.

Kyoko averaged the number of years for Momotarō's journey. "But, Mommy," she said, "by the time Momotarō returned, his parents would be eighty!"

"That's right," said Emi, smiling. "But at least they got to live a comfortable old age."

"Why didn't Heaven send him sooner?" Kyoko persisted. "Why did they wait until they were already so old?"

"I don't know," said Emi. She smoothed Kyoko's hair back from her forehead. "I guess it takes a long time to get from Heaven all the way down to Japan."

"What if he got back from fighting the ogres and they were dead?"

"Kyoko!" Emi looked startled.

"What would he have done with all the treasure then?"

"Okay, that's enough," her mother said. She gave Kyoko a strange look before kissing her good night, leaving the room, and closing the door behind her.

Kyoko stayed up for a long time that night. She imagined Momotarō returning from Ogre Mountain in triumph, with bulging sacks of gold on his back, only to discover the house empty, the hearth cold, everything layered in dust and cobwebs, and around back his parents' graves in the yard, marked by twin mounds of dirt. She remembered crying herself to sleep, sobbing, actually, because she had realized for the first time that one day her parents were going to die and that she would be left alone.

Kornell and Yoshi's
Black Market Dealings

K ornell suspected Yoshi of being part of the yakuza, the Japanese mafia; he certainly had dealings with some shady characters. They would come in in their shiny blue suits and Yoshi would bow and bow, then usher them to the best seats at the bar for omakase, which they would never pay for. One night, when Kornell had stayed at work late, Yoshi had shown him a bag of what looked like coarsely ground flour.

"Burke-san, do you know what is this?" he had asked, giggling. He had been drinking sake with some of the waiters, and his cheeks looked like they had been slapped hard on both sides.

Kornell had shaken his head.

Yoshi giggled harder. He was a jolly drunk and, like many Asians, couldn't hold his liquor. "Very, very special. Good for mans." He had pointed to Kornell's crotch. "Make you very popular!

"In Japan," Yoshi had said, hefting the bag in his hand like a scale, "pay very high price." He had put a finger to his lips to indicate secrecy, and, giggling, he had put the bag away in a drawer.

Kornell had told Kyoko about the late-night deliveries of fish that Yoshi would preside over with the intensity of a mother with a newborn. He would cradle the white craft paper packages, place them gently on the table, and unwrap the swaddling to reveal the homely features only a mother could love—peevishly bug-eyed, slick and slimy, grayish brown with black splotches and a white belly; the highly coveted, outrageously expensive, potentially fatal fugu, or Japanese blowfish.

Again, Yoshi made the giggling gesture toward Kornell's crotch; everything, it seemed, was a male aphrodisiac to the Japanese. Yoshi had told him how customers would pay a hundred dollars for a plate of fugu sashimi, how the skin and guts contained a lethal poison that, if not properly removed, would paralyze you, shutting down your bodily functions, until you choked to death on your own spit. Or this is what Kornell deduced from Yoshi's amusing pantomime, in which he clutched at his throat with both hands, went rigid as a Frankenstein monster, made strangled, choking sounds, and fell limp to one side, with his eyes closed and his tongue lolling out of his mouth.

"Very dangerous, Burke-san," Yoshi said. "You eat and you feel power!" He made a muscle, tapped it with two fingers.

"Unless you die," Kornell said, and Yoshi giggled.

"Unless you die," he said.

Daniel Devises a Plan

Two things increasingly occupied Daniel's time down in the basement. Both seemed equally crucial to his survival though they pulled in opposite directions. The first involved the construction of his WMD, and here Daniel could, in some tangible way, gauge his progress. He waited until after dinner, when he knew The Big Guy wouldn't be coming back down, then dug out the bin in which he kept his specially gathered materials. With an ear cocked for sound from upstairs—footfalls on creaky floorboards, the swoosh of toilet flush, the rattle of old pipes, and the faint, gargling noise of human conversation—Daniel glued, wrapped, bent, and secured, ready to shove the top on the bin and push it back behind the other boxes at the first metallic click of a key in the lock.

Daniel was not particularly good with his hands in other ways than the specific skill set involved with playing the violin—and whether or not he was good at engineering, at conceptualizing something that would actually work, remained to be seen—but he was surprised by how much he enjoyed just the physical making, the handling of the objects, the fastening and the fixing.

The other thing that occupied Daniel was the less tangible project of canvassing his past for mistakes, patterns, and clues. Socrates said the unexamined life was not worth living, and Daniel had to admit that he had lived his life largely without self-scrutiny. If he had had a motto, it would have been something like *carpe diem*, or *tempus fugit*, or *love the one you're with*. He had been too disciplined a musician to be a hedonist, but he had done what he liked—eaten, drunk, and been merry—without much thought for other people's feelings. His moral compass, sadly, had been the kind that circumscribed circles, not the kind that pointed magnetic north. Which is to say that Daniel had been a selfish man and that all roads had led back to him.

Among Emi's things, Daniel had found a self-help book called *Never Too Late: A User's Guide to Personal Growth*, and in the margins, in faint script, he had found some penciled notes. In chapter 1: "Stopping the Negative Feedback Loop," the author had written, "Don't let your negative self-talk fool you. You are a good person." Beside this, someone had written, "How would you know?" In chapter 3, under "Homework," the author had written, "Write a letter to someone in your life that you have hurt and tell them that you are sorry. Try not to rationalize your actions or to assign blame. You don't have to send it. In fact, it's better not to. Just write it, and see how you feel." Beside this, in spiky pencil, "Made me feel worse."

Daniel wondered if it had been Emi's handwriting. He wondered to whom she had written. For his own part, there were far too many people to whom he could write. Sigrid, for one. "Dear Sigrid—I am sorry I ruined your life." That about covered it. No need to go into the details. And Emi. Daniel wasn't sure exactly what he should apologize to her for. But clearly Emi's daughter (if he had guessed correctly) held him accountable for something. And he *was* sorry, not just because he was being held accountable, locked in a mold-filled basement, but precisely because he had no idea what damage he might have caused her.

"Dear Emi—I'm sorry I have thought of you so rarely. I'm sorry I avoided thinking about your suffering. Even when you killed yourself." The words, though honest, sounded alarmingly callous.

Yet the person he thought of more than anyone, the person he felt the deepest need to apologize to, was, of course, Alma. Because the first step toward feeling sorry for the pain you've inflicted on someone else is to feel sorry for the pain that you've inflicted on yourself, in relation to someone else, and on this score, Daniel carried around a deep and permanent wound.

Daniel and Alma Meet Cute

She had walked into Cuppa Joe's, in Boston, and sat down across from him, at a table in the back room. She was wearing a lot of makeup and a black T-shirt cut off at the collar and sleeves, like the muscle shirts guys in the '50s used to wear when they drove their souped-up cars. It had a picture of the Ramones on it—though Daniel had no idea who they were at the time—and her hair was done up in braids, with red plaid ribbons on the ends. She had on this weird, shiny black lipstick that Daniel remembered thinking looked gruesome, as though she had been feasting on carrion. But she . . . she was magnificent.

"You've got to help us," she had said, though she appeared to be alone. Her voice was urgent and surprisingly low. "My name's Alma, and I'm in this band. We need a name, so we're putting it to a vote. Which do you think is better: Cello Vendetta or Cello Kitty?"

Daniel had considered. "They're both good," he said.

"But which is better?" she insisted. Her eyes were downturned at the outer edges, with deep brown centers, and she was looking at him as though the fate of nations hung on his answer.

He pretended to think about it, but really he was taking her in. She was tall and willowy, with high breasts and glowing golden skin. Her cheekbones were high and sharply cut, and she had a cute button nose and small, slightly pointed ears. It was her mouth that he kept returning to, though. Later she would tell him that she considered it her best feature, and it was no wonder. Large and luscious, with a plump top lip that came to a perfect, fleshy point over a generous, pouting lower. Even painted black, it communicated pure carnality.

The conservatory was full of Asian girls, and Daniel had taught his share, but—though many of them were pretty in their way, doll-like, delicate, with gleaming black hair and porcelain skin—he had never quite thought of them individually, as separate entities with diverse personalities and desires. They seemed always to walk around campus in groups, chattering in Chinese or Korean, instrument cases bumping against the sides of their thin legs. In class, they were obedient, but largely passive, listening with wide-eyed attention to his instruction, laughing politely behind their hands at his jokes—and though most were gifted, and some very much so, the overall impression Daniel got was of a bland dutifulness, as though playing the violin were a finishing-school exercise, a cultural accomplishment that a good wife needed to achieve a certain social status, and so he had never before contemplated the relative attractiveness of an individual Asian woman.

But he was contemplating it now, because Alma, whom he had certainly heard about but never seen, was singularly attractive. Beyond this, though, there was something Daniel recognized, an aura, a buzz, a current of excitement that seemed to radiate from Alma like an electric shock, leaving in its wake the twin sensations of light and warmth. Daniel thought of this as "star quality." It was rare. Heifetz had had it. Ma. Zuckerman. Stern, of course. All the great performers. It was a charisma that went far beyond their genius abilities, a presence that could never be fully captured in recordings but that radiated across concert halls, infecting each and every person in the room with a low-level fever. It was intimate and embracing; you felt like you alone had been allowed in. And there was a generosity, too, as though, in being invited, you had been recognized for your best self, your truest and most authentic, and that as long as you remained in the spotlight of her gaze, you would be worthy forever. (Later, when Daniel had heard Alma play, he realized that what he had experienced was no accident. His mentor, Leopold von Stade, used to say that he knew he was in the presence of greatness when a musician made the hairs on the back of his neck stand up, and listening to Alma play Mendelsohn, Daniel had felt it, the tingle, as of extreme cold, at the back of his hairline, each follicle a nerve ending, a reverberating string.)

"Cello Kitty is cute," he said finally, "but Cello Vendetta sounds more punk."

Alma looked delighted and wrote something down on a paper she had on a clipboard. "Thanks," she said. "You were very helpful."

"I'm Daniel Karmody, by the way," he said.

She smiled at him, her teeth showing between those sexy, hideous lips. "I know," she said, and got up and walked away.

A few weeks later, he had been amused to see posters for Cello Vendetta around campus, and he smiled to himself, as though he were in on the joke. He remembered the girl in the black lipstick, with the Pippi Longstocking braids, the provocative mouth, and the radiant presence, and even though he had classes to prepare for, on top of rehearsals and auditions, he found himself that night in a dark, crowded basement on Chasen Street, squinting through a blue haze at Alma and her band. There were three female cellists in black leather and stilettos, and three schleppy-looking guys on drums, guitar, and bass. One of the guys Daniel recognized as Harry Suthers from the Balfour Quartet. He wondered how they found the time to moonlight in this way. Alma sat in the middle, her hair in one long braid across her shoulder. She wore some kind of medieval-looking costume, a bustier, or a corset, with grommets and lace-up ribbons that hoisted her breasts and thrust them forward as she leaned over her cello. She was singing in an oddly pitched and angular alto that was surprisingly appealing, her eyes closed, her red lips poised indecently over a stationary mike. The music was frantic and loud, the amps kept feeding back, bodies kept bumping into him with over-slopping beer and drunken dance moves. In his blue oxford shirt and brown corduroys, Daniel had felt square and out of place.

Later, between sets, Alma had come over; her mascara smeared under one eye, her lipstick faded to orange. She was sucking on a Chloraseptic lozenge, and her tongue, which she stuck out to show him, was a bright, nuclear green.

"Thanks for coming," she shouted in a hoarse, ragged voice. "I have kind of a cold and I'm trying not to fall over."

"You sound great," Daniel said.

"I sound like shit," she said in a neutral tone.

"I'm glad you picked Cello Vendetta," he said.

Alma looked at him blankly for a moment. "Ohhh, yeah." She took his beer from him and drank, leaving a waxy mark on the side of his cup. She made a face. "That tastes terrible with this." She indicated her lozenge. "We put it to a vote," she said. "I wanted Cello Kitty, but it lost." She shrugged.

"Oh," Daniel said, feeling oddly hurt.

"I'm glad you came," she said, and Daniel's spirits rose.

"Me, too," he said.

"Everyone kept mentioning this Daniel Karmody," she said. "How handsome he was. What a hotshot violinist. How great a teacher."

"Did they mention I was faster than a speeding bullet?" he said.

Alma shook her head. "No, but they did say you were single." She smiled at him, and when, a few hours later, he had kissed her, he was so far gone he hoped he *would* catch her cold; he wanted every molecule of her being to merge with his, to trespass his defenses—the astringent mix of Chloraseptic and beer, lipstick and cold germs marking only the beginning, the gateway for the atomic comingling, the woozy-headedness and high fever, that was falling in love.

Alma Soon Ja Lee," Daniel said, the syllables tripping off his tongue. They had just slept together for the first time and were lingering in her bed. "Where does 'Alma' come from?"

"From Alma Mahler."

"Oh, did your parents like Mahler?"

Alma shook her head. "I named myself after her."

"But why? I mean, didn't she cheat on Gustav, have all those affairs with famous artists? Who was it? Gustav Klimt? Oskar Kokoschka?"

"She only kissed Klimt, and Kokoschka came later."

"Oh, well—"

"I named myself after her because I wanted to remind myself not to make the same mistake she did."

"What mistake was that?" asked Daniel, stroking her hip.

Alma smiled. "When she agreed to marry Mahler, he made her promise to give up her career. She was a composer, too, you know. He told her that his work would be enough for both of them, that her job would be to support him."

"Ahhh," Daniel said. "So, you don't want to sacrifice your career for a man?"

"Fat chance of that," Alma said. She shook her head. "No, I don't want to marry a genius."

Daniel couldn't read her expression. Was she smiling, or was she serious? "Well," he said lightly, "I guess that explains what you're doing with me."

Alma and Daniel go to Siena

The day had started disastrously. The weather, which had been dry and hot since they arrived, seemed, that morning, to be changing—the sky low with cloud, the sun partially occluded. Daniel hadn't slept well—he blamed the noise of revelers in the piazza below their hotel—and had woken up with a headache, and he had barked at Alma for not being ready on time.

"Relax, DK," Alma said. "We're taking the weekend off. There's no schedule, no time we need to be anywhere."

"But I've been waiting for you for over an hour," Daniel persisted.

Alma put a dress into her bag and took it out again. "Go down and have another espresso," she said.

Then he gave her the map, though he knew she wasn't good with directions, and they had gotten lost almost immediately, ending up in a drab neighborhood of narrow streets and gray, concrete buildings. The rented Fiat was a piece of shit. The stick shift required an unnatural amount of force, and the clutch kept sticking. The car stalled or lurched into gear like a spastic rabbit, and Alma soon developed a headache of her own.

At some point they had found the highway and had been driving for about an hour when Alma had had to pee, so they had turned off at the next exit. They had seen a sign for a restaurant, but after driving a few miles, there had been nothing but low houses on both sides of a narrow street.

"Turn here," Alma had said. She thought she'd seen a building that looked like a restaurant, or an inn, at the top of the hill, but the road twisted and turned, and whatever she had seen did not materialize, and so they had kept going, up and up, as the road wound between dusty rows of grapevines and olive trees.

"Where is it?" Daniel had demanded. "This can't be right."

Alma unfolded the map across her knees, though it was clearly useless. "I think we should have gone straight back there," she said.

"We couldn't go straight back there! We could only go left or right."

"Well, then turn around."

"Where?" Daniel said, his voice rising. "Do you see anyplace where I can turn around? Christ! The road's disappearing."

And sure enough, the road, which had been paved, then graveled, had petered out into a dirt path, atop a long rise, in the middle of some sort of vineyard.

Daniel shifted into reverse; the car made a sharp whiplash move, lurched backward a few yards, fell off the path and into the side of an olive tree. He slammed on the brakes.

"Slow down!" yelled Alma, white-knuckling it on the dash. "What are you doing?"

"Fuck!" said Daniel. The car stalled. "This piece of crap . . ." He turned the key in the ignition. The car started, then died.

"Do you want me to try?" Alma said.

Daniel turned the key again, whereupon there was a grating metallic sound, like a garbage disposal with a spoon in it, and he pounded his two fists into the steering wheel. "Fuck! Fuck! Fuck!"

"That's helpful," said Alma.

"I don't see you doing anyth—"

"I offered to . . . Look, DK! There's someone!"

From out of nowhere, a woman had appeared. She was short and plump, with white nimbus hair and apple dumpling cheeks, and she was carrying a pair of clippers and a small wicker basket. She came up to Daniel's side of the car and stood patiently, inhibiting his further demonstrations of frustration and anger. He rolled down the window.

"May I assist you?" she said in fluent English.

Her name was Isabella, and she had been an Italian-English translator for a publishing company in Rome. She and her husband owned a small country home just a few hundred yards from where Alma and Daniel had gotten stuck, and after cheerfully navigating them out of the tree and into her driveway, she invited them inside for some lunch.

Her husband was away in the States for business, she said, and she had come up to the country to finish her translation of Mark Twain's *Pudd'nhead Wilson*. "There is no translation for this in Italian," she said, tapping the side of her temple. "'*Pudd'nhead*,' with this connotation of someone slightly soft and stupid, it would have no meaning to Italians. The closest I could come was 'Pumpkin Head.' *Testa di zucca. Pumpkin Head Wilson*." She laughed. "Do you think Mr. Twain would have approved?"

She served them a delicious chickpea soup, with hunks of white bread, and a simple red wine from a neighbor's vineyard. Daniel's mood had improved, as had Alma's own, and they parted company with the woman—loaded up with grapes and a bottle of wine—in the best of spirits, Alma declaring in the car that fate had obviously meant for them to find her, and Daniel agreeing that it had all turned out wonderfully.

The day also had improved, all the gray dissipated into a broader blue, and the sun once again reigning in the sky, and by the time they got to Siena, they were laughing and singing Puccini, Alma with her bare legs up on the dash.

They ate dinner late, alfresco, in the Campo, and stayed for hours, nursing glasses of port. "I'll love you until the day I die, Alma," Daniel declared, and they went back to the hotel, where they made love all night, in every position and on every surface of their room, emerging late in the afternoon of the next day, to climb the stone stairs of the Campanile.

She remembers heat and dust and brown hills everywhere, shimmering with the soft green of olive leaves. She remembers Isabella, in khaki shorts and Birkenstocks, with a deep-cut smile on her plump, pleasant face. *Ceci* soup and hearth bread. Velvet Tuscan wine. Isabella cutting grapes with a pair of snub-nosed clippers, stooping in the soil like a stout lady Bacchus. She remembers in the car, her legs on the dash, the smooth palm of Daniel's hand creeping up underneath her San Lorenzo market-stall skirt. *Vissi d'arte, vissi d'amore!*

And this. Alma remembers sitting at a table in the Campo in

Siena that same evening. The warmth of the day still lingering with the light, but with a premonition of cooler air. A few stars and a sickle of moon. Daniel is a little drunk, and maybe she is, too. They are not touching, but she is aware of his physical proximity, feels it like heat, pulling her closer, tighter, even though neither of them is moving. It is very sexy, this feeling, and she knows that soon they will not be able to keep their hands off each other, but just at the moment, there is a kind of equilibrium, a stillness between desire and impulse, which she is loath to disturb. *This*, she thinks, a thought she will not consciously retain, though the feeling will come back to her—*this is happiness. Right now. In this moment. Here it is.*

DANIEL BUILDS A WMD

Daniel's allergies were worsening. He had had to ask The Big Guy for more tissues, and had been tempted to ask him to get the more expensive brand, because the generic was so rough it was chafing his nose raw. He had petitioned for a razor and shaving cream—his beard was itchy and bits of tissue stuck to it—but so far, nothing. Also, his digestion had been terrible for days. He needed some Kaopectate, or what was the stuff that Sigrid used to buy? Milk of magnesia. Or was that for the other thing? He could never remember.

As Daniel fretted over his health, he worked obsessively on his weapon of mass destruction, which he'd modeled, loosely, on a catapult, crossed with an IED. The problem was that he couldn't conduct a proper test launch. His WMD consisted of crushed glass fragments and both heated and unheated metallic projectiles of several sizes, propelled out of a Ferris wheel arrangement of rubber hemispheres by means of hooked elastic bands. He had been able to test the basic physics of the apparatus with a few paper clips and some heated curlers, but the fragments of Christmas ornament could only be unleashed once, so Daniel had to just take it on faith that the device would work when it needed to.

He did feel a little bad for The Big Guy, who, if his contraption worked, could stand to be blinded or badly cut. Though TBG had never spoken more than a few words and wore his mask the whole time, his brown eyes, peering out from behind narrow eyeholes, had seemed to Daniel to reflect a basic human decency, and once or twice Daniel could have sworn that he had succeeded in getting him to smile.

In a contingency plan, Daniel had decided that if the girl ever showed up again, he would grab her and threaten to poke her in the eyeball with an unfolded paper clip. It was the best he could do with the materials at hand.

Daniel shuffled to the bathroom for the nth time that night, his stomach churning. His situation was clearly a question of survival: fight to leave the dungeon alive or wait to die in it. And unlike one week prior, Daniel knew, with utmost conviction, that he desired to live. He was slowly realizing the extent of his culpability in Emi's suffering—her divorce, the end of her music career, her death—not to mention Alma's—for, banal pleasantries in her Facebook message notwithstanding, she undoubtedly had suffered due to him, and perhaps suffered still. Somehow, these unpleasant realizations made him yearn to live long enough to become . . . different. *Kind*, if he was feeling ambitious. *Decent* would be enough. Would be aspirational. He kept going back to that summer twenty years ago, and the decision he had made (and the one he hadn't), that had led to this—his snot-sniffling-bowel-loosening-weapon-engineering-itchy-bearded-bologna-and-white-bread-eating-damp-basement-dwelling-possibly-life-ending misery.

Alma Busks on the Bridge

Y ou're kidding!"

"I am not. Watch me."

"Alma, you can't be serious . . ."

"Oh, don't be such a stick-in-the-mud!" Alma struggled into the tiny elevator with her cello and fold-up chair and pushed the button. Inside the metal cage, she descended. Daniel ran down the stairs.

"Paolo is going to be pissed," he called.

"Since when do you care about Paolo?"

"I'm just worried you'll exhaust yourself, that's all. It's hot." Daniel turned the corner, hopped the banister, and got to the ground floor before the elevator. He heard the creak of the ancient mechanism. The cage door opened. "Let me carry those for you at least," Daniel said, succumbing, as he always succumbed to Alma's various whims and constant will (for not to succumb was akin to standing in front of an ATAF bus in the middle of Viale Strozzi on a weekday afternoon).

Daniel grabbed the chair with one hand and the cello with the other.

"Be careful!" said Alma sharply.

Daniel knew what the cello was worth. It was a 1732 Francesco Goffriller, on indefinite loan from the National Classical Music Foundation, and it had been in Alma's possession for two months. "I'm fine," he said.

It was early afternoon and the tourists on the Piazza del Duomo staggered out of Santa Maria del Fiore, the Campanile, and the Baptistry, blinking into the sunlight, dazed by their rude reemergence into a modern century. Tour guides held up colored triangular flags to guide their flocks, waving them cheerlessly like heraldic banners after a battle that had been badly lost. Daniel cringed when he recognized a group of Americans, indelibly egregious in floral shirts and unflattering shorts, baseball caps and cross-trainers; ungainly with cameras and backpacks; overweight and pink, talking too loudly in accent-inflected English—Georgia, Boston, Iowa, New Jersey.

"Hey, ya wanna get a gelato?"

Alma put her hand on Daniel's back. "Gel-*at*-o," she repeated, giggling.

"Tourists," Daniel muttered, and they both laughed.

They made their way out of the Duomo traffic and into the funnel leading to the Ponte Vecchio. Daniel noted how the vendors, at their street stalls, looked at Alma, following her with their eyes, like hungry lions. He felt a pride of possession—*she's with me, suckers!*—that was swiftly undercut by uneasiness, a premonition of loss.

"Hey, boss, where we going?" Daniel said.

"You'll see," said Alma.

"Did I happen to mention that this is a bad idea?"

"You did."

"I thought so."

They got to the bridge, which was crowded with people peering into the windows of the shops, at the glittering candy-box assortment of looping gold chains, and pearls, and precious stones, set in earrings, rings, and bracelets, gaudy-colored and multiple. It was one of Alma's favorite places in Florence. "I love the way the buildings are like these little orange and yellow boxes jutting out on both sides— like they were assembled by happy children!" Alma had declared. "And the way that the thick wooden shutters and oversize iron hinges turn the jewelry stores into these huge locked treasure chests at night." Daniel thought the bridge was too touristy, too congested— the crowd on the bridge, another river, moving, like the river below, in a slow stream.

In front of Fratelli Piccini, Alma stopped. Daniel put the cello down between them. He took out his handkerchief and wiped his brow.

"Just in case you're interested," Alma said. "That's the one." She put her forefinger on the glass window, pressed the tip until it bent back.

"What one?" asked Daniel.

"That one."

Daniel saw that she was pointing to a ring with a diamond set in a pentagon of gold, flanked asymmetrically by small sapphires.

"What's the occasion?" he said lightly.

Alma stared in at the window, her forehead almost touching the glass. She shrugged. "There's always an occasion," she said.

They had talked about marriage, of course, and Daniel assumed they would get married someday, but part of him still could not really imagine pointing to one woman, even a woman as amazing as Alma, and saying, "You, and no other, from this day forward." He thought he should say something, to acknowledge what it was Alma intended by pointing the ring out to him, but she had already turned and was walking away. Daniel hurried after her.

Alma stopped abruptly. "Here," she said, indicating a spot to the right of the bust of Benvenuto Cellini. She pulled the chair out of Daniel's hand.

"Here?" Daniel said stupidly. All around them, people were taking pictures, eating gelato, chattering in English, French, German, and what sounded like Japanese.

Alma unfolded the chair and took the cello case next. She moved stiffly, and Daniel could tell that she was mad at him.

The whole thing was crazy—irresponsible, really; she was going to give herself sunstroke or heat exhaustion. They should have been practicing in the air-conditioning or taking a nap. But busking on the street like a two-bit amateur was just the kind of stunt that Alma relished—like moonlighting as a punk rocker, or painting her fingernails red, because other people did not do it or because they said that *she* could not.

Alma had taken the Goffriller out of its case. It was a beautiful instrument, big and warm, with back panels of bird's-eye maple and a top of finely grained spruce. It shone in the Florentine sun like a sacred object; Benvenuto Cellini, looking down from his height, seemed to regard it appreciatively.

The crowd started to get interested as Alma smoothed the back of her skirt and sat down. Their distracted gazes settled on her, expectantly, geared for spectacle. Alma took a deep breath, did a couple of neck rolls. Tuned her instrument. Daniel thought she might look at him, but her eyes were closed. She began to play. The Adagio, from Bach's Toccata, Adagio, and Fugue in C Major.

Daniel stepped back and let the crowd absorb him. He tried to see Alma as the others saw her, as though she were a stranger. A slender young Asian woman, in a black T-shirt and simple black skirt, tanned legs spread wide, each sandaled foot planted assertively on the cobblestones. Long arm drawing bow across strings, long fingers coaxing legato, black hair mysteriously wrapped around itself and away from her face, which was oval and angular and golden. With her eyes closed and her body relaxed—her bow arm flexible, sweeping, almost as though it contained no bones—she looked like she might be dreaming, head nodding and lolling to the music that rose up and out from her—clear, and pure, and aching.

Alma's beauty seemed apiece with the music she made, as ravishing as any work of art Daniel had encountered in Florence—any Madonna, Venus, or Magdalene. More than any musician he knew, Alma could seduce you, tease you into rapt attention, and beyond, to an ardent, prolonged arousal. Elusive, mercurial, she beckoned you hither and backed off, strung you along and pulled back, withholding just enough so that you had to lean forward, at the edge of your seat, every nerve ending attuned to the fulfillment of the promises she had made you—until, finally, at the very last possible moment, she gave it all, every last part—and though you might be surprised, or unsettled, or even perplexed, you would never be disappointed. In the Adagio, she was easy, light within the melancholy, as though recalling a sad dream.

If Daniel hadn't been in love with Alma already, he would have fallen in love with her in this moment, fallen in love, as he sensed all around him men and women were falling—struck dumb in the middle of the Ponte Vecchio, on this day in early June—with spears of sunlight dappling the coffee-colored water and spackled clouds in blue sky—struck dumb by the sadness and the beauty that she had conjured in this moment, this now, a now of collective consciousness that held each of them within it; the sadness and the beauty not so much *in* the music as brought out by it, drifting like smoke up to a heaven they believed in, or to a heaven they believed in now—and Daniel felt a shudder rise in him, so close to ecstasy that it brought intimations of his own death—and it was not love he felt for the music, or for the girl, but a kind of worship; he wanted never to be far from such transcendence, such bright and unalloyed spirit; he wanted never to be separate from it.

Next to Alma, attached to the iron fence surrounding Cellini's bust, there were a number of small padlocks with names on them in Magic Marker. Donna and Oscar. Pietro and Marianne. Alma had told Daniel that couples came from around the world to this spot to fasten their locks and toss the keys in the river, in the belief that this would make their love last forever. Daniel pitied them their faith in iron weight and ancient water, in the ballast of objects and their relevance to fate, when the love he knew could not be clasped or bolted, but floated free, carried in the atmosphere—on a phrase of music, a patch of sunlight, the scent of perfume—in a previous and eternal present beyond human interference.

Kyoko and Kornell
at Holey Shmoley's

*M*iyazaki, Imamura, Kurosawa, Ozu / Kawabata, Hokusai, Utamaro banzaiiii! / Kobo Abe, Hiroshige, Bashō, banzaiii! / Kamikaze, wabi-sabi, origami, hara-kiri, banzaiiiii!" Kyoko delivered her recitation in a strange, breathy contralto, with long stresses in unexpected places—"*Miyazaaaaaaaaki*"—stuttering syllables— "*Uta-ta-ta-maro*"—modulating from a whisper to a growl. Her voice rose and held on the last "*Aiiii!*"—up to E, twice again from middle C. The crowd, hitherto standing around, jumping up and down in place, or headbanging to the beat, erupted in a triumphant cheer, arms raised, as though Kyoko had just crossed the finish line of an Olympic sport.

"*I'm a samurai / I'm a geisha / I'm a samurai / I'm a geisha!*" Kyoko screamed. Kornell delivered his thundering drumroll. "*Hey, hey, hey! / I'm Japanese! / I'm Japanese! / I'm Japanese! / I'm Japaneeeeeeeeese!*" Kyoko, soaking with sweat, worked up and snarly, managed a final wind-milling guitar chord à la Pete Townshend. The lights went up on a

press of shining faces. The sound of clapping rolled over the murmur
of conversation, shrill stadium whistles, and shouts of affirmation.
"Yeah! Ye-yah!"

It was Kyoko's third time playing at Holey Shmoley's, whose
manager she suspected of having a thing for her, plus a few performances in college, in various earlier iterations of the Yukio Mishimas.
But she had never been on the way she'd been tonight.

"Fucking awwwwwesome!" a young boy in a skullcap said to
Kyoko, handing over a damp paper napkin for her to sign. "Dude,
you guys totally rock!" Kyoko just nodded and wiped her forehead
with his napkin. She accepted a beer.

Kornell got up from behind his drum kit, a little stiffly. He gave
Kyoko a nod of approval. "You brought it, Kyo!" he said. "That was
some inspired shit right there!"

Kyoko smiled. A rare, unencumbered smile, childlike, delighted,
with no ironic emphasis. "They liked it," she said.

Emmons was impressed. He was tall and lean, with a porkpie hat
and muttonchop sideburns. He was wearing a shirt of black
satin, with a black satin tie, a black and white herringbone vest, and
skinny, black, hipster jeans. They called him King of the Viral Bands
for his ability to cultivate talent from homemade YouTube videos,
taking them all the way from internet buzz to professional music
videos, to recording contracts, and to live tours. He had been responsible for the seemingly overnight success of the Nocturnal Submissions, turning "Succubus Lullaby" into a slick hit, and a music video
directed by a Hollywood rising star, leading to a million-dollar recording contract with Craven Records.

Introducing himself now, he took Kyoko's hand in both of his own and worked her arm up and down like a water pump. "That was great!" He beamed, displaying long, vulpine teeth. "Just great! You guys killed it! The crowd loved you!"

Kyoko nodded curtly. She was wary of the way Emmons was looking at her. His eyes were a shade of untrustworthy blue, which made Kyoko think of those one-way mirrors on cop shows. You thought it was a mirror, because all you could see was a reflection of your own face, but it was really a window, with invisible people on the other side, watching you.

"That's your first single right there!" Emmons was saying. He cocked his head. "Though . . ." He wagged his finger at Kyoko. "Though . . . you know . . . there's an argument to be made for 'Sep-puku.' Such a great song!" He cocked his head to the other side. "A little dark, maybe," he said. "For a first single. I don't know. But you've got some strong material. You're a little dynamo, you are!"

Kornell sensed Kyoko's unease. She was a different person onstage—a screaming id, he teased her. In fact, Screaming Id had been in contention for their band name early on, but Kyoko had ve-toed it on the grounds that it was too "band name-y." Now that she had reverted back to her quiet, unreadable self, Emmons was disap-pointed. She was still tattooed and pierced, with the electric-blue cox-comb in the spike of short black hair, in her salmon-colored Chuck Taylors and her black leather pants and black Despoilers T-shirt, but all the attitude had gone out of her. Gone were the sneer and the snarl, the roiling, charismatic anger, the sparking glare, and the ra-ging voice that Emmons had already characterized as a Japanese Patti Smith with a little Chrissie Hynde/Courtney Love vibe.

"What's your game, man?" Kornell said. He stood up straighter, pushed his chest into the skinny white man's space. Emmons shifted slightly backward in his stance. He preferred to deal with the girl. She was tiny, with small tits and slim hips, and her intensity level was off the charts. He was willing to bet she was a little monkey in the sack, and his gaze went back to Kornell, in envy and awe. How does *that* happen? he wondered.

"Well . . ." Emmons said, taking a swig of his beer. "The Nocturnal Submissions are about to go on their first cross-country tour this summer. I played Jake 'Seppuku.' He really dug it." He shifted his gaze from Kornell to Kyoko, narrowed his eyes. "If you could get out to the West Coast, San Diego to Seattle, with Portland, San Fran, L.A. . . . we might put you on as an opening act. We . . . I've got a few bands that I'm thinking of putting into a rotation."

Kyoko's heart lurched, but she was outwardly impassive.

"What would it pay?" Kornell said.

Emmons looked at him blankly. "Nothing," he said. "I pay for the venues, publicity, some travel . . . You get out there. Start building a fan base."

"What about an album?"

Emmons nodded impatiently. "We can talk about that later."

Kornell made a noncommittal face. "When's the tour?"

"June 20 to July 17."

"June 20? That's in two weeks!" An image of Daniel in the Naugahyde recliner flashed in Kornell's head.

Emmons nodded unapologetically. "We had a cancellation," he said. "I've got five, six other bands begging me for the favor. Absurdist Boot Camp, The Whoremonger's Wife . . . Good bands. Better-known bands. But I've got a feeling about you guys." He winked at Kyoko. "It's all small venues. Very cool bars, intimate music halls. A little bigger than this . . . The Sunscreen, outside of San Diego. The Polynesian, of course. Perfect for you!" He winked again.

Kornell put his hand on Kyoko's shoulder. "It's such short notice," he said. "We'll have to think about it."

"Well, don't think too long," Emmons said. He had to admit that the big Black guy, paired with the tiny Asian girl, added to the draw. He handed Kyoko his card. "I really hope this works out," he said. "It could be really good for you. Great exposure. Learn the ropes. Jake and the other guys are great people. Generous. Fun. You'll love them!"

"We'll think about it," Kornell said sternly.

"We'll do it," said Kyoko, surprising herself as much as them, ignoring Kornell's anxious but-we-have-a-man-in-the-basement stare.

She still felt the afterglow of the thrilling confidence she'd been awash in moments earlier, the confidence of knowing these songs were the best she'd ever written, of feeling Kornell's steady presence on the drums, holding the architectural bones of the song in place so she could give herself over to the frenzy that filled her. She had never before felt that connection, like an umbilical cord between her and the crowd, the rush of power that made her feel, briefly and wildly, in control of it all—the crowd's mounting energy and excitement, their eager response to her music. And the performance had unlocked in her mind, unbidden, unexpected, another burst of creativity: she now knew the perfect way to dispose of Daniel Karmody.

Baby, are you crazy?" said Kornell when they were back home. "How're we going to get out to California in two weeks, when we've got . . ." He pointed straight down.

Kyoko grinned. "I know exactly what to do. And we'll do it soon."

"Okay, but . . . what about my job? What about Sumo?"

She pursed her lips. "Korny," she said. "When the universe sends such a clear signal, the only answer you can send back is yes."

Kornell looked at her for a moment, then broke into a huge grin. "Damn, girl," he said, "if I didn't know better, I'd think you were an optimist."

"Well, I wouldn't go that far," said Kyoko, but she was smiling.

Daniel and Paolo go at it

She had let Paolo kiss her in front of the Fontana del Bacchino and immediately regretted it, had afterward conflated the tall, handsome impresario with the absurdly fat dwarf on the spitting turtle; the taste of rust and cigarettes and the smell of musky cologne, the lingering manifestations of her repentance. It was, ironically, the kiss that had settled it for her, or so it had seemed at the time, a Judas kiss, then, to mark an end, not a beginning. It surprised Alma to discover how in love with Daniel she really was, to discover—not with her mind, but in her body, in the nerve endings and the spine and the pulsing of blood—that she had already made her choice. She wasn't necessarily pleased to receive this information, walking away from Paolo after this discrete, telegraphing kiss, but pleased or not, she had received it.

Only, despite what she'd realized, or because of it, she was unable to get the memo to Daniel, who, upon hearing that Alma had gone for a walk with Paolo in the Boboli while he and Archie had been in

their meeting with Deutsche Grammophon, promptly began to behave like an asshole.

I t was a walk, for Christ's sake!" Alma said. "A W-A-L-K. Not a
F-U-C-K."

"Did he invite you to visit him in his penthouse apartment on
Central Park West?" Daniel interrogated her. "Did he ask you to
come back by yourself next summer?"

"This is ridiculous," Alma said. "I refuse to talk about this anymore. You're acting like a teenager."

"I'm just trying to understand what you see in the guy," Daniel
said. "I mean, besides his money, his good looks, and his connections.
Oh, and let's not forget that he's royalty!"

"This is all about your jealousy and nothing to do with me," Alma
said. "Fuck you and your fragile male ego. I'm sick and tired of it."

She walked out the door, went down the elevator, and had a couple of drinks at the hotel bar. Archie the pianist was there, and she
spent the next hour crying on his shoulder, even though she knew
that Archie, chaste and fastidious, in his half-moon spectacles and
suit vests, was half in love with Daniel himself, and that he drank too
many vodka gimlets because only alcohol dulled the longing.

The next night was the gala performance at the Teatro Comunale.
Princess Caroline of Monaco had been there with the Italian
prime minister, and there was a reception afterward, in the ballroom
of the hotel. Alma had been besieged by admirers, blue-haired music

appreciators in sequins and tuxedos, the same the world over, praising her playing, asking for her autograph; the women talking up their sons, wanting to match her up with them; the men with their arms around her waist, slipping her their phone numbers.

She had been wearing a black jersey knit dress with a very low back, and while she was talking, she felt something cold pressing against her, right above her ass. She turned around and it was Paolo, looking very dashing in his tux.

"*Cara mia*," he said, "you were magnificent! Come, I must kiss you!"

Alma turned her cheek toward his puckered lips. He kissed her again on the other side. "You look ravishing tonight," he whispered in her ear. "My darling, why do you torture me?"

She laughed. She had had a glass or two of prosecco. It was her night, and she felt triumphant. The Dvořák was still in her head. Her left hand fingered the notes of the most transcendent moment, as she listened to herself chasing the clarinets, spiraling around them, hovering, holding, herding them toward the orchestral climax. It had been one of those performances that dislocated time and space, where her sense of the audience, the musicians, the venue, dissolved, along with any awareness of self, where all the borderlines and all the boundary lines became permeable, opening up and outward, carrying the sound, spewing it, spilling it, driving it forward, until she'd come up blinking into the stage lights and the applause, thrust back into her body, in her dress in the chair—returned to the banal matter of life, like a shipwrecked sailor recovered from drowning. It was a feeling spoken of by musicians with reverence and in awe, this material undoing, this deliquescence—the transcendence of self as the apotheosis of interpretive art, the annihilation of time as its sacrament.

Alma thought back to her argument with Daniel about posterity and art, and was convinced more than ever that she had been right. You could record a performance, as they were going to do in Rome at the end of the tour, but you could never reproduce the currency of the moment in which a performance pulsed and breathed. This was divine, the closest Alma had come, beyond even sex, which was more an emptying out than a pouring in, a draining of self rather than a merging.

P aolo put his hand on her bare back and again Alma started. She turned away from him and felt his arm jerk, jostling her champagne glass, which splashed its contents down the front of her dress, before flying, then falling—Alma tried to catch it—and smashing into pieces on the floor.

There was a collective gasp in the room, and Alma saw, in the space that was opening in front of her, Daniel, with Paolo's immaculate tuxedo shirt gathered in his fist, shoving him back against the flocked velvet wallpaper.

"Fucker," said Daniel.

"Daniel," said Paolo brightly, smiling reassuringly to the crowd.

"Fucking keep your hands off her, you fuck!" Daniel tightened his grip on Paolo's shirtfront. His face was red and his fist was white.

"Daniel!" Alma entreated.

"Is this really necessary, my friend?" said Paolo. "Shall we at least go outside?" Paolo put the flat of his palm against Daniel's chest in a gesture of conciliation, for which he was repaid by a chokehold with two hands that knocked his head back against the wall.

"*Vaffanculo!*" exclaimed Paolo, driving his knee into the vicinity of Daniel's groin.

"Paolo!" said Alma.

"Oof," said Daniel, doubled over in pain.

Paolo dropped his guard, and Daniel drove his head into his stomach, sending both men sprawling to the ground. The precarious tower of champagne glasses, overflowing with prosecco, trembled and shook, but did not fall.

"Ow, son of a bitch!" said Daniel.

"Stop!" said Alma.

Daniel, astride Paolo, hit him in the face with his fist. Paolo grunted. Blood spurted from his nose.

"*Testa di cazzo*," said Paolo, having lost, along with his blood, any vestige of good humor. Grappling, the two men exchanged positions, and Paolo struck Daniel a blow across his ear.

"Cocksucker!"

Bam!

"*Figlio di puttana!*"

Boom!

Around the room there was a commotion of concern—waiters in white with silver trays tucked at their sides; guests calling for help or suggesting someone else go get some; women swooning or threatening to swoon; a hotel employee, a maître d' or concierge, officious in a navy suit with a red kerchief, standing with his hands on his hips, looking on the verge of doing something—all through the room a buzzing of excitement, of curiosity, and the thrill of witnessing a spectacle in which—at last, at last!—the ordinary constraints of civilized human behavior had been shucked, the veil drawn back, and bloodlusty animal instinct restored.

Alma couldn't help feeling a flush of pride at first that she should be thus fought over, like a Guinevere or a Helen. But this passed quickly, and she soon grew embarrassed, then irritated, and finally bored, by the protracted silliness of the fight. She was not a dumb damsel, some pulchritudinous and passive prize whose fate was determined by men's actions. It wasn't even about jealousy, she realized, so much as it was about the male ego, less about the relationship between her and either Paolo or Daniel than it was about their relationship to each other—the complicated cock-blocking, dick-measuring, cojones-proving, score-settling, territorial-pissing, preening, and shooting match that existed between men.

Alma thought of the Medicis who displayed the hanged bodies of their enemies from the windows of the Bargello, of the sculptor Bandinelli who sold Cellini bad marble to sabotage his rival's work, of the century of blood spilled in Florentine streets by the Guelphs and the Ghibellines, all of which began over a broken betrothal. She imagined the whole historical pageant as a series of dicks, one after another, stacked up, laid end to end—the measure of man's achievement.

The scuffling ended in a sheepish draw. Paolo helped Daniel up off the floor. Both men were bleeding about the face. Paolo's famous coif had come uncoiffed; Daniel's jacket was torn from the shoulder. They exchanged a solemn handshake, mumbled their apologies to those in the vicinity, righted a few upended chairs.

Alma turned on her heel and went up to bed, escorted by Archie and the manager of the hotel, leaving a note for Daniel to sleep in the other room and to not dare disturb her.

DANIEL COMMITS

Daniel pressed the buzzer on the door of Fratelli Piccini. Someone buzzed him in, and he opened the door by the handle, which was shaped like a seahorse. Inside the shop, it was cool, quiet, and bright. There were elegant Oriental rugs on the wooden floors, antique desks and cabinets, and casement windows overlooking the Arno toward the Ponte alle Grazie.

A small black dog bustled over to greet him, followed by an attractive young woman with dark hair and freckles and a taut, athletic body. She wore a crisp tailored jacket over jeans and a silky white blouse, and was very short, though she wore the tallest, pointiest black heels Daniel had ever seen.

"Good afternoon," she said. "I'm Sabina Tozzi. How may I help you?"

Daniel, who had never been inside a jewelry store before, was feeling unaccountably panicked, but something about the woman made him feel more at ease. She was young, but carried an easy authority, and her English, almost fluent, was also easy.

"I'd like to see a ring," he said. He could not yet say *buy*. In truth, he just meant to look. "It's over there."

"Show me," she said, moving with him to the front of the store. "Ahh." She smiled. "This is a beauty." She took the ring out of the case in the window and handed it to him.

He held it gingerly. It was the one Alma had pointed to, with small square sapphires on either side of an asymmetrical diamond set in a pentagon. He tried not to wince as he converted the price into dollars, converted the dollars into lessons and gigs. He thought about Paolo, the smarmy bastard, who seemed to shit money, and then he no longer cared about the price.

"For an engagement?" Sabina asked. She was looking at him with interest, her deep brown eyes openly curious. The right side of Daniel's face was swollen, his eye partially shut, and he had a greenish-purple bruise across his right cheek, some scratches along his nose.

Daniel nodded. The ring in his hand sparkled in the light. In the back of the shop a man in a blue suit conversed with an elderly couple in Italian.

"I . . . I think so. I'm . . . Yes," he said.

The woman looked amused. "You are not certain?"

Daniel shrugged and felt foolish. "The other men who come in here," he said. "They're all certain?"

Sabina Tozzi laughed. "Well, anyway, they are less honest with me, if they aren't," she said.

When Daniel thought of marriage, the image that came to mind was of a cliff, of him running at top speed along a beach path and suddenly, abruptly, like the ill-fated coyote in the cartoons, finding himself treading air, before plummeting to earth. He thought about Alma, about her passion and her obstinacy, her sense of humor, the way she kissed him sometimes, at the moment of their parting, with an almost desperate urgency, as though she expected never to see him again. He thought about her naked body stretched beneath him on the bed, his favorite curve along her hip leaning into the dark velvet of her inner thigh. Daniel remembered the first few months after he and Alma had met, experiencing all the time they were not together as a kind of fugue state, his body and brain operating in curious brownout—dragging himself from class to practice to rehearsal, until the sight of her would re-infuse him with a surge of blood and adrenaline. Daniel would pull at her clothes, breathe her hair, climb her body like a jungle gym, inserting as much of himself inside her as possible, wanting nothing so much as to inhabit her wholly. He would think to himself, *Slow down, slow down, remember this moment, make it last*, but even as he thought it, it seemed, she was buttoning her blouse, pulling on her skirt, moving away from him—and the moment, the precious, irretrievable moment, would have passed.

Sabina was looking at him patiently, her little dog lying, with equal patience, at her feet. She was attractive, Daniel thought, and tried to imagine her compact, well-proportioned body without clothes, and he knew that what he was about to do precluded his ever knowing, ever knowing what she, or any other naked woman, would feel like under his hands—and because he was a man, he bemoaned his great sacrifice, and because he was vain, he bemoaned womankind's great deprivation.

"Do you think it's possible," Daniel found himself saying, "to ever be completely certain about such a . . . such a huge thing?"

"Certainty?" said Sabina, pursing her lips in consideration.

"Maybe no. Maybe it's more like religion. A matter of faith. You follow your instinct. What do you Americans say? Your *guts*."

Again, Daniel thought of the coyote in midair, the look on his face as he realized where he was, in the moment just before he fell. He knew that life with Alma would never be easy, that she was strong-willed, hotheaded, and capricious, but he also knew that it would never be dull, that in aligning himself with Alma, he was signing on for a singular life. He speculated that in the moment just before the coyote registered his predicament, before the recollection of gravity and the physical laws, his furry feet furiously pedaling the blue atmosphere, in that semibreve rest before he sank like a stone—for that one glorious, suspended moment—he must have felt like he could fly.

And then he was walking out of the store with the ring in a blue velvet box in his pocket and everything looked different to him, brighter, more defined, the tourists with their cameras and backpacks, the window displays of winking gems, the men in their sculls on the river, the cobblestones under his feet. But it was equally true that the world felt shrunken, reduced. The woman in the tube top with the tattooed rose over her left breast, the one with the pug at the end of a leash, the beautiful Italian schoolgirls who loitered and laughed along the Lungarno Torrigiani—closed off to him forever, sealed behind an invisible curtain of propriety and prohibition—infinitely desirable, endlessly longed for, forever and resoundingly unfuckable, from now until the world's end.

Kornell Steals a Fish

He felt bad about stealing from Yoshi, who had been kind to him, and he felt bad about having to kill Daniel, for whom he had developed a strange kind of affection. (Between the dude's constant banter, clownish antics, and plucky can-do attitude that could not quite mask his soft white-boy whupped-up-on desperation, it would have been impossible not to.) Just this morning, he had come down to find a Twister mat lying out on the cellar floor. "Left hand, red," the dude had called, flicking the arrow on the direction board. "C'mon, Big Guy, let's play!"

But the plan had been set in motion, and there was a narrowing margin of time and opportunity, so Kornell found himself in the walk-in refrigerator at the back of Yoshi's kitchen, at three a.m., having let himself in with the key Yoshi had given him two weeks before. In an orange cooler in the corner, underneath a stack of metal trays, Kornell found what he was looking for.

ALMA MAKES A DISCOVERY

Alma showed off her ring to some of the women in the orchestra, who were standing around the lobby. "He fed it to me in the tiramisu," she was saying, for the umpteenth time, with an aggrieved air that tastefully undercut the boast. "I mean, I almost swallowed it!"

Many of the young women, Alma was aware, had crushes on Daniel, and Daniel had flirted with all of them—a fact that Alma was aware of, and would swear she did not mind, though in truth it bothered her more than a little.

"I picked it out," she continued. "From the oldest jewelry store on the Ponte Vecchio. I saw it in the window and showed it to Daniel, and he went back a few days later without telling me and bought it, the sneak." She did not add, though most of the young women knew, that the altercation at the Grand Hotel between Daniel and Paolo had put the entire enterprise in jeopardy, and a few of the young women now present had rather hoped that Alma would not have found her way to forgiveness.

One of these was Emi Tokugawa, a violinist from Baltimore, who had studied with Daniel at the conservatory. Though already married, with a young daughter, Emi had enjoyed some of Daniel's attention, both in Baltimore and in Italy. She was a quiet woman, with freckles on her face, and thin, blow-away hair, but there was something about her paleness and her fine, delicate features that made her, in certain lights, and on certain days, lovely in the way small children can be lovely, with a dewiness and a fragility—an art-less eroticism that was the more enticing for being unformed.

Now Emi followed Alma's proffered hand with a sick sense of greed. She was three years older than Alma, and was just beginning to have an inkling that the decisions she'd made thus far in her life were not serving her well. No, it was more that she was beginning to understand that she had made no decisions in her life, but had been decided upon, and far from not serving her well, Emi had the grim apprehension that it was all—and very soon now—about to turn to shit.

When she looked upon Alma, the golden girl, the solo cellist, the winner of Daniel Karmody's heart, she saw her alternative self, the way her life could have been, almost was, might have turned out. All the years of solitary practice, the honors and awards, years of competing and winning, of auditions and master classes, string quartets and orchestras, and climbing to the top, and she had fallen just short in every category.

Looking at the sparkling diamond on Alma's finger, Emi saw the vaunted prize flaunted, the glittering, winking, spiteful embodiment of all that she had wanted and not gotten. She had not received a ring upon her engagement—Gen hadn't had the money—and honestly, until this moment, she had not known she had wanted one.

"See you later," Alma was saying now, with one final splay of the hand.

"Bye," chorused the women. "It's so beautiful!" "You're so lucky!"

Alma took herself off, her beauty and luck resounding around her, lingering. Emi could still hear it, reverberating at low frequency, in acoustic half-life.

In a good mood, then, Alma proceeded to go shopping. She decided that a newly engaged woman deserved something special, and she had had her eye on a leather bag in a tony shop on the Via Porta Rossa. The day was overcast, but still hot, and she walked slowly down the Borgo Ognissanti, with her sunglasses on, her head up, her posture proud. There was always a part of Alma that existed a little outside herself, that commented on her actions, her conduct, her emotional temperature, and it was telling her at this moment that she was entirely happy, that nothing, in fact, could be more perfect than this day, at this juncture in her life, that everyone could see it, radiant upon her face, in her carriage-glow, this joyousness—and that by radiating it outward she was exercising her most generous impulse, incumbent as it was on her to share, as she had shared with the girls this morning, her incredible, outsized good fortune.

This fortune extended to her arriving at the shop, bantering in her impeccable though limited Italian, and the shopkeeper's much less impeccable, less limited English, finding the perfect pebbled brown leather bag, soft as butter, with that delicious fine leather smell that reminded Alma of horses and expensive cars. It was sophisticated but cute, and wholly European, something, it seemed to Alma, that no one in the States would carry but that befit a newly engaged and cosmopolitan young woman on her way up in the larger world. It cost more than anything she had ever bought for herself before, which was slightly terrifying, but also, Alma reasoned, appropriate to the occasion, and when the shopkeeper, a fat and amiable middle-aged Italian man, with a face like a basset hound, began to flirt with her, she laughed and played along, flashing her ring as she gave him her credit card, and again when she signed—with a grand, illegible flourish—the receipt.

As she left the store, the contents of her old purse transferred to the new, the old elegantly concealed in a gray cloth bag with cotton drawstrings, Alma felt quite satisfied, and swinging the bag merrily at her side, she decided to stroll through the San Lorenzo market. Here it was swarms of tourists, of course, in groups of two or three, looking, touching, haggling, buying, but nothing could touch Alma's imperturbable happiness, and she smiled as the vendors called out to her. *"Prego, prego!" "Bella, signora."* "Hello!"

She bought a silk scarf from a handsome boy with huge brown eyes, for no other reason than he looked like a painting of Saint Sebastian she had seen in the Uffizi. The boy, in turn, thought Alma the very apparition of beauty. *"Giapponese,"* he whispered to himself, as he lifted her hair out from under the scarf, capturing a silken strand and winding it around his finger. The scarf was black, embroidered with pink roses, and even though it was much too hot now, Alma thought how well it would look against her black wool coat, six months from now, on a snowy day, deep in New England winter.

Making her way back toward the hotel, Alma looked at her watch and saw that it was nearly one o'clock. She wondered what Daniel was doing, whether he had already eaten lunch. They had left it that they would go their separate ways this morning, because she had wanted to go shopping and he had had some errands of his own.

Alma often skipped lunch, but maybe Daniel would want to go to their favorite fish place in the Oltrarno.

On a lark, she stopped in a floral shop on Via del Porcellana and bought a bouquet of bearded irises to put beside the rose bouquets she had collected the night before. The iris was the symbol of Florence, which she had quickly come to think of as her favorite city: the city of her happiness. These irises were a deep purple, darker than any Alma had ever seen, and buying them made her feel sophisticated, as though she really were a grown woman, with a house and a special vase to put flowers in, and she started to hum one of the minuets from Mozart's string trio, which always made her happy, and she was happy that she was happy, because happiness for Alma was always surprising, in the way that it was for perfectionists, who required a particularly stringent aligning of planets to allow it, and for pessimists, for whom happiness was aberration.

The woman at the desk in the hotel lobby smiled at Alma and her irises as Alma swept through on the way to the elevator. *Giapponese,* she thought. *Questi bellissimi fiori.* The bellboy with the empty luggage cart smiled at Alma, too, and eagerly pressed the up button for her. Waiting beside her, he was conscious of the sweet scent of the flowers and the subtler sweet scent of Alma's perfume. *Bella donna,* he thought, and fantasized about following her up to her room, taking off her dress, and laying her down on the big, soft bed, though he had never laid down on a bed in the hotel, and his palms sweat at the thought of doing so, never mind the beautiful woman, who was so far above him, so rich and nice-smelling, that he should not think the things he thought about her, and hoped that it would not show on his face, what he was thinking, as they rode up in the elevator together.

Alma thought the bellboy looked nervous and wanted to say something to him, a little joke or an encouraging remark, to put him at ease, but by the time she had figured out what she might say and translated it in her head—was it *lavore* or *fare?*—the elevator had stopped on her floor, and it was time for her to get out, so she just smiled at him and said, *"Grazie,"* as he held the door.

There was a mirror directly facing the elevator as you got out, and Alma caught a glimpse of herself. Truth be told, she stopped and looked for a number of seconds, and what she saw, her own face reflected back to her, was familiar and strange—her hair in a low ponytail swept to one side, bangs slightly damp on her forehead, oval face flushed with the heat, almond-eyed, plump-lipped, with a shimmer of eye shadow and vestige of lipstick (Cinnamon Spice). Alma had not been allowed to wear makeup in high school, and it was only in the last few years that she had discovered how much fun it could be to treat your face like a canvas, drawing lines, painting colors, employing various trompe l'oeil techniques that the girls in the conservatory had taught her—for making her eyes seem bigger, her lower lip poutier, her cheekbones juttier, her bridgeless nose more bridged.

Now, looking into the mirror on the third floor of the Grand Hotel in Florence, Italy, she recognized that her face was changing. She had always looked younger than she was, the consensus now being that she could easily pass for nineteen, but it seemed to Alma that her eyes looked out at the world with a new maturity, a calmer, more solidified sense of self, that there was in her expression not exactly wisdom—she did not feel wise—but something alert and keen of countenance that might portend wisdom. She had, from the age of seven, been hailed as a prodigy, which for Alma meant only that expectations had been higher for her, earlier, and among more people, until it seemed her whole life, she'd been running the gauntlet of her own potential. At last, she thought, gauging the truth as she gazed at her face, the clear intelligence in her eyes seemed borne of experience and not of precocity.

She flashed her hand with the ring, and the hand with the flowers, in front of the mirror and, smiling brightly at herself one last time, proceeded to the door of room 318, whereupon she set down the flowers, the cloth bag containing her old purse, and the plastic bag with the silk scarf, and dug into her new purse to find her room card. Sliding the card in the door, she took note of the green light and pushed, only to be stymied by the chain, which prevented the door from opening more than about a foot into space.

Oh, good, Daniel is home, she thought. She knocked, bent down to gather her things from the floor. "Daniel," she called. "DK, it's me."

But still no one came. She took hold of the doorknob, causing the chain to rattle. "Daniel!" she called, knocking more forcefully this time. She listened for the sound of his violin, or for the television, or the radio. *He must be napping*, she thought. Through the gap between the door and the inside of the doorframe, she could see the table in the foyer with the bouquets of roses, beside which she wanted to put the irises—she made a note to call down for a vase, which she'd forgotten to get on the way up—and on the glass tabletop she saw Daniel's overstuffed wallet, his keys, his ChapStick and a handful of change.

Beyond this she could see the antique table decorated with ormolu and marble, and the orange sofa with the taffeta cushions, beneath the heavy gold drapes. Resting on the sofa, almost at the edge of her peripheral vision, Alma saw a purse. Not as elegant or new a purse as the one she had just purchased, and not as large, either. Just a regular, run-of-the-mill woman's purse, small, brown leather, shaped like a piece of melon, with a zipper up the front and a thin buckled strap.

Alma listened at the door for any sound. She thought she heard voices from deep within the suite, where the bedroom lay, beyond the drawing room, but then she thought she had imagined them. She glanced down the hallway on one side and down the L-shaped corridor on the other. Clutching her flowers and her packages stupidly, Alma stood outside her own room and wondered what to do. The mind was slow to process what the eye had taken in, or perhaps not slow, but unwilling. Maybe one of the blue-haired ex-pats from the other night had come to call, and Daniel was . . . Daniel was humoring her in the other room; or she'd taken ill, and he had her laid out in their bed, was right this minute calling the doctor . . . Maybe.

Alma knocked again. "Daniel," she tried to call, but could not seem to summon her voice. She felt a sharp pain in her chest, which she interpreted as regret. She should have stuck to her routine and stayed at the theater, should have worked on the Dvořák, on her intonation in the coda of the second movement, the slow, easy section that Alma had not quite nailed the other night. Maestro Offerman used to scold her. "You sound like you're just waiting to get to the hard stuff," he'd say, and it was true, for her the hard stuff was easy, the virtuosic, the soaring, climbing, pitching, sliding; and the easy, the quiet, even, simple parts, were difficult.

She should have stayed then and practiced, worked on the Dvořák, controlling each exposed note, securing it, going over it again and again, and the "Archduke," the Bach, the Schumann fantasies, should have played scales, played Elgar, Saint-Saëns, Franck, her entire cello repertoire, played for hours, played all night, until her neck and shoulders froze, her fingers swelled and bled, and her arms became like blocks of wood. She should never stop playing, in fact, should forever wrap her loins around her cello, burying herself deeper inside the notes, inside the science and the solace of the music that, though it was suffused with feeling, imbued with it, was not, finally, the feeling itself, but a mitigation of feeling, a yoking, a fueling—a way out.

Alma thought she might faint, or fall down, or have some kind of fit, but before she could do any of these things, Daniel had come to the door and was fiddling with the chain.

"Sorry, babe, sorry," he mumbled. "I was in the bathroom and I didn't hear the door." His shirt was wrinkled, and his hair was sticking up around the cowlicks at the side of his head. He kissed her on the cheek.

Whatever doubt might have remained was gone in that instant. His very casualness was a lie—that he would even try to lie to her was so galling she could spit. The purse was no longer on the couch, and this flipped a switch in her head.

"How was your morning, babe?" Daniel said, smiling, confident still that he could salvage the situation, though he wasn't, just now, sure how. He had taken a risk, but like most inveterate gamblers, he had never gambled on losing.

Alma swept past him without speaking, into the bedroom, where she stood looking around for a moment, though there was nothing recognizably out of place. She opened the bathroom door, the closets, Daniel trailing after her like an anxious real estate agent.

She was in control now. It was her show, and she made Daniel suffer for it. She threw the irises in the wastepaper basket in the bedroom. Daniel winced at the thump they made against the metal, like a brutal, final drumbeat. She went into the second bedroom, which they had not used except to store their instruments and to hang up their concert clothes. She was surprised to see the sun streaming in through the open windows. Dust danced in the buttery shafts that fell like searchlights on the patterned rug. She realized that the bedroom had always been dark, its heavy drapes closed. Daniel's violin case lay on the wide velvet seat of a chair. Some of Daniel's shirts, encased in a dry-cleaning bag, were laid out over the back. She noted that the bed looked hastily made, the bedspread summarily pulled smooth over rumpled sheets.

She walked toward the closet, but Daniel beat her to it, put his hand against the door. "Alma," he said. He looked into her face and she saw his weakness, his sorrow. *Save me from myself,* it seemed to say. *Even though I know I don't deserve it. Save us both.*

"Out of my way," she said, and flung open the door.

And there was little Emi Tokugawa leaning back against the wall, wearing a white blouse and a blue skirt, looking for all the world like a secretary waiting for a city bus, her eyes cast down upon the floor.

Alma, who should have been prepared, was shocked by the corporeal reality of her discovery. Emi Tokugawa was not a worthy rival in Alma's estimation, and that it should be her—not flashy Louise Ahn, or Nienlin Chiou, who did such a marvelous job with her clarinet solo, or even Marisa Fong, who had big tits—made Alma feel curiously let down, as though it reflected badly on her and on Daniel, whose taste must be called into question. Ha! *Once Asian, never again Caucasian.* Alma recalled her words to Daniel, her foolish clever words, as if joking about being racially interchangeable could protect her from it, as if being right had ever protected anyone from anything. For here in this closet, here was the reality, in the person of mousy second violinist Emi Tokugawa, who didn't have the decency to look her in the eye or say anything in her own defense, just three days after Daniel had proposed. All this stuck in Alma's craw, gave her a headache, made her want to take a nap for about a month. She felt, absurdly, like a character in a Restoration comedy, and she decided to behave accordingly.

"Get the fuck out of here, you stupid bitch!" Alma yelled. But as Emi started to scurry out, Alma held her hand up, like a traffic cop. "No," she said. "You stay. I'll go."

Alma kept moving. Her brain had shut down to everything except the small, clear voice that spoke to her. It said it didn't matter. It would not. She would not allow it. She did not know this man. He could not touch her. She would not allow it. The only thing that mattered was for her to get out of here, out of this room, this building, and as far away as she could from this person who was nothing to her.

Now she must turn. She must walk. She crossed to the foyer, slowly and with dignity, picked up her purse where she had dropped it.

"Alma, don't go," Daniel said. "Look, *I'll* go. You stay here." He reached for her, but she jerked away so violently that he came up short.

Alma was aware of the power she contained in this moment, the power of her reticence, of her withholding. Though the situation surrounding her was sordid and debased, she remained unaffected. In full possession of her dignity and self-value, she could not be brought down.

In this spirit, she walked out the door (did not slam it behind her), went down in the elevator, and through the lobby. It wasn't until she was outside that she realized she'd left her sunglasses behind. Her eyes watered in the bright light, but she was not crying. Not for that sorry motherfucker, no. It was incomprehensible to Alma that Daniel had done this to her. And with mealy-mouthed Emi Tokugawa, who had a husband already, and a child, and couldn't speak up for herself or even stand up straight.

The sun had broken through the clouds, and Alma walked faster in the profound heat, sweating, blind to the tourist hive that buzzed louder as she headed toward the Ponte Vecchio, because Alma felt the constriction of the ring on her finger, the blazing lie of it, the mockery, and she meant to take it back.

There is nothing harsher than the interrogating light of disillusion, and it was easy now for Alma to see all of Daniel's deficiencies and to reevaluate his former positive attributes as flaws. She should have seen that he was nothing special, just one in a long, boring line of fetishists—white boys with wider notions, who got hard whenever a slant-eyed, slim-hipped Asian girl went by. Well, lucky Danny, fox in the henhouse, white man in an endless orchestra of Oriental girl musicians. They could have him, Emi Tokugawa and all her ilk. Could have his cheating, lying, rice king self. She was well out of it now. Here she bumped into a large man laden with camera equipment, eating a giant ice cream cone with a spoon. "Look out!" she said, and the man scowled after her, half of his ice cream now imprinted on his shirt.

And here she was at the door of Fratelli Piccini, buzzing the buzzer four times without answer, pulling on the seahorse-shaped handle twice, before believing the sign–CHIUSO–that said it was closed. Which was ridiculous since all the other shops on the bridge seemed to be open. Alma struggled to take the ring from her finger. It was hot and her finger must have swollen, because she had to pull hard and then twist before it came off. She held it between thumb and forefinger, and felt a moment of weakness. It was so beautiful. Maybe she could keep it. Too bad for Daniel, he had given it to her. Maybe this was the price to be paid for fucking little mousy mouse

Emi Tokugawa. The price to be paid for being a scumbag. Alma shoved the ring back on, but on her right hand this time. She would wear it as a reminder that all men were liars and cheats, and every time she started to think otherwise, she would only have to look down and see the ring, and she would remember.

Alma looked up, wondering what to do now, where to go, when she caught sight of Daniel's head, bobbing in tourist waters, looking for her. She tried to duck, but he'd seen her. She saw his mouth form the shapes of her name—open, closed, then open again—saw his familiar face, square head under a wavy mass of brown hair; those stupid sunglasses he had insisted on buying in the Sant'Ambrogio market their first full day in Florence, even though she'd told him that they were going to be here for two months and he might want to shop around first; his too-big nose that they'd joked was the reciprocal of her small one, inclined toward sunburn, pink now from always forgetting sunblock; his cleft chin, that she had initially thought was funny-looking, describing it to her friend Sheila as a "butt chin," but that she had grown used to, then liked, and now thought funny-looking again. It was the face of a traitor, a fuck face, she thought. Why hadn't she seen it sooner?

He was heading toward her, dodging and weaving in the crowd, which seemed mostly to be going the other way. Alma started to run, heading for the other side of the river. The paving stones were bumpy under her sandaled feet, her new handbag bumped up and down against her hip.

"Alma! Wait!" Daniel yelled.

Alma tried to run faster, but just at that moment, her toe caught and she tripped, lost her balance, regained it, sideswiped a woman eating a piece of pizza, bounced off a student wearing a University of Minnesota T-shirt, lurched forward, and fell, ending up on her hands and knees on the uneven stones, almost exactly at the spot on the terrace, in front of the bust of Cellini, where—a year ago now, it seemed—she had set up her cello on a sunny afternoon, full up with the feeling that nothing could ever go wrong, that everything she ever did would be done in bright sunshine, with the adoration of a crowd and the love of a man with whom she thought she would be spending the rest of her life. And that same man, oh, so changed in just a handful of days, was leaning over her now, attempting to help her up off the ground, onto which, as far as she was concerned, he had hurled her, as surely as if he had dropped her from the top of Giotto's bell tower.

"Easy," he said, with one hand on her arm. She was bleeding from somewhere, a knee, but not badly. The fall had disoriented her. She rose slowly, shakily. She wanted to walk, but Daniel had hold of her.

"Don't try to move yet," he said. "Wait a minute. Get your breath back." She inhaled his good, clean smell, so familiar—the smell of Kirk's coconut castile soap, which she equated with old-fashioned American masculinity, and which, she was sorry to say, she still found incredibly alluring.

"Are you all right?" he asked. His voice was husky with tenderness.

Alma nodded. "I think so." She took a sudden deep breath. She felt a dizzying, almost unbearable sense of loss. It would be so easy to forgive him, to accept whatever lame-ass excuse he offered up for having to fuck Emi Tokugawa. *Sorry, hon, I thought she was you. You know you all look alike.* So easy to fall into his arms, let him take her back to the hotel to spend the night in sweet reconciliation, all tears and kisses, making love with their eyes open, pledging their troth anew. She would own him then. He would spend the rest of his life making it up to her, but he would grow resentful, and she would be suspicious, and Alma knew that the whole thing was ruined, and she hated him the more for ruining it, for taking something pure and good and shitting all over it, turning it into trash.

So she shook herself free of him and took a couple of steps backward. "Fuck you, Daniel Karmody!" she said, surprised by her vehemence. "*Fuck* you!"

He made a move toward her.

"No, no, no! You stay away from me." She had backed up into the railing that ran around Cellini's high pedestal. People all around were watching. They were making quite a spectacle.

"Come on, baby," Daniel coaxed, talking to Alma as though she were an animal he was taming. "Come on, now. Let's go home. You can hate me. I deserve it. You never have to speak to me again, but let's go home."

"Shut up!" Alma said. "Shut the fuck up!" She brushed at her tears with her palm. Why, why was she crying when she was so angry? It made her seem weak, when she really felt strong, the anger hard as muscle inside her, like a clenched fist rising from her rib cage.

Behind Alma, padlocks studded the railing. Lovers from around the world had fastened them there and then thrown the keys into the Arno, in the absurd belief that doing so would make their love last forever. How many of them had grown disillusioned? Alma wondered. How many now wished they could take a hacksaw to their own stupidity, to their optimism and their innocence, their foolish romantic notions? She, for one, suspected thousands.

Alma was crying freely now. The tears on her face felt stiff and hot. Her hair was wild, and her knee throbbed. She had retreated behind the railing to the terrace wall. A small crowd had gathered around them, as eager for diversion as they had been the other day when she had played her cello. But Alma was beyond caring.

"You asshole," she said.

"I'm so, so sorry," said Daniel sincerely, and Alma knew he was, but it didn't change a thing. "I love you," he said. "I don't know what happened—"

"Oh, like you were just standing there and her pussy landed on your cock? Is that what you mean, you don't know what happened?"

"I fucked up," he said. "There's no justification for it."

"That's for sure," Alma said. She pulled the ring from her finger.

"Alma, don't . . . Let's talk. Come back with me, and we'll talk."

Alma shook her head. "You fucking asshole," she said quietly. She looked down at the ring. "You broke my heart."

She pitched it then, tossed it over the side of the bridge like a spent cigarette. "No!" Daniel shouted, lunging stupidly.

Then time seemed to slow as the ring spiraled upward, flipping end over end, winking with white and blue light, winking and flipping, before falling, with barely a ripple, into the dark river—the same river that had absorbed countless victims of flood and plague, the bodies of Christian martyrs, and the burnt remains of the fanatic Savonarola; where Brunelleschi transported marble upstream for the construction of the Duomo.

And beneath the surface of the water, the ring continued to fall, blinking in the drowning sunlight—past two fish, medieval in appearance, gray, ugly, and gape-mouthed, that struck out at and missed the shining thing as it descended—bouncing once and settling at the bottom, winking no more, under the murk, the sand, and the sediment of history—coming to rest finally beside a burial mound of tiny iron keys.

DANIEL AND EMI

A nd here was the moment, at the hinge between what was and what might have been, the coulda-woulda-shoulda-shimmy-shimmy-coco-puff—Daniel Karmody's most fervent regret.

T here he had been, back in the sunshine with the ring in his pocket. "Maybe it's a matter of faith," Sabina Tozzi had said, and Daniel had felt himself raised up, like a repentant sinner at a tent revival. *Can I get an amen?* He loved Alma. He wanted to marry her. These were the facts that were never in doubt. It had been these facts, in fact, that had precipitated his fall, for if he loved Alma and wanted to marry her, had even, in his possession, the ring that proved it so—then what matter a brief, final fling, a goodbye-to-all-that?—if an opportunity were to present itself, and as long as Alma never found out.

As if preordained then, whom should Daniel run into as he walked back from Fratelli Piccini that afternoon but Emi Tokugawa? He had known her for years; they had been classmates at the conservatory. He was the one who had recommended her for the Maggio. She was a petite woman, with a sweet, heart-shaped face and a surprisingly full figure, and though she played the violin with an intensity that Daniel admired, in person, she seemed to hold herself back, coming across as extremely shy or ill at ease.

"Ahh, Emi, how are you?" Daniel had said, really noticing, for the first time, the constellation of freckles across her cheeks. He couldn't remember ever having seen an Asian woman with freckles. In his current state of mind, Daniel saw this as a sign—Emi's pale face, bright with stars, her strangeness, her blankness, her *not* Almaness, opening out before him like a new galaxy.

"Daniel, hi," Emi had answered, as if she had been expecting him. "I was just wondering . . . I'm having trouble with a passage in the second movement of the Dvořák."

Which was how he found himself in a practice room with Emi at the Scuola di Musica about an hour later. To Daniel's surprise, she had initiated the whole thing, her small hand encircling his wrist, drawing him into the soundproof room. She had pushed him into a chair and unzipped his fly, and Daniel had closed his eyes, lifted his hips so she could work his pants down, and when he'd felt her warm mouth on him, the unfamiliar tongue, he had let himself float free from conscience or consequence, knowing only pleasure.

It should have ended there. It should have never begun. But it had begun. And it did not end there.

They met at the practice room, three, maybe four times. Each time, Daniel was surprised by Emi's assertiveness, her almost desperate passion, which moved him in some way he didn't fully understand. First, he thought it was just because she wasn't Alma, that it was the novelty he responded to, but then, as the novelty wore off, he realized it was something more than this. Daniel suspected that he and Emi were similar in ways that he and Alma were not, and never would be—that what moved him was not the novelty, but this sense of the familiar. He would return from being with Emi, and he would take the blue velvet box from its hiding place in his sock drawer. He would stare at the beautiful object inside, the winking diamond, its twin sapphires, and he could see his future, a glittering, precious thing—he and Alma together, the life they would have—and he would put it away again, thinking *not yet*.

Finally, to force his own hand, Daniel had told Emi it was over.

"You are an amazing, beautiful woman," he'd said, squeezing Emi's hand tight in his, "and I've loved every minute of my time with you, but I'm afraid we can't see each other this way anymore, because I'm going to ask Alma to marry me, and you have to go back to your family, where you belong." He had expected tears, protests, but Emi had just looked at him, gravely, and said nothing.

That night, he took Alma out to dinner, alfresco, at a restaurant in the Piazza di Madonna degli Aldobrandini, in the shadow of the Medici Chapels. There was a bit of a breeze, and Daniel draped his suit coat across Alma's bare shoulders. She wore a black dress with braided gold straps, and the navy blue jacket on top made her look vulnerable, like a child playing dress-up. Her hair, which she usually wore up, and which usually slid down in wisps and tendrils throughout the day, was soft and loose and fell just below her breasts. Daniel thought she had never looked so beautiful; his heart swelled with the sight of her.

He had arranged with the restaurant beforehand, and when dessert came—tiramisu, Alma's favorite—Daniel looked expectantly after every bite.

"Don't you want any?" Alma asked, offering a spoonful.

Daniel shook his head. He was starting to worry, when Alma put her hand up to her mouth. "Ow!" She spit out a mouthful of sponge cake and mascarpone. "What's this?"

"I don't know," said Daniel innocently, "what does it look like?"

It took a while for Alma to register what she had retrieved in her napkin. "Oh my God!" she said. "Is this . . . Oh my God! Daniel! I can't believe . . . I almost chipped my tooth! I could have swallowed it!" She was half scolding, half laughing, still not fully comprehending. "It's the one from Fratelli Piccini!"

Daniel nodded. "Well?" he said, smiling.

"Well?" said Alma, looking at him significantly.

Daniel cocked his head.

Alma straightened in her chair and pointed at the ground.

"Ohhhh!" Daniel took the sticky ring from her and got awkwardly down on one knee. "Alma Soon Ja Lee, is it possible that you could find it in your heart to marry the poor, undeserving man who kneels before you—"

"Daniel Brendan Karmody, I will not be proposed to in the third person," Alma interrupted him. "Be serious."

Daniel tried again. It seemed corny to him, and he felt self-conscious; nevertheless, there was a lump in his throat. "Alma," he said. "Please, will you marry me?" He slipped the ring onto her finger.

"What do you think?" she said, leaning down to kiss him.

———

Then came the day when Emi had come looking for him. There was a knock at the door, and Daniel had opened it, expecting Alma, who sometimes left her key behind.

"Emi!" he said. "You can't . . ." He glanced nervously down the corridor.

"I need to talk to you," she said. She looked like she hadn't slept in a while; her eyes were bloodshot and the dark circles underneath them looked like bruises against her pale skin.

"Umm . . . not here," Daniel said. "Let me get my . . . I'll meet you in the coffee shop. Just give me two minutes, okay?"

Whereupon Emi burst into loud sobs and Daniel had no choice but to let her in. Once inside, she threw herself on him, kissing him through her tears, mumbling words, none of which he understood beyond "I love you," which was the recurring refrain. Daniel pried himself from her arms and sat her down beside him on the couch in the sitting room. He held her hand, and did nothing more than say "Shhh, shhh," "There, now," and "It's going to be okay" for a full ten minutes. He knew because there was an ornate clock on the table next to her that he couldn't stop himself from watching.

Daniel eventually succeeded in calming her down, or anyway, she had exhausted herself from crying, and once she was reduced to an occasional sniffle, he told her that he cared about her and that it pained him to see her so distraught. "You're a wonderful, wonderful woman, Emi," Daniel said. "And I'm a total jerk for confusing you, I'm so, so sorry, I got confused myself. But you have a family who needs you, and I have Alma, and I love her, and I'm going to marry her, but I will always feel so grateful to you for the time we spent together."

Emi gave him the same grave stare that she had given him when he'd made a variation of this speech a few days earlier. She seemed suddenly calm. "I called Gen this morning," she said. "I told him all about us. I told him I want a divorce."

Daniel thought he might have a heart attack, but he forced himself to stay calm. He told her that he was sure Gen would understand when she called him back to say she'd changed her mind, that it had all been a horrible mistake. He stressed how he had never meant to mislead her, how devoted he was to Alma. His words rang hollow even to his own ears, and he was close to weeping himself, from his own deep stupidity and rottenness, and how badly he had fucked things up.

It occurred to Daniel, not for the first time, that he did not deserve a woman like Alma, that he had been bound to lose her, in any case—and he felt a strange sense of relief that perhaps he had fucked things up on purpose, just to get it over with, so that he could get on with the life he was meant to live. Being with Alma had felt to Daniel like a spillover fortune, as though he had found a wallet thick with money just lying in the street. It was nothing he had earned or was worthy of—maybe he was simply meant to give it back.

Daniel looked at Emi differently, in this new light, remembering the way she had shivered uncontrollably after he had made her come that first time, how it had gone on for minutes, her whole body trembling against his. She had been embarrassed by it, and Daniel had made some dumb joke about having that effect on women just to make her laugh, but he had felt such a strange tenderness for her in that moment, more than tenderness, a shock of recognition, as though he knew her, knew her deeply, as he knew himself, and he had been suddenly uncertain whose body trembled, because he felt the tremor rising as if from his own blood.

———————

Then the panic had returned and Daniel had coaxed and cajoled and dissembled with renewed urgency, glancing at the clock and making his frantic calculations. And just at the point where Emi seemed to be persuaded, appearing to accept Daniel's abject apology and his vision of a moral order restored, she had thrown herself across his lap and started kissing him passionately. "Please," she said. "Please, Danny, just once. Just this once. Let's lie down in bed together."

Somewhere, from far away, Daniel heard himself say no, that really she must stop, that she must go. More than this, he seemed to recall an emergency beacon, strobing beams of red light, and a circle of *carabinieri* in plumed Napoleonic hats, standing in front of a concrete barricade painted yellow and black, with their hands up—but despite all this, or because of it, Daniel could not stop.

Daniel led her to the second bedroom—the one they did not use—and onto the bed, where she undressed him and then herself, peeling off her thin blue dress in one graceful motion. He lay back as she slowly lowered herself on top of him, let all his blood go to the one spot, while his depleted brain rested like a cabbage upon the pillow, devoid of will or thought. She pressed both palms on his chest, and in the darkened bedroom, with the drawn shades, Daniel conjured the image of a succubus—lithe Lilith, the demon lover, succulent sucker, devoid of succor, sucker and licker—and he could not resist her, became her succumber, succumbing to her—for her will was far greater—in this, she was not, after all, so different from Alma—and she was so surprisingly powerful, hunched down on her haunches above him, compact and swaying, the small pads of her palms pressing against his heart—the sensation of being inside her was like a tight squeezing into wet velvet, like a silk purse encasement, and with his eyes closed, Daniel was lost to the rocking and the winding, the combining, combustible grinding, and he forgot who he was, or where they were, or anything other than the mechanics of this heat-stoked engine that went such a far distance on mournfulness and longing.

And then she came, moaning low and foreign in her throat, jack-knifing onto his chest like some folded-up origami figure, and Daniel followed, bucking and flailing, like an epileptic in a grand mal seizure. It was painful, this release, terrifying—he shuddered as his cock kept pumping, a veritable geyser (but not Old Faithful). And from somewhere deep inside his cabbage-brain, he heard a knocking.

ALMA DREAMS

Alma dream-remembers the same memory-dream. She is wearing a pale blue dress with a velvet bodice and organdy sleeves. She walks onstage with Archie Gantz. The audience applauds. Archie sits down at the piano, and Alma settles herself on her chair. She gathers Franny into the cove of her spread skirt and brings her bow arm into position. She nods, and he begins.

It is always the Franck. The opening, soft. The short first note, followed by the first extension. Soft, fluttering vibrato. In the manner of dreams, she is both playing and watching herself play. The woman onstage is strong in her movements, decisive, but delicate—her lines are fluid, her arms relaxed, with tension concentrated in the fingers. There is no wasted effort. Her head is now tilted toward her instrument, confiding, tête-à-tête, now bowed, coaxing it, now turned slightly away, as though listening to it sing. Franny's tone is rich and deep. The opening movement is enigmatic, brooding, but refined. Alma experiences it as restrained longing. She imagines an elegant older woman who has lived with her sadness for so long that she has learned to carry it gracefully, though the pain, over all the years, has not diminished.

From the start—in dream, as in memory—Alma knows that something is off. She knows this because she is *thinking* that something is off. Which means a part of her has remained separate from the music. Alma experiences her playing as relinquishment, like falling into a rushing river—the music, which is the river, comes from a place far distant and flows infinitely forward; it is what distinguishes Alma's playing, that she is able to fall into it, to ride it, with enough skill not to be dashed to pieces, but with enough grace to seem simply to be borne along. The effect on her listeners is of having slipped into something deeper, far larger than the present moment, so that even as the music ends, it seems to stay with them, seems to have been with them always. At a certain point of mastery, all of Alma's art had become a process of loosening, of lessening control, of becoming small and still, and letting the music run.

But in the variations of her dream-memory, she remains outside the flow. She is thinking the music. From the first extension, the fanning out of her fingers to reach up a major third, elbow moving forward, the weight of her arm shifting to support her pinkie finger, in its smooth, sad vibrato. Contracting, stretching. The tiny shift down, the long ascent of the perfect fourth, F-sharp to B. Chasing Archie's gently rocking line.

Alma feels a buzzing, as though a cloud of bees were swarming above her head. She starts to tense as the sound increases, grows louder, bigger, faster. Something is happening. The music builds, and she struggles to keep up. She listens for Archie. The embellished recapitulation, the opening reprised. Her fingers fishtail on the strings, feel sloppy and drunken. Coming into the second movement, Alma is afraid. She holds her breath. She is fighting for each note. Pushing it. And then . . . the unthinkable happens, the unimaginable thing. Alma's body goes numb, goes limp. Her bow arm skitters off the strings, and the music flattens and goes silent. She goes pigeon-toed, twists sideways off her chair, and down. The back of her hip scudder-thuds to the stage floor. Alma paws impotently at the ground like a lamed horse.

Then the dream goes wild. The houselights go up. They blink and go out again. A trapdoor opens and she falls through it. There is a call for a doctor. Daniel runs across the stage. Paolo reaches for her hand. Her cello is broken into pieces like Humpty-Dumpty. It plays Elgar, its strings sprung like mattress coils. She presses her cheek against the hardwood floor. "Get up," says Daniel. "Not that way," says Paolo. Alma screams and screams and does not stop.

All the variations begin the same way, with the blue gown, and the Franck, the buzzing of bees, and the falling, but the endings are pure surrealism, random generator of sounds and images—nuns holding chickens and flautists with bowling balls, pieces of Haydn and Brahms played by women wearing white gloves, and babies with toy hammers, in diapers and chain mail. Daniel is always there, and Paolo, and her father. Archie, Kristophe, and Rickey. All the men in Alma's life are there. None are able to help her. All the women are blank-faced and forbidding, with 1950s hairstyles. The babies are helium-headed, troubled by heat rash. It is always hot, and bright, and crowded, and noisy.

And in each variation, comatose Alma (comma), coma-tossed, knows, in her coma-toes, that—in life, as in dreams—her long run of good luck is over.

KYOKO'S DISH

K yoko wondered if, indeed, revenge was a dish best served cold, or if room temperature might be better. She supposed it didn't matter either way since the end result would be the same, and under these circumstances, one needn't worry about spoilage. She regarded the fish, which was brown and gray with black spots. Unpuffed, it seemed lumpish and unremarkable.

"It doesn't look deadly," she said.

"Oh, but it is," Kornell said. "Better keep Sumo away." For the cat was pacing under the table, banging into their shins with the broadside of her fat, furry body. Kyoko scooped her up and put her in the bedroom, closing the door.

"Did Yoshi do that?" Kyoko said, indicating the deep cut that divided the fish along its midsection.

"No, baby, I did," said Kornell proudly.

"And you're sure the poison hasn't already been removed?"

"No chance," said Kornell. "That's hundred percent tetrodotoxin right there. Be careful with it."

Kyoko looked closely at the plate, at the thin pieces of white, translucent meat that were laid out inside the whole fish, like a cutaway diagram. She felt an urge to try some, to dare a tiny toxic taste, wondered if she would feel the soft buzz of paralysis immediately, a tingling in her spine and head.

The truth was that Kyoko already felt a buzzing in her head and a fizzy, funny feeling in her stomach, which she attributed to nervousness, and being so very close to accomplishing her longtime goal. She felt like her whole life up until now had gone along in slow motion, with discrete moments that seemed almost static in her memory, like an Ozu movie—long hours of stillness, the only sound her pencil on paper, or the plucking of guitar strings, or her mother weeping in the other room. And suddenly, in the last two weeks, time had sped up, and everything was happening all at once—the band, the trip, the kidnapping. Kyoko wasn't used to so much action. It confused her, made her dizzy. She took a deep breath and thought of her childhood tai chi lessons, consciously lowered her stance.

"Let's do this," she said, though Kornell had already left the room.

DANIEL, DEFEATED

Hollowness. Hurt. Denial. Daniel, denied. It was a cliché. It was pathetic. The lover downcast. The lover spurned. The lover who, hoping to get away with twice what he had, had ended up with nothing. Daniel knew that he had no one but himself to blame, his misery of his own manufacture, but that did not make it false, did not make it less painful.

The rest of the summer had been a fog of rehearsals and concerts, travel arrangements, and recording sessions. Alma had refused to speak to him, but once, in rehearsal, she had thrown a metronome at his head, and he'd had to have five stitches above his right eyebrow.

Paolo became a fixture at Alma's side, with his prissy Italian ways, his stifling cologne and phony aristocratic air, which was no less phony for being authentic. There were more tears from Emi, more scenes and pleading. She couldn't understand why the breaking off of Daniel's engagement to Alma did not immediately translate to his pledging himself to her.

Mostly what Daniel remembers is being alone, walking the side streets to avoid the tourists; sitting on a shaded step off Piazza Sant'Ambrogio and eating a *lampredotto* sandwich; drinking Peroni till late in a small bar near Santa Maria Novella and listening to the trains. He started revisiting all the places that he and Alma had gone together—the usual spots, but especially the Duomo, with Michelino's fabulous fresco of Dante and his beloved city of Florence, from which he had been exiled for the last twenty years of his life.

Daniel and Alma had had an argument once, after Daniel said he thought Dante had been foolish not to return to Florence once a general amnesty had been declared. "I mean, that was his chance," he'd said. "He could have gone back then."

"But he couldn't have, don't you see?" Alma had said. "He would have had to make a big public apology. They wanted him to grovel."

"So?" Daniel had shrugged. "A little groveling is a small price to pay for getting to return to the city you love."

This had incensed Alma. "I can't believe you would say that!" she had said. "Don't you understand? It's a matter of principle, standing up for what you believe in!"

"There's principle, and then there's practicality," Daniel had said. "You can stand by your principles, and be miserable and exiled, or you can just say whatever they want you to say and come home."

Alma had given him a look of disgust.

Standing in front of the fresco without Alma, Daniel wondered whether that had been his problem, that when it came right down to it, he had no principles to stand by. What was it that he believed in resolutely? That he would defend to the death? Not love. Not art. Alma always said he wasn't single-minded enough; he was too easily distracted, she said, by other choices, other paths. The idea of deliberate sacrifice was difficult for him. He had wanted Alma, but he had wanted Emi, too. Not because he valued Emi as highly, but because he had valued her at all.

You shall leave everything you love most dearly: this is the arrow that the bow of exile shoots first. You are to know the bitter taste of others' bread, how salt it is, and know how hard a path it is for one who goes descending and ascending others' stairs.

Dante envisioned the lowest circle of Hell as a frozen waste, reserved for traitors and killers of kin. There he placed Count Ugolino and Archbishop Ruggieri. In life, Ruggieri had locked Ugolino up in a tower with his sons and grandsons, and had the keys thrown into the Arno. In Dante's *Inferno*, the two are trapped in ice up to their necks, side by side, Ugolino gnawing on his enemy's skull for all eternity. Daniel had imagined Paolo's perfectly coiffed head within range of his eyeteeth. He would have gladly crunched down on that bit of flesh and bone, if it had meant extracting the bitter juice of his rival's triumph.

Twenty years later, from the perspective of his own captivity, it was Daniel's own numb skull he wanted to gnaw on, the bitterness of his most shameful memory that he wished to extract. He had felt, those last weeks in Florence, like an exile from a city within a city. For, although he was free to walk the streets, to enter any building, pass over any bridge, he was no longer free to do so with Alma, and it had made no difference, all his groveling and apology, for he did not win her pardon.

DANIEL GETS HIS JUST DESERTS

I n the dark corner of the basement, Daniel hid behind two storage boxes, his WMD primed and ready. The tricky part was aiming it quickly and accurately as soon as The Big Guy came down the stairs. Daniel hoped the surprise factor, coupled with the barrage of shrapnel, would overcome his captor enough to enable Daniel to escape up the stairs and out of the house. He knew he had no chance against TBG in terms of strength, but he thought he might be able to outrun him in the open. He wished, though, that he knew what was out there, if there were other houses nearby or if it was heavily wooded. From the tiny ground-level window, he was only able to see a patch of crabgrass with some dandelions and beyond it a few trees. The sound of cars was intermittent, and not very loud; Daniel estimated they were at least twenty minutes from the city.

―――――――

K ornell unlocked the padlock, and the two dead bolts, at the top of the stairs. The basement was dark. There was a switch at the top of the stairs and a switch at the bottom, around the corner, by the bathroom. Kornell just assumed Daniel had turned the lights off and was napping, so he did not flip the light switch on again. Instead, he descended, in the semidarkness, with a bologna sandwich and a glass of SunnyD on a tray.

N *ot yet, not yet. Now!* Daniel popped his head up from behind the boxes and turned his weapon toward Kornell, who was standing at the base of the stairs with a dinner tray in his hands. Aiming for the head, in particular the eyes, Daniel pressed back on the first lever and let loose with a spray of broken glass and sharp metal. *Fire one! Fire two! Fire three!* Without waiting to see the effects of his attack, Daniel jumped out from his hiding place, grabbed the base of his weapon, and swung it at TBG's head with all his force.

S hit!" Kornell put his arms up to defend himself against the bombardment of porcupine needles that struck his face and chest, some of them hot and stinging. There was a loud roar, then something heavy clobbered him on the side of the head. Kornell grabbed at it. It appeared to be a telescoping tripod, or some kind of retractable metal cane; it collapsed in Kornell's hands. A shadowed figure passed him up the stairs, and Kornell lunged to grab it, latched onto a piece of fabric, twisted, and pulled. There was a muffled *oooff*, and a thud, and the shadowed figure slipped down a few steps, landing in a heap at Kornell's feet. The shadowed figure was, of course, Daniel Karmody, and when Kornell saw him, curled like a paisley at the bottom of the stairs, he started to laugh. He couldn't help himself. He turned on the light and surveyed the room, which was littered with tiny mirrorlike shards that winked and glittered, and metal fragments, oblong objects of unknown provenance, pieces of elastic, and lengths of coiled green wire. "Shiiiiit," he said, still chuckling. "Homey got himself an art project."

What . . . ?!" Kyoko came rushing down the stairs, stopped halfway. "What the fuck just happened?" she said, looking down at Daniel Karmody, who lay on the floor with his hands covering his face.

Kornell, who had been so careful up until now, took off his mask and laughed. "Dude tried to escape," he said, indicating the debris spread out across the floor. "Look at all this shit! Can you believe it?"

Kyoko stared at the pieces of glass and metal, then pursed her lips. Daniel had not moved from the bottom of the stairs. "Hey, you!" she called. "Get up!"

Daniel opened his eyes slowly. He was more humiliated than hurt, aware that he had blown his one big opportunity, that all his hours of work and ingenuity had ended up glancing ineffectually, like Lilliputian arrows, off TBG's upper torso, but he was curious to come face-to-face with Emi Tokugawa's daughter, and this was what finally roused him from his abject position. Kornell helped him into the recliner, where Daniel collapsed against his Snugli blanket.

She was smaller than Daniel remembered from the night he had been abducted, with Emi's high forehead and porcelain complexion. Her hair was short, spiky, with a blue streak in the middle, and Daniel noted a tiny gold barbell through one eyebrow and a ring through her nose. She was dressed all in black, even her boots, which were the kind bikers wore, with large silver buckles. She had her mother's grave expression, the look of restraint, which in Emi's case had been a lie, but instead of Emi's sad smile, the girl had a look of slight annoyance.

"Do you know who I—"

"I know who you—"

They both paused. The girl began again. "Do you know why you're here?"

Daniel cleared his throat. He had to be very careful. "I presume," he said, "that it has something to do with your mother."

"You know who my mother is?"

"I figured it out," he said. He pointed to the magazine on the cot, at the address label.

The girl was clearly flustered, but Daniel wasn't sure whether this was to his advantage. "And what do you know about my mother?" she said. Her voice was raspy, deeper than he'd imagined, coming from that tiny frame, and Daniel knew for certain now that it had been her voice he had heard, caterwauling in the night, to the accompaniment of wailing guitar and crashing drums.

"I know that she was a wonderful woman," he said. "A talented musician. A kind and sensitive—"

"Cut the crap! Like you cared!"

"I did."

"You fucked her! You knew she was married and had a kid, but you fucked her anyway! That's all you cared about."

Daniel winced. "It wasn't . . . It was more . . . I mean, yes. We did have a brief . . ." He rubbed his palms along the armrests. His heart was doing its own caterwauling, and his hands were damp. "A brief . . . affair. Which I regret very much."

"You know what happened to her?" The girl's gaze was un-flinching. Daniel flinched.

He lowered his voice. "I heard, yes."

"What did you hear?"

"That she had . . . That . . . that it was suicide."

"Wrong!" Kyoko seemed to launch herself at Daniel, coming up onto the toes of her boots. "Wrong! Wrong! Wrong!" Daniel smelled garlic on the girl's breath, a vinegar sourness. "I was there. I know. You killed her. You seduced her, you broke up her marriage, you abandoned her, and you killed her!"

"I . . . I . . ." Daniel closed his mouth. What could he possibly say? He lowered his head. "I'm sorry," he said.

There was a long silence. The fluorescent light flickered and hissed. Kyoko looked at Kornell, who turned and went back up the stairs.

"You're sorry?" Kyoko repeated. "You're sorry?"

She had to admit that he did look sorry—sorry, and small and weak, with his scrub-brush beard and dirty, disheveled hair, in his torn shirt and too-small pants. For the first time, Kyoko considered the idea that Daniel Karmody might be a creature capable of re-morse, of some true feeling—and just as immediately, she rejected it. She felt the corrosive heat rise from her stomach, into her chest and throat, and she spat it out, onto Daniel's sorry head.

"You're sorry? You fucking asshole!" She kicked Daniel in the vicinity of his shins.

"I—" Daniel began.

"Shut up! Shut up!" The girl was kicking him repeatedly now, and as he brought his arms down to protect his legs, she kicked his arms. "You don't get it. You think we're all the same. Little dolls for you to fuck."

Daniel half stood, but tripped on the blanket, and fell over. Kyoko was crying and kicking Daniel harder, in the side and stomach. He tried to use the blanket to pad her blows, but it made it harder to elude them.

"You asshole!" she yelled. "You don't care that you ended her marriage"—kick—"ended her life!" Kick. "You fucked her"— kick—"forgot about her"—kick—"and went on fucking other women who 'look just like' her!" Kick. "That's all it was to you!"

As the violence continued, Daniel concentrated on its rhythm, which was kick, *oof*, pain, kick, *oof*, pain—a slight delay after registering the toe of the boot on his body, slight anticipation in the ejaculation, *oof*, before the full, breathtaking sensation of pain.

K yoko was sobbing now, and could not see what she was kicking, could only feel the doorstop weight of him at the end of her boot. Each solid connection of her foot to Daniel's body felt good, though she wished she wasn't crying—that he would not see her crying—but the crying, too, felt good. "You killed her, you asshole!" she said, and saying it felt good. Her body spasmed as she kicked and screamed, and she was briefly flooded with the same wild power she'd felt onstage at Holey Shmoley's two days ago.

———

She stopped when Kornell came back downstairs holding a plate. Daniel, balled up, relaxed slightly. Food was good. Food meant that they were going to keep him around longer.

"You killed her, and you deserve to die," Kyoko said in a quieter tone. There was some movement, but Daniel didn't dare look to see what was happening. His body was electric with pain, lit up with a tenderness that ran deep and hot. She was right, he thought tiredly, he deserved it. Deserved it and desired it. Whatever it was that she had in mind for him.

Which was . . . a gagging surprise. Something soft and spreading mushed against his face. Fishy taste, slimy texture. Daniel's reflexes took over as he struggled to keep his mouth closed, his teeth drawbridge-clenched, but the stuff had pushed up inside his nostrils, and he couldn't breathe. He coughed, snorted, gasped, gagged. The girl's small hands pressed against his face. In pain from his beating, after thirteen days of captivity, Daniel's mind was not functioning maximally, but to the best of his reckoning, as he braced himself against the fishy onslaught, it seemed that he was to be force-fed to death. He pictured himself blowing up like a balloon, his distended stomach exploding across the room in bits of flesh and viscera. It was an unpleasant image, even if it seemed farfetched.

Kyoko grabbed handfuls of fugu and stuffed it into Daniel's mouth. She had sunk to her knees and was crying so hard she couldn't see. "Fucking die!" she kept saying, though her words were smeared with tears and snot. She kept the image of her mother in her mind, not just the image of her lying on the bathroom floor, but the image of her in full glory, in her red evening gown, with rhinestone clips in her hair—her eyes lined in Cleopatra kohl, shining with expectant light.

Other images of her mother. Sitting at the kitchen table in her robe and slippers. Playing a duet with a student. Smiling. Crying. Nodding. All the ordinary, everyday ways that her mother had been, but that, Kyoko hated to admit, were fading in her memory, growing muddier, grainier—becoming less and less like images from real life and more like photographs, like newspaper photographs printed long ago. She wondered how long it took for the tetrodotoxin to take effect. She was battering Daniel's face with the flat of her hands, most of the fish having been pulverized or gone wayward of his mouth.

"Ouch!" Kyoko grabbed her hands away. Daniel had bitten her hard on the middle and index fingers of her right hand; she could see the U-shaped line of teeth marks dotted along the tips. Without thinking, she put them into her mouth, and it was the taste that reminded her. "Shit!" she said.

Kornell leaned over her. "Spit!" he said, and she spat. Several times.

"Shit! Shit! Shit!" she said.

Then it dawned on Daniel. Poison! And he spat, too. Several times. Kyoko, whose pale face was flat white, rubbed her tongue on the sleeve of her shirt. "I got . . . Some went in my . . . Oh, shit . . . Korny."

"It's okay, baby." Kornell took his ski mask out of his back pocket and swabbed at Kyoko's mouth with it. "Don't worry. It's okay."

Daniel, on his hands and knees, tried to make himself throw up, but could only manage a dry heaving. He slumped against the recliner in exhaustion, slumped farther into a modified child's pose. He felt the fish drying stiffly across his face, the heat and sting of his injuries moving up and down his body like a berserk elevator. He was still alive, he knew, because he felt like shit, but he wasn't sure for how much longer.

"How is it okay?" he heard his former tormenter say in a small scared voice.

"Because I took the poison out," Kornell said. "I took it out ahead of time. The fish is harmless."

Daniel, in his slumped position, was beginning to feel overcome by fatigue. He struggled to keep his eyes open, wondering if the girl would react with anger.

"Good," she said simply. "Oh, Korny. That's good."

And, forgotten by his captors for the moment, Daniel managed to fall asleep.

redemption

(or what passes for it)

FORGIVENESS

There is a form of forgiveness called absolution, by which an offender is freed from guilt or obligation. You could buy absolution from the church back in the day, spend a few coins, and receive your golden ticket to heaven. This was not the kind of forgiveness Kyoko offered Daniel Karmody, in the aftermath of the great fugu debacle. "Fugu-veness," quipped Daniel's delirious brain.

It was the sort of forgiveness that only followed punishment. After the pummeling Kyoko gave Daniel. After the blowfish she smushed into his face. And it was not just a one-way process, because Daniel had to mediate his own forgiveness, for Kyoko and Kornell had deprived him of his liberty, plotted to kill him, and fed him processed meats on white bread for thirteen days, causing him not just physical but emotional and psychic injury.

And it was not even intentional, this forgiving. Certainly, Kyoko would have never voluntarily extended it. It was just that, lying there—sobbed out, exhausted, her hands greased with fish slime—she had looked over at Daniel, whose body lay crumpled on the floor beside her, and felt no anger, no hatred, nothing except a hollowness in her chest that felt both empty and light, as though whatever had once resided there had flowed out, drained off, leaving behind only unaccustomed buoyancy. She realized she had never really wanted to kill Daniel and that Kornell had known this before she did, and these realizations felt good and right.

And when Daniel regained consciousness, he was so glad not to be dead that he surprised himself. Like Kyoko, he felt a lightness, which in his case contained the absence of guilt. Daniel had done bad things, terrible things, things with painful consequences for other people, things he had done without thinking, selfish, careless things, things he could not undo—and all of it was inexcusable, and all of it he owned up to, and he *was* sorry, though he understood that this was not an end point, nor really a beginning, but part of a process that would continue, now that he had been allowed to go on—and this absence of guilt, this lightness, was a kind of self-forgiving—not because he deserved forgiveness, but because he desperately needed it.

Daniel Rereads the Message

The first thing Daniel was allowed to do was check his phone. There wasn't much on it because everyone knew he was on vacation. He went straight to Facebook and reread Alma's message.

DK—

I hope you're happy and that things are going well for you. I don't know if you'll get this. You probably heard about my MS from Archie, or Sophea, or one of the old crew. (You always said it was like the mafia.) I'm living in California—about 20 minutes outside San Diego, three blocks from the ocean. I can see dolphins jumping from my front deck. I'm no longer able to play, but I teach an occasional master class. Woohoo. I just wanted you to know that I think about you sometimes, and wonder how you're doing. I did get the letters you sent through Kristophe. I think you know why I never replied. I don't want you to think I didn't want to. You're a good man, DK, and I'm not angry with you anymore. For what that's worth. (Probably very little.) Congratulations, belatedly, on your marriage. Guess I was wrong. Thanatos, huh? I hear you kill every night. (Wow, that was almost as bad as one of yours!) Well, take care.

—A.

Daniel read it over a few times, feeling so far removed from the version of him who had first read it, and been injured by it, two long weeks ago. This time around—benefiting from the clearheadedness that can result from being kidnapped and nearly murdered—two things struck him hard. That even after all these years, her voice came back to him, low and sweet, sounding in his ear like a bedtime confidence. And that something was very wrong. *I hope you're happy and that things are going well . . . I just wanted you to know . . .*

With a rising sense of alarm, Daniel registered the brittle blandness for what it was: weariness, the relinquishing of hope. An exhausted goodbye.

Daniel had, of course, heard about her MS from a number of people, and from newspaper articles when he'd googled her. The articles were fond of drawing a comparison between Alma and Jacqueline du Pré, which he knew would infuriate her. Why hadn't he tried to contact her all these years? He had certainly wanted to. Now it might be too late.

Though somehow, deep in his sentimental Irish heart, he believed it wasn't too late, believed he could psychically feel Alma's still-beating heart, her continued presence on this earth, albeit on the other side of the country.

_____

Did you say you were headed to California next week for your tour?" Daniel asked Kyoko. "I know this is weird, but do you think you could give me a ride?"

Kyoko, still bewildered by the way things had transpired, just stared at him.

"I mean . . . I'd chip in for food, gas . . ."

"To California?" she repeated. "Why?"

"Um, I—maybe you know, there was a cellist. Alma."

Kyoko stiffened.

"I know," Daniel said. "I know. But here's one thing I can try to fix. I hurt her, like I hurt your mom. I'd like to try to . . . to . . . I think she may need help."

"No, I don't think—" Kyoko began.

"All right, man," Kornell said. "We'll take you. Absolutely."

And so they had driven back to Daniel's house, in the same white Econoline Kyoko and Kornell had driven up in two weeks earlier, though it seemed a year ago to Daniel. While Kyoko and Kornell waited in the van, Daniel went inside to make some calls, pack a couple of bags, collect his violin, his computer, his eyeglasses, his vitamins, and his electric shaver, and just before he was about to leave, he took a last backward look into the living room, at the white couch that looked stylish but had never been comfortable, at the chrome and the carpet, and the bare places where Sigrid's things had been, and it was a relief to realize that he had never felt at home here, had never fit into Sigrid's house, her life, or her world. She had valued objects, not for themselves but because other people valued them—the beauty in the commodity, not in the thing itself. Daniel thought that she had valued him similarly, not because of who he was but because other women had wanted him. He looked at the blank space where Milo Kretz's *Untitled #172* used to hang, and as he stared, Daniel felt the space widen, growing whiter and blanker in front of his eyes, but instead of feeling loss, or reduction, he felt himself drawn in—the blankness advancing, the wall itself growing less substantial—until it seemed to him that he could pass right through it.

Daniel turned his back and closed the front door. Kyoko and Kornell had kept the motor running.

Daniel, headed west

He sat at the approximate center of a rose-colored bowl, surrounded by red rock formations—precariously shaped spires, looming walls, and turrets—a cathedral made of clay. The sky was pale blue, with a shaving of moon still, though it was now morning, and the sun cast everything in a soft, contemplative light, blunting the edges of the world.

Daniel had no idea the country could be so beautiful, so strange and open and brightly colored. He'd been out west many times, but always on planes, and only to university campuses or concert halls. What he had been missing! Up ahead, Kyoko and Kornell were walking Sumo on her thin red leash. From the picnic table where Daniel sat, he could just make out Sumo's gray tail, like a fat little feather waving on the horizon.

It was the fourth day of their trip, and now that they had the Midwest behind them, Daniel had convinced K&K (as he now called them) to take a slower, more scenic route. He closed his eyes and took a deep breath of cold air that prickled in his nostrils and smelled faintly of campfire. He knew soon enough it would be hot again. That he was here at all, in Kodachrome Basin State Park, somewhere in southern Utah, was astounding to Daniel. Incredible. And with his kidnappers as traveling companions! Daniel shook his head and laughed out loud at the absurdity. And yet here he was, puny but alive, among the centuries-old rocks in the vastness of a landscape that would have been unimaginable to him even a few days before.

Daniel got along well with Kornell, who, it turned out, liked a bad pun or joke as much as he did, and seemed, in general, like a solid, all-around nice guy. Kyoko was still prickly, and Daniel tried to keep out of her way as much as possible (as much as one could on a cross-country car trip with almost 24/7 contact). He didn't get their relationship—Kyoko seemed dour and extremely introverted, while Kornell was friendly and open, even with people who narrowed their eyes at him or seemed physically stung by his presence. But something must have worked, because, through the walls of his motel room the last three nights, Daniel could hear their lovemaking, which was loud and long and seismic. It annoyed Daniel, who tried holding a pillow over his head, but then it made him wistful—he remembered making love like that—and finally, he was happy for them, for their youth and their stamina, their exploration and their eagerness, for the intensity of their feeling, without filter or caution—without experience to check it or pain to distort it—and for the innocence of believing that it would always be thus, this capacity for merging, this burning, this suspension of solitude, this solace, this moment, this being.

RICKEY ACTS AS HOST

Rickey passed through the lobby and saw them talking to Dennis. A Black man, an Asian girl, and a white guy.

"Can you tell us what hospital she's in?" the white guy asked.

"I'm afraid I can't do that, sir," Dennis was saying. He looked up at Rickey and nodded.

Rickey somehow knew right away that the white guy was Daniel. Alma had described him perfectly. He was tall and handsome. Piercing blue eyes. Pale complexion, but with pink cheeks and nose. Dark hair—though it was more salt-and-peppery now. A full mop of it. Poet's hair, Rickey thought, thick and roguishly disheveled, the kind women liked. Hey, men, too. He was dignified-looking, held himself well, good posture, with broad shoulders.

"Well, who *can* tell me, then?"

Dennis shook his head. "I surely don't know, sir," he said.

The dude was getting frustrated, but he was holding it in. The younger two hung back, detached. "Look, we've driven all the way across the country just to see her. I'm an old friend. We haven't seen each other in twenty years. Could you at least find some way to let her know I'm here?"

"I'm Rickey Marchand, Alma's neighbor. Can I help you?"

Daniel and Dennis both looked relieved. "Thank you, Rickey. I'm Daniel Karmody. This is Kyoko Tokugawa and Kornell Burke."

Rickey smiled. "I'll take them up, Dennis," he said.

"Okay, Mr. M., if you're willing to take responsibility."

"I am, Dennis. It's okay." Rickey shifted his bag from his right arm to the left and indicated for them to follow him toward the bank of elevators. "Sorry about that," he said. "Dennis can be the soul of discretion. Also, he's a little . . ." Rickey mouthed the last word, "stupid."

Inside Rickey's apartment, the young people sat, while Daniel stood, with his hands behind his back, taking in the decor. It was obvious that Rickey was gay, which relieved Daniel, since there were photos of Alma on his bookcase. Besides which, he was way too young. Why it mattered to Daniel that Alma's relationship with Rickey could not be sexual, he hardly knew, but it made him feel better, less open to ridicule. Had Rickey been Alma's boyfriend, one of the poseur European types she seemed to prefer, it would have been harder to explain himself—who he had been to her, why he was there, but, now, surrounded by the same minimalist white furniture that Sigrid had loved, with zebra-print throw pillows and swooping, chrome-armed lamps, Daniel felt sturdy, masculine, ready to take charge.

———

S o, how long has she been in a coma?" Daniel asked.
"Twenty-two days."

"Brought on by . . ."

Rickey hesitated.

"She sent me a message," Daniel said. "I think it was that night. I'm here because she sounded like she might have . . . might have been thinking about doing something to herself."

Rickey wondered what the couple was there for, what relation they could have to Daniel. They seemed so incongruous, the tiny grumpy-looking girl with her spiky blue hair, her piercings and tattoos, and the huge, calm, bald man. Kyoko was looking at Rickey's books, while Kornell sat, politely, on the edge of one of Rickey's Thayer Coggin lounge chairs, contemplating the view out over the bluff and into the Pacific Ocean.

Daniel was trying not to let his gaze fall too long on the photo of Rickey and Alma at the racetrack. It cracked Rickey up the way heterosexual men puffed themselves up, like rain-forest toads. There was a certain way that straight guys tried to play it with gay guys, simultaneously indicating that they didn't care if you were gay and making it clear that they weren't. Only, of course, what they were really signaling was that you had been removed from the list of penis-bearers, with whom they competed for all the great prizes, the women, and the glory, forever hallelujah. It disappointed Rickey that Alma had fallen for this guy, but then he was always being disappointed by straight men. It was a habit he'd acquired young.

"So, Kyoko, Kornell—right?" Rickey said. "What can I get for you? A glass of water? Some lunch? I could make some lemonade."

Kyoko shook her head. Kornell smiled. Rickey thought he looked amused. "Thanks, man. We're good."

Rickey turned to Daniel.

"A glass of water. Please."

Rickey went to the refrigerator. "Yeah," he said. "Alma took some pills." He poured a glass of water from the Brita pitcher. He spoke carefully, not wanting to betray Alma's privacy.

"When was this?" Daniel pulled out a barstool and sat down at the kitchen island.

Rickey put the glass down. "Same night she went into the coma," he said. *Obviously*, he did not add. "May 26?"

The same night. Daniel had been convinced of it. The same night he had been sitting in his car, listening to Alma play Bach—the same night he had been interrupted at his own suicide by two masked figures—had been the very night Alma had sat down to a bottle of pills. Surely it must mean something, this strange confluence. If it had led to him sitting here now, in Del Mar, California.

"What do the doctors say?"

Rickey shrugged. "She could come out of it. She could not. Possibility of severe brain damage. Possibility of partial or full paralysis."

Daniel took this in. He held the glass of water, but he did not drink. For a moment, there was no sound except the scolding of gulls and the soft *whuush* of traffic below. And then there was another noise, that Rickey had a hard time placing. It sounded like breathing, but it rose in volume, ragged and arrhythmic. Rickey looked over at Daniel, who was hunched over his glass, and it took a moment to register that he was sobbing.

———

Afterward, it was determined that Daniel would stay in Alma's apartment and that Rickey would take care of Sumo for Kyoko and Kornell, who split for L.A.

"Don't fuck this up," Kyoko had told Daniel in parting. "I could've killed you, but I didn't. So make it count." She had walked off before Daniel could reply.

Each day Rickey would come back from work with Thai take-out, or Daniel would make some pasta or chicken, and they would eat a quick dinner before heading out to the hospital.

"Did Alma really throw a metronome at you?" Rickey had to ask.

"Right here." Daniel pointed to his forehead, just above his right eyebrow, where a tiny half-moon scar was visible, like an inverted comma.

Rickey laughed. "Sorry, but it's pretty easy to picture. That girl is crazy! Once, I came home, and she had stuffed all her clothes—I mean, everything—into trash bags, and she wanted me to take them down to Goodwill, said she was sick of all of it."

"Did you take them?"

"I made her put most of it back. She had all these beautiful evening gowns. You know . . . Yves Saint Laurent, Christian Dior . . . Beautiful, beautiful dresses! Must have been worth a fortune!"

It felt strange to Rickey, but also familiar, to be having dinner at Alma's place, drinking Sonoma's finest pinot, looking out at the same but different ocean view from her kitchen window, and laughing. Only here was Daniel Karmody, the love of Alma's life, sitting in the seat where Alma usually sat, passing the salt and pepper, telling Rickey versions of the same stories he had heard from Alma's point of view so many times.

And at the hospital, Rickey watched Daniel sit beside Alma,

holding her hand, talking to her as if twenty years, thousands of miles, and a bitter breakup hadn't separated them for a minute, and it just about broke his heart. Cynical Rickey, protective Rickey, half in love with Alma himself . . . he had no choice but to recognize the genuine feeling—to recognize, and to honor, and to do everything in his power to help it along.

DANIEL AND ALMA, REUNITED

A lma?" Daniel held his breath.

They had gotten the call last night that she had regained consciousness, but they hadn't been allowed to see her until this morning. Rickey had, tactfully, gone to the cafeteria to get some coffee.

Alma looked at him blankly. She had been so long dreaming that she didn't trust she was awake. "DK?" she said.

Daniel nodded. "Bet you didn't expect to see me here," he said.

Alma considered. She had not. And yet her thoughts had been so full of him that it was not as odd as it might have been. He was a little thicker, with white in his hair, and he was getting that old man's nose, bulbous and dark-pored. There were lines around his eyes that fanned out at the outer ends, lines at the corners of his mouth, but it was recognizably Daniel, the man who had betrayed her so many years ago.

"I'm still mad at you," she said.

"Okay," said Daniel.

ALMA IS RELEASED

The day they released Alma from the hospital, Daniel wheeled her out, with her lap full of flowers, and Rickey carried her bags, hurrying ahead to open the car doors. "My men," she had taken to calling them, after the nurses on the floor started referring to them that way. "Your men are here," they would say. "Look at what your men brought you today!"

It was, somehow, a natural alliance—the gay friend and the ex-lover—and the two men had grown genuinely fond of each other, having bonded over their mutual love and concern for the same woman. But it was equally true that their first rivalrous instincts had not been altogether extinguished and a competitive impulse still lurked beneath the cooperative surface, like a cruising shark's fin.

Rickey reminded Daniel of Archie, the only other gay man he had ever known well, though, in truth, Archie had been a bit of an enigma—he had shared very little of his personal life with Daniel, and had weathered the various storms of Daniel and Alma's relationship with the utmost discretion. Nevertheless, they were both small, punctilious men, with an acute sense of the absurd and a very particular and exacting relationship to the world of objects. Both, as far as Daniel knew, had disastrous romantic histories and prolonged states of celibacy.

Daniel reminded Rickey of practically every attractive straight man he had ever known—the nervousness that was homophobia masking itself as tolerance, the moments of relaxation followed immediately by the re-erection (ha!) of their guard, the tendency to dwell on matters relating to girlfriends, wives, and the girls they picked up once in some bar, in some city, when they were away on business.

Both thought they had primacy over the other—Rickey, because he had been Alma's best and only true friend for the last three years; Daniel, because he had known Alma first, and more intimately, all those years ago.

What all this amounted to—to Alma's amusement and immediate benefit—was a veritable comedy of solicitude, a Keystone Kops display of altruistic one-upmanship.

"Let me get that," Rickey said now, positioning himself between the car door and the seat, so that he could help ease Alma from her wheelchair to the car.

"I got it, I got it!" Daniel said, lifting Alma into his arms. "You get the chair!"

Rickey was about to protest, but he saw that Daniel had already picked her up and that he was now in their way. He moved clumsily aside. "Watch out," he said. "Careful of her head!"

To Alma, who was blinded by sunlight, and confused still by

drugs and the sudden changes her life had taken, the performance was humorous, but distant, like a sitcom she'd been watching on her TV in the hospital. She still couldn't quite believe that Daniel was here, that she wasn't still floating in a deep dream. "My men," she murmured lightly. "My men."

I was thinking, the bed here." Rickey indicated the space now occupied by the couch. "We move the end table out here." A parallel indication. "And we move the couch over to here." He waved his forearms outward, like a traffic cop.

"Why not just move the dining room table into the bedroom, swap out the bed, and put it here, so Alma can look out at the ocean?" said Daniel.

Rickey put his hands on his hips. "But she's farther from the bathroom then."

"I can sleep on the couch," Daniel said. "I can help her, if she has to get up in the middle of the night."

"Umm, hello?" Alma said from her portable throne, which Rickey had festooned with gold-star-studded wire and a multicolored crown made from pipe cleaners. "I'm right here. Don't I get a say?"

Rickey and Daniel both turned to look at her.

"I want to stay in the bedroom," she said.

"But . . . it's too small," said Daniel. "We already decided that with the wheelchair and all the stuff from the hospital—"

"—and it's easier for me to check in on you," said Rickey.

Alma shook her head. "I want to stay in the bedroom," she

repeated. "And I want Daniel to stay with me." She blushed. "In the guest room."

"Of course," said Daniel.

Rickey frowned. "Are you sure?"

Alma smiled, held out her hand to him. "I'm sure, sweetie," she said, squeezing his palm.

Daniel, Rickey, and Alma

Did you ever notice that all the bad things come from Asia?"
said Alma.

Rickey looked up from his section of the newspaper.
"Like what?" he said. Beside him on the couch, Daniel poured tea.

"Diseases." Alma took the mug that Daniel offered. "Thanks."
She was lying on the white chaise longue that she called "the barge."
Head propped by pillows, most of which Rickey had bought for
her—crushed red velvet, fringed gold velour, indigo corduroy—her
lower half swathed in leopard-spotted microfleece, she looked like
an ailing monarch, Cleopatra on the Nile, asp-bitten and glamorous.
Rickey loved seeing her like this, flushed and relaxed, brimming with
mock outrage. He could watch her all day.

"You've got your Hong Kong flu, your Asian flu, your bird flu.
Cholera. Malaria. SARS," Alma said. "Did you know that the bu-
bonic plague originated in Mongolia?"

Daniel smiled. "I did *not* know that," he said.

"I knew this biologist in Atlanta," Alma said. "She was studying invasive plants, and she told me about a vine called the Oriental bittersweet that spreads like wildfire. It grows on trees, winds all around them, and eventually chokes them to death."

"Diabolical," said Rickey.

Alma nodded. "Right? And Asian carp are killing all the fish in the Great Lakes. They brought them over to eat algae, but it turns out they eat everything."

"I heard about them," Daniel said. "Don't they grow to be more than a hundred pounds and five feet across?"

"You see?" Alma said. "All the bad things."

"Now, now," said Rickey. "Let's not be so self-hating, my dear."

He was looking at her with love, and, Alma knew, intended the comment merely as amusing repartee. But she recognized the word from her online wanderings; she had seen forums where Asian Americans accused one another of this—self-hatred, internalized racism, complicity.

"Not all bad," she agreed, grinning to displace her slight unease. "Because I'm one of them."

"A carp?" said Daniel.

"An invasive species."

Daniel and Alma go for an outing

D aniel had a hard time folding up the wheelchair. The footrests kept getting in the way. "Fuck! Goddammit!" Finally, he just threw the thing in the back of the van, partially open.

When he climbed into the driver's seat, Alma was laughing at him. She put her hand up to his cheek. "Poor baby," she said, "your face is all red."

"Oh, so that's what I get for my chivalry?" Daniel feigned indignation. "Scorn? Mockery?"

Alma smiled sadly. "Chivalry?" she said. "More like nursing." She hated the idea of being in a wheelchair, but the doctor had insisted. "Just until you get some muscle tone back," he had said. "Gain some more weight. Then we can reevaluate."

Daniel knew that she was worried that the doctor had been lying. "More like wrestling a bear trap," he said.

Daniel had planned the whole day. They were driving to Dixon Lake, where they were going to go for a boat ride and have a picnic on the beach. He'd made chicken sandwiches on baguettes, with avocado and red peppers, lemon mayonnaise, and stone-ground mustard. There was a fat bunch of red grapes, a small wheel of Brie, and—he was looking forward to this—a bottle of crisp California Chardonnay stashed on ice in a red Igloo cooler.

"Here we go!" said Daniel, putting the van in first gear and releasing the clutch. There was a sound of metal grinding and the van lurched and stalled. He restarted the engine and tried again, this time foot heavy on the accelerator, and they jerked into motion. "Umm . . . sorry about that," he said. "Haven't driven a standard in a while."

Alma laughed. "You never could, DK," she said. She looked at him sidelong. "And you were otherwise so good with your hands."

"There's a difference between handling a car and a violin," Daniel said.

"Or a woman."

"Or a woman," he agreed.

"Come to think of it, you were a bit heavy-handed. You always came in too early."

"Are we talking violins or women?" Daniel said.

Alma smiled ambiguously out the windshield. Her face, beneath the mask of her illness, was startlingly familiar to him, her smile, at once provoking and intimate. He loved—had loved—this sparring, this friction, a double helix of desire and resistance.

"It was you, my love, who always came in late," he said. "Why do you think we called you the 'Drag Queen'?" Daniel waited, wondering if he'd pushed it too far, but Alma put her hand, briefly, on his thigh.

"But wasn't I worth waiting for?" she said.

And it was true. In their dim apartment in the Back Bay, with the mattress on the floor and dripping faucets, Daniel had waited for her, and at restaurants and movie theaters, in the backstages of concert halls, in the corridors of college music buildings, on sidewalks, and in friends' houses. Anyplace you could wait, he had waited, and eventually she had appeared—a tall, sulky beauty, tipping slightly backward as she walked, as though to delay her arrival even further, her cello invariably leaning against her in its hard case like an inebriated friend.

Once, wanting to give Alma a taste of her own medicine, Daniel had purposely told her to meet him an hour before he wanted her to show up. He had hidden behind a newspaper kiosk and watched as—nearly forty minutes after the time he had specified—Alma had arrived, waited for maybe two minutes, and then started to go. Catching up to her, Daniel had asked why she was leaving already. "You're never late," she had said serenely, "I assumed you were dead."

Daniel laughed, recalling it now. Alma was looking at him curiously. "You were always worth waiting for," he said. "Every time."

On the lake, Daniel took his time, rowing and resting, letting the boat drift.

"So, before I came here," he said, "a young woman kind of cornered me. She beat me up, then tried to kill me by shoving blowfish in my face, fugu, which has a deadly poison." He hoped to offer up the story as an amusing distraction for Alma, hoped to tell her just enough to intrigue and entertain her. But his voice was shaky.

"The thing is," he pressed on, "the woman was Emi's daughter, Kyoko. She's in her twenties now. She wanted to kill me as revenge, for her mother. She's in a punk band," he added, babbling nervously.

"Vocals, guitar. With her boyfriend on drums. They're touring the West Coast right now, hoping to make it big."

"Emi's daughter?" Daniel felt Alma's interest perk up, as he'd hoped. "She wanted revenge," Alma said slowly, "for how you treated Emi?"

"Yes," Daniel said.

"There's something you're not telling me," Alma said. "She 'cornered' you—how?"

"Well . . ." A bit wounding to the male ego, this part. But he had her full attention. How good it felt to see her engaged and present. Even if it was at his expense. "Actually, they kidnapped me. She and her boyfriend. They came to my house in ski masks, tied me up, threw me in a van, then brought me to their house—which turned out to be Emi's house—and kept me locked in the basement for almost two weeks. Then did the thing with the fish."

Alma looked at him incredulously for a moment, then laughed in low chortles through her nose.

"They fed me white bread and bologna before that," Daniel said, gratified by her laughter and seeking to prolong it. "Did horrors to my stomach. I developed a mold allergy and had a constant runny nose. I grew out an itchy beard. I talked to myself to stay sane."

"You can't be serious, DK," Alma said, her laughter subsiding.

"Oh, I am. And right before she shoved the fish in my face, Kyoko said I was an asshole who saw Asian women as 'little dolls.' She said I saw them as all the same." Daniel's voice cracked, and he felt, oddly, like a Catholic boy giving confession, though he had only done that twice, when he was eight years old.

"Emi's daughter said all that?" Alma seemed to consider this. "Why didn't the poison work? Why didn't she kill you?"

"Hey, don't sound so disappointed," Daniel joked. He picked up the oars and started rowing, aiming for a picnic spot to the right of the dam. "Her boyfriend, Kornell, took the poison out ahead of time. To make sure she wouldn't be guilty of murder."

"Only kidnapping, wrongful imprisonment, and assault," Alma said lightly.

"Yes, only that."

"And *did* you? See them as all the same?" There was a familiar edge to her voice.

Daniel stopped rowing and took in Alma's face, the ineffable force of her, the dark brown eyes that turned slightly downward at their ends, the small nose, the full, sensual lips that he had first seen painted black. Around her, the water glittered under a cloudless sky.

"I agree with her," he said carefully. Remembering the percussive pain of Kyoko's boot in his side. "She called me an asshole, and I am. I mean, I was. Over and over, to everyone. Especially women."

"Especially Asian women?" Alma asked, sounding genuinely curious.

"Well, yes, after you, except for Sigrid, they were all—yes." Daniel blushed and wondered why on earth he'd brought this up. His mind filled with memories of twenty-nine-year-old Alma arguing with him about Yellow Fever and colonizers and power, face flushed, danger sparkling in her eyes.

Forty-nine-year-old Alma regarded him for a moment, then tilted her face up to the sun and closed her eyes. The only sounds were the sloshing of lake water on the sides of the boat and the trilling of a distant bird.

"Only you would come visit me at the ocean and drive to a lake," Alma said, after a long silence.

"You complaining?"

"Absolutely not," she said.

He began rowing again. On the shore they had left behind, the faint outline of Alma's wheelchair stood stoically, like a last, lingering well-wisher waving bon voyage. Alma leaned to the side and dangled one hand in the water. "Thank you," she said. "Thank you for this, Daniel."

Daniel rowed in steady strokes. *"Prego,"* he said. The boat picked up speed, gliding swiftly across the lake, which was smooth as paper.

"Tell me again about this new gig of yours," Alma said, when they were eating their lunch.

"Music thanatology," said Daniel. "Playing for the dying, at hospice centers and in their homes."

"Money in that?"

"Some."

"Recession-proof, I'd imagine," she said.

"People are always dying," he agreed, then added hastily, "I mean, business is steady."

Daniel had called Roger and, without going into details, arranged for him to take over for the next few months. José-Carlos Vaz would fill in for him, and Roger had someone new in mind at second violin. Randall Trask had died, Roger informed him, and Daniel had been sorry to hear it.

"And what do they like to listen to?" Alma asked. "These clients of yours."

"Oh . . ." he said breezily, "'Dance of the Blessed Spirits,' *Death and the Maiden*. Bach's prelude to the Suite in G Major. Lots of Bach."

She nodded. "Predictable."

"Usually."

Alma looked at him. "What would you want to die listening to?" she asked.

Daniel was taken aback. He hadn't told her about sitting in his car listening to her play Bach's second Suite with the motor running, on the same night that she had been sitting with her pills. He wondered if she had been listening to music, and if so, what, but he could not ask her.

"I don't know," he said. "It would depend on my mood." He shrugged. "Beethoven. Any of his string quartets. Mozart. The Jupiter. Mahler's Third."

Alma made a face. "No one should die to Mahler," she said.

"What about you?"

She thought for a moment. "I want Janis Joplin," she said. "'Get It While You Can.'"

Daniel thought about all the people they had played for, the people who were now dead—Cicely Rubenstein, who had loved Vivaldi. Jerry Kannen. Archer Pope. Mac Mackenzie, who had died of ALS and loved Saint-Saëns; Julie Chen, who favored Brahms and had died of breast cancer; Winnie Eckersley and her Pachelbel; Randall Trask and *Death and the Maiden*—all of them, to the end, holding fast to beauty, to the life that beauty sustained. Daniel hoped that he had helped them, that the music had truly—consoled, thrilled, or distracted, Daniel wasn't sure—but he hoped it had given them something good, something holy, a thread to swing across, from infinite to infinite, from life to . . . after-life. It was the closest to religion Daniel would allow himself.

"Is it a good quartet?" Alma asked now.

Daniel nodded, squinting out at the canvas-colored water. "The viola is great," he said. "We're currently replacing our second violin."

Alma smirked. "Of course you are," she said.

Daniel shifted uncomfortably on the bedspread he'd brought to picnic on.

"And the cello?"

He brightened. "She's not you."

"Ahh," Alma said. "Of course not."

There was a whirr of motorboats, a slapping of sails. Leisured sounds on a summer afternoon. Daniel felt pleasantly drowsy.

"Remember," Alma said, "that time we went to Siena? When we got lost, and met that nice woman?"

"Antoinetta!"

"No," Alma said. "Isabella."

"Are you sure?" Daniel frowned. "I'm pretty sure her name was Antoinetta."

"Isabella," Alma said. "Definitely."

"Hmm . . . Anyway, she was a translator," Daniel said.

"Yes," said Alma. *"Pudd'nhead Wilson."*

"That's right!"

"And she gave us that great bottle of red wine," Alma said.

"I don't remember that," said Daniel.

"Yeah, you do! We drank it that night. It was from her neighbor's vineyard, remember? You said it tasted like Chianti, and I said it was too sweet, and we found out later that I was right, it was a Cabernet!"

Daniel laughed. "Oh, I remember now," he said, though he did not.

DANIEL AND ALMA DISCUSS THE PAST

Later, while Alma slept, Daniel played scales. Mr. Segrest, his first violin teacher, had said that scales came from God. "They are perfect," he said, a soft hand on Daniel's shoulder. "Play them exactly, and you touch the Creator." Daniel hadn't understood what he meant, but years later it had struck him—the order was sublime, one note in sequence following another, always the same, and yet somehow ever-changing. A finite number of scales, an infinite number of expressive possibilities—a miracle of musical DNA.

Afterward, he played for hours—Mozart's Sonata in B-flat; the Bach *Chaconne*; the Méditation from *Thaïs*. It felt so wonderful to play Rocky again, after so many days away. Daniel realized the last time he had gone three weeks without playing the violin he'd had a bad case of mono, in the eleventh grade.

———

In the middle of the night, Alma called to him. Her cheeks were flushed, and the pillow had left a crimped impression on the left side of her face, like the pattern of a fossil. "Your phrasing was weird," she said. "It sounded like you were holding your breath."

He climbed into bed with her, placed his face close to hers on the pillow. "Ever the critic," he said.

She started to cry, and he stroked her arm.

"Alma, what's the matter?"

Alma shook her head, crying harder.

"Are you in pain?"

She shook her head more vehemently. "Leave me alone," she said.

"No," said Daniel.

She turned to face him, her eyes a brilliant dark brown, her beauty wrecked but still evident, like a pagan temple. Daniel felt the old thrill. It raced in his blood, stirred in him a potent mixture of sadness and desire.

"Alma," he said. He started to say something, about how glad he was to see her, how much he had loved her, but something in her expression stopped him.

"You thought you'd come play for me, didn't you, DK?" she said. "All that 'easing the passage to the next world' New Age bullshit. Dance of the Fucking Blessed Spirits! You take that crap right out of my house, do you hear me, Daniel Karmody? You take it and shove it right up your ass!" She turned away and wept into the pillow.

"Sshh," Daniel whispered, "it's okay." Under his hand, her body bucked and heaved, but her sobs were stifled, almost silent. He could feel the vertebrae of her back, a curving snake of notched bone.

Alma sat up abruptly. Her eyes were swollen, and her hair was flying everywhere. "You cheated on me," she said.

Daniel was taken aback but tried not to show it. "I did," he said. "I'm sorry."

Alma looked at him as though he had not spoken. "Why? Why did you do it?" she said. "Didn't you love me?"

Daniel opened his mouth, closed it. He knew it was important to get it right. Everything depended on the truth. But what was it? He hadn't known it then. Did he know it now? Was there always a reason for the things one did? Daniel did not think it was facetious to ask this question. He had thought the one definitive action of his life would be to marry Alma; instead it had been to lose her.

"Daniel?"

"I absolutely loved you, Alma," Daniel said. "With all my heart. I can't tell you how much—"

"Then why?" Alma's expression was cold, her tone sharp. Daniel remembered that look, that tone.

"The easy answer is that I was stupid," he said. "I thought getting married was a kind of end to something—youth or, possibility, choices . . . I don't know . . . and there was Emi, and I was vain, and I guess I thought I deserved one last fling before I fully committed."

Alma pounced. "'Deserved'? Really?" She glared at him.

"I'm trying to be honest here, Alma. I'm not saying it wasn't low."

"Well, good!" Alma snorted. "Because, frankly, that would be a hard sell."

Daniel felt his face redden. "I *said* it was stupid," he said.

"No, you said *you* were stupid."

"I did. I was. Totally, and without question. Stupid, stupid, with stupid dressing on top." Daniel looked to see if Alma cracked a smile. She did not.

"You said that was the easy answer," she said. "So what's the hard one?"

Daniel hesitated. "It's just . . . I guess . . . It was always like this between us," he said. "Like we are now. We fought about everything. Like in Italy, remember? Not just in rehearsal, but about the art, the architecture, the entire history of Florence—Dante, the Medicis, all those Virgins, Brunelleschi, and . . . what's his name?"

"Paolo?"

Daniel laughed. "Never mind Paolo. No, I meant the other artist, the guy with the doors."

"Ghiberti."

"That's right. You thought Brunelleschi's were better, the ones that lost. Anyway, it was exhausting, all that fighting. I don't think you realized how hard it was sometimes to be with you."

"Oh, so it was *my* fault you cheated on me?" Alma sat up straighter, her posture suddenly rigid, as though an iron spike had replaced her spine.

"I didn't say that, Alma. Stop twisting my words."

"You said I was difficult! That it was exhausting to be around me!"

Daniel sighed. For a moment, he missed the solitude of Kyoko's basement. Where was his Snugli blanket? His beanbag neck pillow? "Honestly, Alma, I'm not sure this is such a good idea," he said. He touched the sheet that covered her knee. "It's ancient history by now. We've been having such a good time, what good can it do to get back into it?"

Alma stared at Daniel's hand as if it were a disembodied object. She looked suddenly subdued, and her voice, when she spoke, was drained of sarcasm. "I don't know what good it can do," she said. "But I'd like to hear it."

"You were such a force of nature," Daniel said. "So intense and passionate and smart. And so extraordinarily talented! The most naturally gifted musician I've ever known." Alma didn't say anything, but Daniel could tell she was struggling not to look pleased. "Everything mattered to you," he went on. "Everything was crucial. What food we ate, what movie we watched . . . You had such a strong opinion about everything. And God forbid I shouldn't have one. Remember? You got furious at me because I said I didn't have an opinion about Ted Turner colorizing black-and-white movies."

"He was desecrating an original art form!"

"You see?"

"He didn't even—"

"—I think I just got scared," Daniel said. "I saw a lifetime of arguing about what pictures to hang on the walls, and where to go for dinner, and who came in early or late, and which was better, Florence or Rome."

"Was I really that bad?" Alma asked, but her tone was tranquil.

"I was worried I would lose myself in your slipstream," he said. "Like what you once said about Gustav and Alma Mahler. How you didn't want to be in anyone's shadow. Only, it turns out, I was Alma."

"So that's what it was?" Alma said quietly.

"I think so." Daniel's voice broke. "And you're just the same now, every bit as fierce. I love that about you."

Alma settled herself back against Daniel's chest. He stroked her hair. It seemed to Daniel that everything that had happened in the last few weeks had led to this—Alma's head on his chest, his arm around her shoulders—so strange, and yet so natural, as though the past had just now caught up to the present.

Strange, too, how the present commandeered the past, marshaling it for its own purposes, its own artful arrangements. Daniel knew that what he had told Alma was true. He remembered several years ago, sitting at the back of Friedberg Hall, listening to a seventeen-year-old audition for the conservatory. Daniel had been worn out from an afternoon's worth of auditions, and starting to think about supper, when he had looked up from his doodling and really begun to listen to what the kid was doing, and what he was doing was playing Bach beautifully, playing it richly, with a poignancy and technique that were superbly matched. Unlike so many young prodigies' performances, which relied on uncanny mimicry or bluffed emotion, this boy's playing was fresh but mature, subtle, modulated, without affectation—and Daniel realized that he would never play Bach as feelingly—not that he wouldn't play it differently, because every musician played a piece differently—but that he would never play it as purely, as profoundly, or as well. It had probably been true for a while, that his abilities as a violinist had been surpassed by his abilities as a teacher, and he had certainly understood that his career had reached a plateau, but listening to this skinny teenager, gangly-limbed, acne-pocked, with his stalk-like neck and his hair sticking out like dandelion seeds, Daniel had felt it in the very pith and marrow of his soul: obsolescence.

Only weeks ago this memory had driven Daniel to despair, the notion of his own insufficiency, but now it no longer seemed to bother him. The truth recast. Daniel could not know what difference it would have made had he stayed with Alma, whether he would have basked in her reflected glory or been obliterated by it, like an ant under a magnifying glass. He had told Alma that this was why he had cheated on her with Emi Tokugawa, out of fear of his own diminishment, but he mistrusted his manipulations. The past was not a fixed point, and neither was the truth, and telling the truth about the past was like trying to hit a bull's-eye with a shotgun. Daniel's ordeal in the basement had taught him that much.

"I'm sorry," he said to her now. "I'm sorry, Alma."

She drew away from him. "DK?" she said.

"Yeah, baby?"

"Play something for me, will you? I'm going to try to go to sleep now."

"Sure thing," Daniel said. He got up and smoothed the covers up around Alma's shoulders. She closed her eyes.

H e played part of the first movement from Alban Berg's Violin Concerto, a favorite of Alma's, in part because Daniel had been playing it with the New England Orchestra the season they had met. The piece bears the dedication "To the memory of an angel," a reference to Alma Mahler's daughter, who died at age eighteen. Berg had captured something of a young girl's grace in a folk dance melody that gave way, in the end, to a darker, more oppressive rhythm. Daniel hadn't played it in a long time, but it hardly mattered—when you knew a thing by heart, it meant more than just by memory—it meant that *it* knew you, that it had found its way inside you, abiding there, and could always be reclaimed.

When he had finished, Alma was asleep. Her mouth was slightly open, and her breathing was deep and even. Daniel didn't know how long he would be able to stay and take care of her, but he wished it could be forever. He felt such a deep tenderness for her, tenderness and a surprising sense of responsibility. And maybe it came from guilt, or penance, or because he was at loose ends in his own life—he didn't care.

———

He went into the bathroom to brush his teeth and was stricken by the sight of Alma's medicine bottles, lined two deep on the shelf like chess pieces: Medrol, Topamax, Ambien, Wellbutrin, Dilantin, Xanax. Just to be safe, he threw out all the ones he could identify as tranquilizers or sleeping pills, sweeping them into the wastebasket with the flat of his hand. Daniel looked in the mirror and was shocked by how old he looked, jowly and red-faced, like a drunken peasant in a painting by Bruegel. It was a selfish face, Daniel saw, dissipated by indulgence and the fear of not getting his share, but he recognized something redeemable in his expression, or wanted to anyway, and he ducked a last, quick nod at that shining, passable thing.

Kyoko and Kornell
in an Oregon diner

Kyoko was surprised by how much she liked the members of the Noctural Submissions—Jake, their lead singer and guitarist; Bennie, the bald keyboardist; the bass player, Martin; and Pony, their drummer, who was as big as Kornell, but white and long-haired.

"*Toro* is the fatty tuna," Kornell was explaining to Jake, who shared his enthusiasm for Japanese cuisine. "My favorite. Salmon and yellowtail are good, too."

"*Unagi* is my favorite," Jake said. "That sauce! Oh my God!"

"Raw fish, man!" said Pony, squinching up his face. He shook his head. "Can't do it. The texture . . . Ewww . . ."

Just then the waitress brought out their orders. She set down a plate of eggs, sunny side up, in front of Pony. Kornell slapped Pony on the shoulder and started laughing. Pony looked down at his plate and started laughing, too. "At least it's cooked!" he protested.

"Yeah," said Kornell, "but that shit comes out of a chicken's kootchie."

"Thanks, man," Pony said. "I really appreciate it. No, really! Thanks." He pierced the yolks with his fork.

It surprised Kyoko how much Kornell seemed to enjoy interacting with other people. She hadn't really noticed it before, and she realized, guiltily, that this was because she herself was so antisocial, so hermetic, that, out of love for her, Kornell had simply folded his world down. That he had never once shown the slightest sign of resentment or unhappiness amazed Kyoko. How could a person like Kornell love her? She, who was so awkward with people, so aloof.

But it seemed she might be changing. Scrunched into a booth, with Kornell on one side and Bennie on the other, surrounded by breakfast plates and cups of coffee, Kyoko helped herself to some home fries and listened to their banter. She thought about her mother, about the last few years of her life, when no one came to the house and she never went out, and Kyoko had kept her company, had watched TV with her while she drew or figured out chord progressions on the guitar. It had not seemed strange to her that this had been their life; she had loved her mother and had wanted to make her happy. Even after her death, Kyoko had stayed there, in the small space that they had inhabited together, her growing obsession with Daniel Karmody occupying the place her mother had left. And now that the obsession had lifted, now that she'd delivered Daniel to a chance for happiness—with Alma, no less—without rancor, Kyoko felt a curious sense of lightheadedness, as though what she had taken to be the ceiling had suddenly revealed itself to be the sky, opening onto a vast expanse. It wasn't an entirely pleasant feeling, this dizziness, this sensation of unbalance, but it wasn't wholly bad, either. It reminded Kyoko of the moment in tai chi when you relinquished your center, offering it up—your stability, your root—just before coming into it again, twofold. Because loss only looked like weakness, when many times it was its opposite: strength in the surrender, in the act of giving up freely what was yours to take.

"Hey, babe, you doing all right?" Kornell reached his arm across the back of her shoulders.

Kyoko smiled. "Yeah," she said.

WHERE YOU PUT THE END

I t ends like this: Kyoko singing, *"I'm a samurai! I'm a geisha!"* in a
hot fog of silhouettes in a club in Portland, Oregon. Her voice is
hoarse from two weeks on the road, and she rasps the chorus, her
fingers so slick with sweat that they keep slipping off the notes. But
the audience sings along, buoying Kyoko, carrying her aloft. *"I'm
Japanese! I'm Japanese!"* And Kornell's righteous drumbeat pounding.
Everything is in motion, the room alive with bodies—thrashing, jumping, dancing, in a spastic rhythm that is like a machine pumping—
blood or oxygen, some essential thing, to feed the organism that
breathes in this moment, in this place—new, and young, and alive—
in the enduring and forever present.

A nd like this: Alma and Daniel sitting side by side on the white
chaise longue. On the coffee table in front of them, Alma's
laptop plays a YouTube video of the Yukio Mishimas performing

several days ago at a bar in Sacramento. Alma holds Daniel's upper arm in both her hands, squeezing gently. She taps a bare foot to Kornell's drumbeat. Kyoko's frenetic dancing and harsh vocals make Daniel remember getting kicked and called an asshole on the basement floor. But he doesn't mind much. Because Alma is squeezing his arm and murmuring sounds of surprise, approval, and unselfconscious delight, her eyes rapt and unblinking on Kyoko's rage-filled ecstasy. As the crunch of the last chord lingers, spreading, breaking up into piercing echoes of feedback that wander and fade, Alma's eyes glisten with tears.

DANIEL AND THE RETAINER

Long before Alma, though, there had been Gracie Han, and even though Daniel would tell you he does not remember her, she hangs upside down from the rafters of his unconscious, flitting across his brain in soft shadow, tickling at the outer reaches of his memory like a shy dream.

They had been classical music prodigies, two of a hundred or more in the greater metropolitan area—all disciples of a handful of haughty European immigrant teachers, who competed for the same top spots every year, accumulating busts of composers and beribboned certificates of commendation, who practiced their instruments four or five hours a day and attended music camp in New England or upstate New York instead of spending their summers playing baseball or horsing around by the pool.

Daniel was turning fourteen that year, and Gracie must have been a year younger. Both played the violin, Daniel in the coveted concertmaster position, and Gracie, third chair. The rest of their cohort were fourteen-to-eighteen-year-olds, lurking adolescents with the obvious markers of puberty, which they carried awkwardly, the way they carried their instrument cases and music stands, their canvas bags and backpacks filled with sheet music and composition paper.

Daniel was all Adam's apple and knobs, and large feet, with a giraffe-like build, and a way of annoying the older kids with his banter and his eagerness. He had been an aspiring magician and would try out his tricks at the picnic tables where they ate lunch—pulling streams of colored handkerchiefs from his pocket, attaching and detaching metal hoops, dematerializing coins from his hand and discovering them again in a pretty girl's ear.

"How'd you do that?" the girl would ask breathlessly. But before Daniel could bask in her attentions, an older boy with a five-o'clock shadow, looking as thuggish as a kid who played the French horn was able, would scoff, grabbing the girl around the shoulders. "I can show you a magic trick," he'd whisper sotto voce, cutting his eyes to his crotch.

Gracie never socialized with the others. She was so small and underdeveloped that she looked like a fourth grader, though she had the gravity of a much older person. She always wore cardigan sweaters, no matter how hot the weather, over white blouses, and capris. On her feet, she wore white sneakers with ankle socks, the lacy tops of which seemed to itch terribly, for she was always scratching at her ankles, one leg crossed atop the other, raising long red welts with her fingernails.

Daniel first noticed Gracie one day at lunch. Rebuffed by the older kids, he was sitting alone practicing a trick that had somehow gone wrong, involving different lengths of rope. She was sitting facing him a little way down the table, scratching an ankle absently, opening a rectangular Tupperware container packed with tiny white circles rimmed in black, speckled with green and yellow.

Having performed his trick successfully a couple of times, one length of rope seemingly cut into unequal thirds, re-forming into a whole piece again, Daniel paused and noticed, without noticing (in the desultory way we do sometimes, especially as children), Gracie pulling apart a pair of wooden chopsticks, rubbing the two pieces together, one in each hand, with surprising vigor, as though she were setting up a magic trick of her own, then transferring them to the same hand and expertly clacking the tips a few times. Just as she seemed about to have at her curious lunch, she stopped and, with one deft motion of her thumb, removed her retainer from the roof of her mouth and set it on a napkin.

Daniel noticed, and did not notice, the delicacy and the expertise of this movement, the grace of it (the Gracieness), also the grossness—the transparent pink plastic molded to the roof of her mouth, attached to a thin bracket of wire, the whole of it pulling away with a string of silver saliva, to nestle in the rough, white textured napkin. And in this half-conscious observation, Daniel felt a quickening, a sudden and confounding sensation, as of twin hearts beating, one in his chest and one, strangely and simultaneously, between his legs.

"What is that?" he ventured, indicating her lunch, not her retainer.

Gracie regarded him. "*Gimbap*," she said. "Rice wrapped in seaweed."

"What's inside?"

Gracie held one up, clamped between her chopsticks. "Cucumber. Scrambled egg. Spinach," she recited, as though only just noticing. "Want one?" She held it out to him.

Daniel became aware of the older kids sitting behind them. He shook his head. "Yuck," he said, and taking up his lengths of rope, he left her.

Whatever consciousness Daniel might have retained of Gracie Han was submerged by the shame of what happened next. There is a kind of magic trick of memory, a sleight of mind, which allows us to forget what is mortifying or traumatic, or even what is pleasurable, if the pleasure itself is shot through with enough discomfort.

It became important to Daniel, somehow, to witness Gracie's ritual of retainer removal each day at lunchtime. He would find a way to sit near enough to her, or to be poised at the periphery at just the right time, and when he saw her put her thumb in her mouth, for a moment looking like she meant to suck it, he felt that extra beat in the measure of his pants, and waited until she withdrew the retainer and placed it on her napkin. If Daniel noticed anything else about Gracie at that time—the severity of her haircut (angry bangs, blunt bob), the planes of her prepubescent chest and hips, the thin dowels of leg showing between the hem of her pedal pushers and the top of her socks, the parallel pink lines of aggrieved scratches clustered around her ankles—it did not register much beyond surface contempt for the "little Oriental girl" who sat behind him in the violin section.

One day, toward the end of that season—the orchestra had been rehearsing for their upcoming concert (Sibelius's Fifth Symphony)—they were all hanging out dejectedly at lunch, having just been scolded by Maestro Zurick for their sloppy playing and careless attitude, and Daniel was distracted by his own sense of failure, for Maestro Zurick had singled him out for criticism. "Are you zee leader, Daniel?" he had said. "Zo, you must lead!"

Because Daniel was younger, the older kids resented him. Martin Chang, in particular, thought he had been robbed of the concertmaster's chair. Daniel didn't think Maestro Zurick appreciated how difficult it was to get the other kids—all of whom went to different schools, from numerous districts, suburbs, and neighborhoods, across a one-thousand-square-mile radius—to listen to him. He was trying to think of a joke he could tell to gain their respect, something off-color enough to make the older kids laugh, but not so raunchy that it would get him in trouble. He was thinking of one in particular, involving a doctor's office and a newlywed, a joke he didn't fully understand, but that seemed sophisticated and implicating, when there was a series of short screams (F-sharp) and little Gracie Han jumped up from the picnic table and ran down the path toward the parking lot, waving her hands in the air above her head. In the process of panicking, she had upset her lunch on the grass. A dozen or so of her rounds of rice and seaweed lay, like spare mandalas, in symbolic disarray. Someone went to get a grown-up. The others laughed and made fun of her, eager for bright diversion. Daniel spotted the napkin under the picnic bench, imprinted with the damp U-shaped outline of Gracie's retainer. He picked it up and put it in his pocket.

It turned out Gracie had been stung by a yellow jacket, on the pointer finger of her bow hand, and since she was allergic, she swelled up and had to go to the ER, where she was released before the end of the day. A search ensued for her lost retainer, but it was mysteriously never found.

In the sanctuary of his bedroom that night, Daniel retrieved the thing, gently brushing away stray pieces of wet napkin and dirt. It was a weird texture, the garish pink of it partly slimy and partly smooth. It felt to Daniel like a living part of the dark, secret cave of Gracie's mouth. Gracie, who was not Gracie, but all feminine mystery: hidden, wet, and coax-able. Daniel slipped the retainer into his own mouth, but there were no spaces for the wires to fit between his teeth, and the convexity at the top did not match the roof of his mouth, which seemed larger and less arced. It tasted foreign, a little plasticky, but also salty and a bit sour, as though the inside of Gracie's mouth had recently contained lemons and potato chips. Daniel plunged his tongue into the rosy, hollowed cove, and was made dizzy by the transgression.

From there it was a mere matter of days before he turned his attention from object to subject, from flimsy piece of pink plastic to girl herself, who—miracle of miracles—had acquired a new retainer and a fleshy Band-Aid for her swollen forefinger. The Band-Aid was, in fact, a few shades paler than her skin, which was the color, with her summer tan, of warm honey. She had gone to the beach earlier that summer and still wore the ghostly markings of a bathing suit, pale yoke peeking from the edges of her cardigan, coming together at a hidden point at the back of her neck, which was long and slender and downy with soft hairs. Her dark eyes, pupil indistinguishable from iris, seemed always cast down—in maidenly modesty, Daniel wondered, or scouting warily for bees? Her mouth, engulfing the pink apparatus that replicated the one he kept in a sock in the back of his top dresser drawer, was thin on top and full on the bottom. Indeed, perhaps aided by the slight protrusion of the retainer, Gracie's lower lip puffed petulantly, permanently pouted, adding to her overall look an air of contradiction, of childishness and womanhood, of bratty tantrum and sulky sensuality.

Even with all this, Daniel did not retain conscious memories of Gracie Han (did not retain 'er!), except to recall a mousy girl who had once been stung by a yellow jacket. The fact that Gracie had been Asian would have hovered in the background of his memory, like that yellow jacket, but would not sting him into any sort of awareness until sixteen years later, when he met Alma Soon Ja Lee, whose green tongue, stained from Chloraseptic for a sore throat, had inserted itself into his own mouth, and whose lissome beauty reactivated some disturbance in him, some distant reverberation of desire that encompassed Gracie Han, but went beyond her, to the molten discovery of priapic pleasure and a first taste of the foreign, the Other, the Un-self, opening his palate to all manner of dark and forbidden flavors.

AFTERWORD

I.

Mom was not the most practical person. She saw this as a badge of honor. "I'm terrible at math," she'd humble-brag. Or: "I don't understand a thing about the stock market." Or: "I hate doing my taxes—even the word gives me a rash."

Her impracticality was a deep claiming of power over her life. Mom knew how she wanted to live, and she would not, for a second, allow anyone to shame her for it or distract her from her priorities. She desired a wild and precious life devoted to art. Learning about math or the stock market or taxes would slow her down. Life was too short. Mom always used to half joke that she planned to die young.

Her impracticality was also rebellion. Her grandfather was a stern, formidable school principal back in Seoul. Her father became a science professor in the U.S. Her mother made a brief, brilliant foray into the world of banking. Mom chose a different path. Family lore has it she knew by age six she wanted to be a writer.

Her rebellion stems from a family tragedy. Mom had a younger brother who was born with health problems and died as a toddler when Mom was four. Her parents were stoic in their grief, immigrants in a small town in upstate New York, far from extended family. Mom's childhood included isolation, silence, and unacknowledged sorrow. And so, she was called to creative writing—a way to break silences. I think many writers are driven by a terror of important things going unsaid. Mom liked to repeat the oft-quoted last words of Socrates before his execution: *The unexamined life is not worth living.*

Impracticality, rebelliousness, and, the final ingredient, stubbornness. I think Mom shared this trait with all writers. Non-writers sometimes point out that creative writing is difficult to do well, unlikely to ever pay much, and doomed to heaps of failure and rejection. They're not wrong. So our only defense is to be stubborn as hell. To simply insist, as Mom did, that, yes, I will drudge up my most painful memories to turn them into stories. Yes, I will devote years to this, without any guarantee of recognition. Damn right! And no one can stop me!

II.

I grew up in a small town in central New Hampshire. My parents, both fiction writers, chose it for the low cost of living. They worked at the local college: Mom as editor of the alumni magazine, my dad as consultant for, then director of, the writing center—day jobs to support their writing. When I think back to my childhood, I remember the town almost as a villain—a center of boredom, mediocrity, and conformity that my parents often complained about feeling stuck in.

Mom and I escaped into epic movie marathons with buttered popcorn every weekend. We'd stop at McDonald's for French fries on the way home from Shop 'n Save to reward ourselves after the tedium of grocery shopping. I remember hours lounging on her bed, taking turns reading aloud, sometimes from her novel-in-progress, sometimes from her favorite books.

She chose *Crime and Punishment* (we loved it all the way through but bemoaned the sentimental ending) and *Anna Karenina* (we skipped the long, boring passages where characters discuss the state of agriculture). We read *Mrs. Dalloway*, then *The Hours*. We read *Madame Bovary. Heart of Darkness.* John Irving's *The World According to Garp* and *A Prayer for Owen Meany.* Morrison's *Song of Solomon.* Hardy's *Far from the Madding Crowd.* We bought the audiobook—on cassette tapes!—of Jeremy Irons reading *Lolita* and listened together. Mom liked intense, unconventional characters and beautiful prose. She wanted to share her love of these books with me, partly because she worried I wasn't being challenged enough at school.

She was right. I was often bored and lonely at school. But reading these novels on Mom's bed, I felt curious and engaged, connected to humanity in all its complexity. I was even moved to write myself, scribbling stories in notebooks, trying to re-create the feeling that reading gave me. Sometimes I showed them to Mom, and she offered me a mix of praise and thoughtful questions.

What Mom loved most in the novels we read together were moments of transcendent power, when narrative time stops and the language becomes intense—sentences lengthening, or else shortening—as an essential truth about the human condition is revealed. She called them "moments of amplification."

"You have to sprinkle them in sparingly," she'd say, somewhat regretfully. "You have to earn them. But for me, they're what it's all about." As she read aloud, she sometimes stopped to mark one, to copy later into her notebook. She had a few such passages hand-written in her almost illegible chicken-scratch on scraps of paper and taped up around her writing desk—one from *Lolita* about blue light filtering through Venetian blinds as the protagonist observes the ebb and flow of his monstrous lust and regret; another from *To the Lighthouse* about yearning to know the meaning of life.

Perhaps it's surprising how rarely I remember Mom being busy writing. When she wrote, it was in intense spurts—especially while at artist residencies.

In 2005, Mom's novel *Secondhand World* was bought by Knopf. It was the story of a Korean American teenager in the 1970s who clashes with her immigrant parents. Though not the first novel she'd written, it was the first that would be published—her lifelong dream. "It's going to be a Borzoi book!" she said, her face flushed with excitement. (She explained that Borzoi books were famous for thoughtful design and bindings and typography, including—she was especially excited about this part—deckled edges.)

I was nineteen and had just completed my first year of college. Mom insisted on using her advance to take me, my brother, and my dad to Paris for two weeks that summer. We rented a beautiful apartment with a balcony in the bohemian Eleventh Arrondissement. Our days were a magnificent blur: savoring golden pastries in the morning, wandering wide-eyed through art museums for hours, cooling down with gelato every afternoon. Mom had some French friends she knew from artist residencies. We met up with them for aperitifs and long delicious dinners. One of them had a son my age; Mom arranged for him and me to go out to dinner, just the two of us. He turned out to be painfully shy, but still it was a thrill to be out in Paris with a French guy, without my family. I think Mom set up the dinner to challenge me, to encourage me to be more engaged, to expand my sense of the possible—the same reasons she read novels with me. There was beauty and transcendence in that trip to Paris. Like living inside one of Mom's beloved "moments of amplification."

Finances were stressfully tight the following spring. Mom had neglected to save the percentage of her advance that was due as taxes. We had spent it all in Paris.

III.

The next several years brought many changes. *Secondhand World* received good reviews and was one of two finalists for the PEN/ Bingham Prize. Mom got a tenure-track position teaching writing and literature at the University of North Carolina, Asheville. My parents got divorced. Mom fell in love with Greg, a multitalented punk rocker, baker, and carpenter. I graduated from college and ended up in New Orleans, working whatever jobs crossed my path: office assistant, waitress, ESL teacher. I often felt aimless and lonely. Talking to Mom always made me feel better. She valued my opinions, especially about novels, which we often discussed. And I loved hearing about her own writing.

"My new novel is very different from *Secondhand World*," she told me excitedly on the phone. "It's going to have many characters, omniscient narration. Lots of shit is going to happen—suicide, kidnapping, attempted murder. It'll be arch and clever but also heartfelt; I'm gonna channel Nabokov. And part of it takes place in Florence, so I have to go there as research." (As it turned out, she would have to identify the loveliest jewelry store on the Ponte Vecchio and buy herself a diamond ring, also as research.)

She emailed me chapters now and then. Sometimes she told me she realized this or that section didn't, in fact, belong in the novel. That's the kind of writer Mom was: unable to go on to the second sentence until she had painstakingly shaped the first, unable to start a new chapter until she had made the current one shine. "Well-pruned trails leading nowhere," she called the beautiful sections that ended up getting deleted. She called herself a "word wanker." A self-aware insight, a cheerful self-deprecation. And, I believe, a way of saying *Bugger off!* to anyone who might dare suggest she embrace the often-touted "bad-first-drafts" approach. She wanted to do things her way, practicality be damned.

Sometime in 2013, Mom completed a draft of *The Fetishist*. I assumed she'd pass it to me when she was ready. But she was still revising, polishing.

IV.

By March 2014, Mom was a tenured professor in North Carolina, still happily polishing *The Fetishist*. One day she called to say she felt a large rectangular lump in her breast that she could've sworn wasn't there the day before. She scheduled an appointment. It was breast cancer.

It was Stage III at first, then it spread, becoming Stage IV. The recommended treatment was chemo, surgery, radiation, then more chemo. Unlike in the movies, doctors were cagey about life expectancy, unwilling to provide a number. But when we googled (and googled and googled), it seemed like several years was the best guess.

I experienced deep terror and dread. I tried not to think about it, but I was constantly thinking about it. The idea that I would continue to exist after Mom was gone struck me as impossible. I sensed that the biggest, most painful challenge I would ever face was on its way.

Soon after her diagnosis, Mom declared she was done with fiction. The artifice of constructing an elaborate imagined world felt wrong to her now. Instead, she was working on a nonfiction collection. "I need to spend the time I have left understanding myself, my life, and the world around me, unadorned," she said. She started sending me powerful, stripped-down personal essays instead of novel chapters. Some of them we read aloud together when I visited her in Asheville, which I started doing every few months.

She never looked back. When anyone asked about *The Fetishist*, Mom would say "I'm done with fiction," in the same tone she would say "I'm a word wanker" or "I'm terrible at math." Matter-of-fact, with a dash of defiant pride. She didn't refer to *The Fetishist* as an "unfinished" novel. She called it "abandoned." I never pressed her, never asked to read it. It felt more respectful to support her turn to nonfiction.

Mom seemed calmer, happier, than before. She wrote more regularly than I'd ever seen her do, working on her essays every day. "There's something so great about just being able to say: this is me, this is it, I know myself," she said more than once, with a peaceful smile.

My heart would ache when she said this. I was happy for her, of course. But it also highlighted a truth I'd been ignoring for years, since well before Mom's illness: I was hiding from myself. I didn't know myself, and my friends in New Orleans didn't know me either. I wasn't engaged or connected; I had things to say but didn't know how to say them. Observing Mom's quest for self-understanding slowly forced me to realize this most basic fact: I was miserable.

Then, in early 2019, Mom was really dying. As in, she went to the hospital for acute pneumonia, was pronounced a goner, surprised everyone by recovering enough to sit up, then got transferred to a hospice center. I took an indefinite leave of absence from my job and went to Asheville.

In the month or so before she began losing lucidity, Mom kept working on her essays. She wrote vulnerable posts on Facebook—often shot through with dark humor—about her dying process, which friends of hers still today tell me helped them in their own process of understanding and accepting death.

We discussed the playlist for her memorial celebration. The Clash's "Should I Stay or Should I Go." DeVotchKa's "How It Ends." Of course, Janice Joplin's "Get It While You Can." We discussed where her remaining bits of money should go. "Don't save your share for retirement!" she implored me. "Spend it on something exciting—jewelry, a purse, killer outfits. Something fun!" We discussed her most urgent wish for me—that I would learn to put myself out there more, that I would believe in myself and dare to share my "badassery" with the world.

What we did not discuss in the hospice center was her abandoned novel. Or her essay collection. Or anything related to posthumous publishing. She said nothing about her wishes for her unpublished work.

V.

Sitting by Mom's bed in her final days, the solution to my self-constructed misery announced itself in my mind, unbidden, obvious, surprising: *Start writing.* After her death, I did. I went back to New Orleans and changed my life. I started writing essays and stories, many of them about Mom. I started breaking the silences about myself, in order to know myself. It felt so good.

My uncle established a fellowship in Mom's name at MacDowell, an artist residency program that Mom loved, to support Asian American writers. For the first fellowship celebration event, in the spring of 2021, I invited the poet and essayist Cathy Park Hong to read. I had read her *Minor Feelings* and loved its bold exploration of Asian American womanhood and artist-hood before I even realized something so obvious: Mom and Cathy had been friends.

At the event, I read a raucous excerpt of *The Fetishist* (the chapter that categorizes the different types of Asian fetishists; you know the one). The response was thunderously positive and energized. People asked when they could read the whole novel. Several Asian American women from the audience told me they felt deeply seen by Mom's work. Being sexually fetishized as an Asian woman is a difficult topic—thorny, complicated, likely to offend. That Mom was able to articulate what it feels like, from the perspective of the fetishized, with nuance, humor, and aplomb, with a bold yet considered fearlessness, is a liberating, literature-affirming triumph. It felt amazing to share that with others.

After the event, I started having conversations with my brother and stepdad. Wouldn't it be amazing if we could get Mom's unpublished work—both *The Fetishist* and her essay collection—out into the world?

I asked Cathy Park Hong for advice. She offered to pass Mom's manuscript on to her agent.

Caught off guard by her generosity (I had only expected general advice), I found myself scanning Mom's voluminous files on the laptop that had been hers and was now mine. Her files were a mess. I found about a million called *The Fetishist* followed by a date or a random number or words like "first bit" or "newer." I panicked, scrolled. The most recently opened version was from late February 2014—shortly before her diagnosis. She literally never worked on the novel again after that. Never even opened the file.

Looking at the manuscript, I realized I'd already read many of the sections while the work was in progress, but Mom had sent them to me out of order. I didn't know how the whole thing fit together. How could I have forgotten that I'd never read a complete draft? I wasn't going to send the agent a document I hadn't read. So I plunged in. I read it in two sittings. After two years without her, it felt joyful and intense to be so immersed in Mom's words, her beautifully crafted sentences, the entertaining and emotionally hard-hitting POVs spanning two decades, the characters' couplings and yearnings and strivings, their violence toward self and other, their sort-of redemptions.

I could see that Alma and Kyoko represented two different sides of Mom as an artist. Alma the classical cellist, who had an illustrious career interpreting the canon of revered white male composers, represented the side of Mom that cherished Nabokov and Hardy and Conrad, that scribbled their words in her notebooks and studied them. In contrast, Kyoko the punk rocker, who named her band the Yukio Mishimas (look up how he died and why; Mom chose that name for a reason), represented the side of Mom that was angry about old white men ruling the world, angry at the exclusion of women and people of color from the canon, the side of Mom that announced, through her writing, "Step aside, Nabokov; I got something to say!"

I was astonished by how complete the novel felt. And by its intimate exploration of terminal illness, though Mom wrote it entirely before her diagnosis. I reveled in how much *Mom* was packed in its pages, not only in Alma the diva and Kyoko the rebel, but also in Emi's reckless impulsivity and desire for transcendence, in Daniel's wry humor and love of puns. I saw a bit of my relationship to Mom in Kyoko's daughterly devotion—a pure devotion, fierce, expansive, ever-evolving. I saw Mom in all of the characters' stubbornness and pride and painful/sublime self-awareness, and in the omniscient narration's elegant, layered, heartfelt intelligence.

So much Mom, in every sentence. I was reminded of our hours reading aloud together, her chicken-scratch copied passages, her deeply held values of courageous self-awareness and the examined life. Which were now my values, too.

Reading Mom's novel reminded me of my newfound identity as a writer, of what an honor it is to be part of this world—those who make the brave, impractical, stubborn decision to devote their lives to trying to create good stories, to not leave anything important unsaid.

VI.

Things happened quickly after I sent the manuscript. The agent, PJ Mark, responded, calling the novel "funny, smart, and wildly contemporary." He found an editor who wanted to publish it: Sally Kim, a highly successful pioneering Korean American woman in a mostly white industry, just like Mom.

We had a call, the three of us. I was so nervous, worried I could somehow say the wrong thing and ruin everything. But I took a deep breath and reminded myself to be brave.

Sally said she had read *Secondhand World* recently, and the ending made her cry. She talked about how *Secondhand World* and *The Fetishist* go boldly into intensely sad, painful territory, yet both end on a note of lightness and hope that feels earned.

PJ and Sally talked about how to do promotion, tricky with posthumous publications. In lieu of author readings and interviews, they suggested we organize events where writers could discuss the novel together. I realized they saw great potential for the novel's ability to find a wide audience, and to start important conversations.

After the call, it struck me that, in the five years between diagnosis and death, Mom could have published *The Fetishist* in her lifetime. Her illness could have been part of the urgency, could've added poignancy to her readings and interviews. She could have been fêted in bookstores and bars across the country, her goodbye tour. Though I'm overjoyed all of this is happening for *The Fetishist* now, it feels tragic that Mom never got to see the world responding to it.

Sometimes, like while waiting to hear from PJ, or while working on the edits for Sally, I found it hard to unclench my stomach. Because failure in this case wouldn't be the failure of my own work (virtually guaranteed for novices like me). No, it would be my failure to advocate for Mom. To properly honor her after her death, to get her work the attention it deserves. Other times, what knotted my stomach was the way engaging with Mom's writing made her feel so present, which emphasized her absence.

Presence and absence, healing and pain. Every time I receive good news for *The Fetishist*, I feel so simultaneously happy and sad that I burst into tears while beaming. The first time, it startled me. Now I just refer to it as "happy-crying." Consistent with Buddhist beliefs about yin and yang and the balanced duality of everything. Consistent with being a writer, which requires the ability to explore ambivalence and contradiction. When I happy-cry, I feel like a mess and I feel connected to my truth. I feel connected to Mom.

I am so happy Mom's beautiful novel is being published; I am so sad she's not here to see it happen. I'm happy *The Fetishist*'s publication process is helping me grow as a writer and person; I'm sad Mom's death is the reason I'm playing this role. I suppose I no longer conceptualize joy and sorrow as opposites, because everything related to *The Fetishist*'s publication makes me feel flooded with both at once.

VII.

When I began therapy in 2017, my therapist recommended I ask Mom to write a letter describing what she saw in me, so I could have it always after she died. I mentioned the idea to Mom and she seemed interested. But no letter materialized, and we didn't discuss it again.

Then, in January 2019, as Mom was dying but before she began losing lucidity, I was surprised to receive an email from her. It was her letter. Though I'd been sitting by her side in the hospice center each day, I hadn't realized she'd been writing it.

In her letter, Mom describes in great detail what she sees in me, why she loves me. I still cry from relief/happiness/longing/grief when I read it. But what's on my mind as I write this afterword is this part:

"I do not know how to unconnect with you now, or anytime, so I won't, can't, don't. I feel very much like you and I have infinitely more to do/to say/to experience together, and that the next levels will be interesting in new and other ways. More great mystery, more love, more joy. More connectedness. I know this sounds very woo-woo crazy, but maybe not. I just know it's not the end. I will, in all important ways, be here for you always and whenever you need me. We'll find a way. I believe this."

Mom and I were never writers at the same time. She never knew me as a writer, not in my adulthood. But here I am, almost four years after her death, writing words that will appear with her words in a book. Bringing *The Fetishist* to the world has been an explosion of great mystery, love, joy, and connectedness. I believe Mom and I are experiencing it together. We are connecting in new and interesting ways. And I'm learning to overcome my silences, to say what needs to be said, to engage with my inherent "badassery." This was both Mom's dying wish for me and, in ways that are still being revealed, her dying gift to me. (Excuse me while I happy-cry.)

KAYLA MIN ANDREWS
New Orleans
February 2023

ACKNOWLEDGMENTS

Mom didn't write acknowledgments for *The Fetishist* before she died, so I (Kayla) would like to thank, on her behalf, the following people who helped get this novel out into the world:

My stepdad, Greg, who provided so many excellent ideas and encouraged me with conviction throughout the publication process and beyond. Backing up a bit: as Mom's partner over the years she wrote this novel, Greg provided stability and love, held space for her, and generally made her life conducive to art-making. This novel, in so many ways, exists because of his love and strength.

My brother, Clay, for his love, support, humor, and generous worldview.

My uncle Kollin, for having the vision and determination to set up the MacDowell Fellowship in Mom's name. Thanks for being a great brother to Mom and son to Halmoni and Haraboji, as well as uncle to me and Clay.

Kongki and Yungwha Min, Mom's parents. Thanks for raising an

amazing daughter and rooting for her in her writing career. Your support meant so much to her. (Kongki Min died December 23, 2022, as I
was writing these acknowledgments. We love and miss you, Haraboji.
Saranghaeyo.)

Cathy Park Hong, for believing in the beauty of Mom's work, and
being willing to fight for it.

Alex Chee, for his encouragement, efforts, and time championing
Mom's work.

Laura Catherine Brown, for invaluable advice, writerly feedback,
deep conversations, and artistic inspiration. You were a great friend to
Mom and are a great friend to me. Thank you.

PJ Mark of Janklow and Nesbit, for seeing the value of Mom's work
early on, for being a kind human as well as a thoughtful and effective
advocate, and for making the process less scary. Thanks also to everyone
at Janklow and Nesbit, including Emma Leong in the UK.

Sally Kim of Putnam, for her vision and drive, her amazing feedback regarding edits, her generosity of spirit, and her determination to
honor Mom's legacy. Sally was absolutely the perfect person to take on
this novel. I've been in awe of my good fortune in working with her.
Thanks also to everyone on the team at Putnam, including Sally's assistant, Tarini.

Michael Kannen, classical cellist and music professor at the Peabody
Conservatory at Johns Hopkins. Michael was Mom's friend and reference
person for all things music-related, starting early in her process of writing *The Fetishist*. Then I reached out to Michael and continued the work
with him, checking and correcting details so we could fulfill Mom's wish
of having the novel feel accurate to classical musicians. Michael's collaboration was rigorous, joyful, and vital. I can't thank him enough.

My friends and mentors who helped me grow as a writer and
person, such that I was up to the challenge of getting *The Fetishist* out

into the world; who warmly listened and advised as I stressed at various points along the way; who cheered me on and shared in the overwhelming joy of it all. These amazing people include but are not limited to: Maurice Carlos Ruffin, Emilie Staat Strong, Karisma Price, Annell López, Stephanie Knapp, Liz Brina, Chris Romaguera, J.Ed Marston, Tom Andes, Chad Lange, Allison Alsup, Max Ciolino, Serena Chaudhry, Carey Lamprecht, Erika Pettersen, Lucille Jun.

Jenny, Gina, Brett, Stacy, and everyone on the team at MacDowell who helped us set up an annual Katherine Min Fellowship to support Asian American writers. In a sense, it was at the first Katherine Min Fellowship celebration with Cathy Park Hong that this magical publication journey got started.

The many residencies that gave Mom space and time to write: Yaddo, Hambidge, the Millay Colony, Ledig House, the Sewanee Writers' Conference, the Virginia Center for the Creative Arts, Jentel, Ucross, and especially MacDowell. Residencies were invaluable to Mom's writing process, a source of artistic growth and joy and friendship. Thank you for the important work you do to empower artists.

The writers of Fourth Kingdom, a Korean American writers' group that makes a point of meeting up for a good Korean dinner every year at AWP. Mom so loved spending time with you, being part of a community with all of you. Special thanks to Marie Myung-Ok Lee for her friendship with Mom, for her vital work supporting this community, and for introducing me to Fourth Kingdom and their AWP dinners, which I now look forward to every year myself.

The students and faculty at the University of North Carolina Asheville, where Mom taught while writing *The Fetishist*.

And finally, thanks to all the new voices out there, coming out now, coming out soon. Mom was so genuinely excited to encourage newer writers, and to read what they had to say. Please keep telling your stories.